WITH A LITTL

It was Andrea
Andrea, who w ... o
be a good wife

She had always felt, in her humble way, that she had been lucky to be included in with the clever, swinging, golden set, with Jilly who was brilliant and Carol who was artistic and Penny who was ambitious. Andrea was none of these things but she could organize a nice reunion, with nice food, and nice things. So she wrote the letters and thought what fun it would be to see them all again.

She had no idea what a catalyst her reunion would be — what turmoil would erupt into their lives as a result.

WITH A LITTLE HELP FROM MY FRIENDS

Patricia Burns

CORGI BOOKS

WITH A LITTLE HELP FROM MY FRIENDS

A CORGI BOOK 0 552 13320 5

First publication in Great Britain

PRINTING HISTORY

Corgi edition published 1988

This book is set in 10/11 pt Clarendon

Corgi Books are published by Transworld Publishers Ltd., 61–63 Uxbridge Road, Ealing, London W5 5SA, in Australia by Transworld Publishers (Australia) Pty. Ltd., 15–23 Helles Avenue, Moorebank, NSW 2170, and in New Zealand by Transworld Publishers (N.Z.) Ltd., Cnr. Moselle and Waipareira Avenues, Henderson, Auckland.

Reproduced, printed and bound in Great Britain by
Hazell Watson & Viney Limited
Member of BPCC plc
Aylesbury, Bucks, England

WITH A LITTLE HELP FROM MY FRIENDS

CHAPTER ONE

The article caught Penny's eye as she was trying to get her son ready for his father's Reasonable Access day.

'Unreasonable bloody Access, if you ask me,' she muttered, flicking through the pages of the Sunday colour supplement in search of some distraction from the bad-tempered thumping around in Justin's room.

'Half-past nine. Nobody else in the building is awake, let alone up.'

And then she saw the photograph, under the headline 'The New Right', and her attention sharpened. She knew that face. Swept with a sudden aching nostalgia for the time when life was simple and uncomplicated, she looked at the caption for confirmation.

'Mrs Jill Lovesey, Member for Standingleigh East, with her husband, Mark, and two children, Robin and Emily.'

'Good God,' she said out loud. 'Jill the Red's gone over to the other side.'

If it was the same person. She stared at the face in the photograph, smiling so confidently at the camera, and surrounded by the symbols of her achievement, her handsome family, a couple of sleek ponies, a stockbrokerish house. Jill never could stand horses, or horsey people. But there was no mistaking that level gaze, that square jaw, that defiant stance. It had all been softened now, of course, by success and the intervening years. No longer was Jill the scruffy eighteen-year-old in flared jeans and embroidered afghan coat, half hidden behind a veil of waist-length hair. Gone was the fisherman's smock and the flat sandals. J-boots, Penny thought, with a smile of reminiscence. Instead the Member for Standingleigh East was as well groomed as her children's ponies, quietly stylish in Jaeger and an expert cut and perm.

Instinctively, Penny glanced in the red-framed mirror by the notice board. Appearance was so vital in her profession. She ran her fingers through her hair and nodded at her reflection, satisfied. Yes, the new streaks did work. Pink was not too young, nor too outrageous. She was only thirty-six, after all. It was not so very long ago that she and Jill and the others were all living in each other's pockets, sharing each other's lives and dreams and ambitions. It seemed like only yesterday. Yesterday, and yet it was another age.

'Mum!' Justin erupted from his room in his pyjama top and football shorts, his thin face thunderous. 'Where are my Liverpool shirt and my tracksuit?'

Penny swallowed the rising irritation. It was always the same when he was going to meet his father. He could never find what he wanted, got annoyed and blamed it all on her. And she, who hated to let him go away from her love, her influence, tried so hard not to cling that she usually ended up shouting at him.

'Where did you leave them?' she said.

Her son glared at her, a fair, lanky replica of herself, with thirteen years of frustration gathered in his blue-grey eyes.

'I dunno, do I? In my room. But they were dirty.'

On any other day, Penny would have asked him why the hell he hadn't put them out to be washed, why he couldn't use his brain for a change. But today was access day, so she used her strongest defence and made herself play a part. Perfect, patient mother. Being an actress did have some advantages.

'Let's go and have a look, shall we?' she suggested, sweetly reasonable.

With Justin scowling and muttering behind her, she poked around in the disaster area that was his room. Good God, what would her mother have said to such a tip? When she was thirteen, Penny was keeping most of the house clean, not just her own room. She had always envied Jill, whose mother employed a cleaning lady, and who was never expected to do a hand's turn. Not that she had ever let Jill know it. The ability to act came in useful even then. Jill had never guessed how intimidated Penny always felt, going to that gracious, immaculate house with its careless abundance of food and drink, fresh flowers and electrical gadgetry.

The tracksuit, still muddy from school sports last Wednesday, was buried under a heap of magazines and computer tapes. So was the Liverpool shirt. Holding down a now almost overwhelming urge to let fly at him over the state of his room and his inability to do the least thing for himself, Penny held the revolting garments at arm's length.

'There you are. It's far too late to do anything about them now. If you still want to wear them, the most I can do is give them a good brush.'

Justin kicked the bed.

'Wendy always has my things washed and put away by the next day,' he informed her.

'Well perhaps— ' Penny began, her voice loaded with venom. And stopped just in time. Perhaps you'd like to go and live with Bloody Wonderful Wendy and your dear darling father, she was going to say. And supposing he said yes, he would like to do just that? She couldn't bear it. For all the worry of bringing up a teenage boy, for all his sulks and silences and constant demands for money, she loved Justin to distraction. He was all she had. 'Perhaps you won't need your football gear,' she substituted. 'Did your father actually say he was taking you out?'

Justin mumbled something about going with the kids to the park, and Penny guessed that he wanted to show off to his two young half-brothers. Unbidden, the picture of Jill and her reliable-looking husband and two nice clean children rose in her mind's eye. Jill didn't have to cope single-handed against a whole family pulling her son away from her.

'It's going to rain,' she pointed out, desperation beginning to edge her voice. 'You'll probably stay in and watch the box.'

And eat wholesome home-made cakes in front of an open fire.

'Oh all *right*. I'll just have to leave it, I suppose.' Justin dragged a pair of jeans from the tangle on the end of his unmade bed. 'I'll get changed,' he said pointedly.

Penny left him to it. Long gone were the days when they both wandered about the flat in various states of undress. Justin was growing up. Soon his voice would begin to break. What if he decided then that he wanted to live with Mike and Wonderful Wendy and they applied for custody? Would the court say that an adolescent boy should be with his father, especially as his mother was periodically away filming? She wandered back into the kitchen and picked up the colour supplement again to banish the thought of the empty echoing flat. There was the Member for Standingleigh East, smiling fearlessly back at her. Jill must be away from home just as much as she was. She probably had a flat here in London where she stayed when Parliament was sitting, and then travelled back at weekends. But was she accused of being a neglectful mother, pursuing her own career at the expense of her children's security? Penny doubted it. There was the solid, capable husband always at hand, and probably an au pair or housekeeper, even a nanny when the children were younger. No searching for a relief childminder, or ringing up friends who were never there at the last minute before catching a train to some Godforsaken spot for location work. No nagging worry or guilt, wondering if he was all right, not pining or unhappy, or simply resenting her absence. Oh no, Jill would have it all superbly organised, with the help and support of her husband. Her eyes flicked down the columns of print, searching for information on him.

'Mark Lovesey, whom she married in 1969 . . . Managing Director of family firm . . . machine tools and precision engineering . . . noted sportsman . . .' A real Mr Perfection. And no doubt devoted to his clever wife.

'What's the time?' Justin appeared once more, dressed after a fashion.

The red and grey sweatshirt was one that Wendy had bought for him. It was saggy round the bottom now from when Penny had put it in too hot a wash. Deliberately? She could not remember, but Justin still wore it, whether out of defiance or because he simply did not notice how awful it looked, she did not know. Penny resisted the temptation to tell him to put on something better. God knew, she bought him enough clothes. Really trendy stuff, the sort of thing other boys might envy. She might just as well have dressed him from jumble sales for all he cared, but her own teenage memories forbade it. The humiliation of those second-hand dresses and let-down skirts was still sharp. A whole wall of fitted wardrobes could not contain her clothes now.

She glanced at the kitchen clock.

'A quarter to ten.'

Justin swore under his breath.

'I wanted to be ready by now. Dad'll be waiting.'

Let him wait, Penny thought. She said, 'Well, you are ready, aren't you?'

No answer. Still scowling, Justin stumped into the hall, grabbed his parka and lunged towards the door. Penny trailed after him, wanting to hold on till the very last moment.

' 'Bye darling,' she fought to keep her tone light. 'Have a nice day.'

' 'Bye.'

A slam of the front door, and he was gone.

Penny leaned against the wall and closed her eyes. Why did she always get it wrong? Whichever way she played it, Justin always went off to see his father in a bad mood, leaving her feeling either washed-out or furious. She knew how it would be now. She would be haunted for the rest of the day by the conviction that Justin would bounce back the moment he met Mike, the charming and cheerful side of his personality rising to the top, so that he would associate the days with his father with the happy times, and life in general with her as one long battle. She must make more effort to do things with him, she decided. When this new series was in the can, she would take Justin on a really super holiday, just the two of them. She built a sunny little daydream round the idea, imagining them on a palm-fringed beach by a glinting sea, herself cultivating a nut-brown tan while Justin skimmed across the bay on a sailboard . . . then she sighed. Justin would complain that there was nobody to talk to. He would be far happier at a holiday camp.

Justin would be at the street door by now. Unable to resist the masochistic desire to see him with Mike, Penny went into the living-room and pulled aside the long royal blue curtains. Sheltering behind one of them, she peered down the three storeys into the road. Yes, there he was, just emerging onto the pavement. And there was Mike's ageing Cortina parked on the other side, and Mike just getting out, looking as downtrodden and ineffectual as ever. Her heart twisted painfully as she saw the spring in Justin's steps as he crossed the road to meet his father, and the eager way in which he scrambled into the car. It was staringly obvious that going to Mike and Wendy's for the day was the highlight of his week. Penny watched as Mike fussed over Justin's seatbelt, struggled with the car – it took three pulls to get it started – and finally drove off out of sight round the corner. For several minutes, Penny stood gazing at the empty Sunday street, vaguely seeing litter blowing in the chill February wind, a lone cat sneaking into an alleyway between two buildings. Behind her, the immaculate flat felt like a howling wilderness.

But the fighting spirit that had brought her so far was there still. Buried, maybe, beneath the problems of being a lone parent and a bad fit of the mid-winter blues, but beating strong at the heart of her tenacious personality.

'Snap out of it,' she told herself, speaking out loud as she often did when there was nobody else around to give her the good talking-to she needed. 'Make another pot of coffee, you didn't have time to enjoy the last one.'

Good advice, she decided, and made her way purposefully back into the kitchen. Waiting for the water to filter through, she considered all the things she ought to do today. First and foremost, the new script. A good supporting role in an eight-week television drama series. It was the best break she had had in years, and yet Penny could not quite work up the right degree of enthusiasm.

'I'm getting old and blaśe,' she told herself. But she knew it was not that. She needed someone to share it with, someone to be pleased for her, to encourage and criticise. Justin was quite good, and took an interest in the progress of her career, but it was not the same. She was tired of being on her own, of having to be the strong, responsible grown-up. She wanted someone to lean on every now and again. Not often, for she was certainly not the clinging type, but just once in a while it would be so good to know that there was someone there who cared.

The coffee pot filled, steaming and fragrant.

'Oh sod it,' Penny said. 'I'll read it later.'

She cleared a space at the kitchen table, sat on one of the chrome and perspex chairs and put her feet up on another. Pouring out a cup of coffee and adding milk and sugar – to hell with the diet – she looked round the room, searching for something to stop the downward spiral into dejection. The kitchen rarely failed to help. She had had it refitted with the rerun money from a comedy series, and was delighted with its clean, shiny high-tech lines. The black and white units with the chrome fittings, the pillarbox red wire racks and accessories had entirely matched her mood at the time – cheerful, efficient, successful. She had been on her way up, and no-one was going to stop her. As she took in the clean, co-ordinated effect, something of her old optimism seeped back. She was still on her way up. She had not even asked for this new part, the producer had insisted on her playing it. Dickie Forrester had worked with her before, respected her abilities and knew she was just right for the role. If the series was a success, and she was a success with it, then they would be queueing at the door with lovely juicy parts for her to choose from. Keeping this prospect firmly in mind, she reached behind the cereal packets for the colour magazine. She would see what Jill had been up to during all those years since they were at school together.

The article was more concerned with the new MP's political life and philosophy than her background, but Penny managed to cull the major events. After that traumatic summer when they were all eighteen, Jill had gone to university. That much Penny knew already. Of the four of them, all with A levels under their belts, Jill was the only one who actually made it to college. Penny thought of the tense filling-in of application forms, the nail-biting wait, the interviews, the disappointments, the conditional acceptances. Andrea came back from her interview at Exeter in floods of tears, convinced she had fluffed it. Carol was told by some helpful person at the Slade that only one applicant in three hundred was successful. It had all seemed so fraught at the time, yet looking back on it now, it was really quite magically easy. They had the world at their feet then, in the mid-sixties. They were young when youth was in fashion, they were clever, they were talented.

Where had it got them? It had taken Jill all the way to the House of Commons. Penny read the tale of her career. A degree in Philosophy, Politics and Economics, marriage to Mark Lovesey, whom she met at university, three years working at the Lovesey engineering firm, then the birth of two children, a boy first and then a girl, nicely spaced with two and a half years in between. All very neat and well planned. At the same time there was the interest in local party affairs, and soon after Robin was born, her first term as a local councillor. A few years later the jump up to national level, fighting and losing a strong Labour seat, and finally the chance of contesting a marginal. Standingleigh East fell to the Tories and Jill in the landslide victory of '83.

Penny skipped through the political bit. Party politics left her cold. She only bothered to vote out of a feeling of gratitude to those amazing suffragettes, fighting for their rights and being force-fed for their convictions at a time when women were supposed to be vapid and self-effacing. One part jumped up at her, though. It was a straight quotation from Jill.

'As a mother, I know that children need to be firmly guided. I think the people of this country appreciate that same firm touch. We were a great nation under Elizabeth the First and Victoria. We can be a great nation again.'

It was not the patronising statement that took her breath away, although it was pretty staggering. No, it was the picture it painted of the woman Jill had become. Penny could hardly believe that this was the same person she had once been so close to. What had happened to her? She read all through the article again, searching for clues, but there was nothing. It must all stem back to the reservoir, to the drowning . . . not a word about that in the magazine, of course. Nothing about beautiful, brilliant Jennifer, in whose shadow Jill had lived, or the parents who pinned all their hopes on their remarkable elder daughter. Penny sat frowning at the frustratingly uniformative print. It told her nothing about how and why the rebellious, left-wing, anti-establishment girl had turned into this model of conservatism.

Of course, Jill would be anxious to hush up that turbulent part of her life, and journalists always latched onto the aspect they wanted to present. Penny knew this from bitter experience. Not that she ever warranted a piece in a serious Sunday paper. The scurrilous tabloids had been more her mark. Nothing about her acting ability, of course, or about the solid work and step-by-step progress she had made over the years. All they were interested in was her affair with Gerry. She squeezed her eyes shut, shuddering as she remembered the horrendous publicity. That was when Justin started to turn against her.

She wrenched her thoughts away. She would not

go over it all again. Gerry was gone, he was part of the past, it was over. She fixed her eyes on the magazine article and let her mind wander back over those other newspaper headlines, eighteen years ago, half a lifetime way. Neither Sunday heavy nor muck-raking tabloid this time, but the sober local weekly of their London suburb.

'Reservoir Tragedy: Local Girl Drowned' and then, in the next issue, 'Drowning: Sister Questioned'. Nothing ever came of it, of course. Nobody seriously considered that it was anything more sinister than an appalling accident. Poor Jill was in a state of shock for days, and no wonder. To see her sister die before her eyes like that, to try and save her but fail, it was enough to send anyone half out of their mind. They all four of them had to grow up very fast that week, to face the stark realities of life and death.

'But it did clear the way for you, didn't it?' Penny murmured, staring at the cool, collected face in the photograph. Looking back on it now, with the wisdom and the cynicism of the intervening years colouring her judgement, it was clear that Jennifer's death brought nothing but good for Jill. No longer was she the underdog, the misunderstood, forever trailing in the shadow of her stunning sister. With Jennifer out of the way, she was the pampered and privileged one, the focus of all her parents' hopes. Oh yes, that was when the change must have started, when the anarchist began to see that the Establishment did have something to offer after all.

Penny tipped the last drop of coffee into her cup and sat with it cradled in her hands, pondering. They had come a long way since then, she and Jill. They had both succeeded in their chosen careers, were both poised to rise to even greater heights. There was no limit to where Jill might fly to.

Another eighteen years could see her knocking on the door of Number Ten. And for herself? The old dream of Hollywood beckoned her, tantalising. Anything was possible in this volatile business. Next year could see her breaking into the movies or reduced to bit-parts in adverts, but she had to admit that it was a whole lot easier to slip down than step up. The books of the theatrical agents were bursting with moderately talented people who were out of work more than they were in.

But politicians can be brought down as well, an evil little voice whispered. It happens all the time. A slightly shady business deal, a whiff of a homosexual relationship, an affair . . . however fraudulent or immoral they might be in their own lives, the British public expected their leaders to adhere to a sterner code. Looking at the self-possessed features of the Member for Standingleigh East, nobody would ever guess that once there had been a question mark over her head.

Why would anyone want to guess? she asked herself. What did it matter? The past was gone, there was no earthly reason why Jill should have a promising career ruined by something that happened when she was hardly more than a child. She thought again of that long summer, the year they all left school. Did it really blaze all August long, or was it just the sunny days she remembered? They certainly spent every available moment at the reservoir, sailing or just hanging about the boats, and the boys . . . Jill, Carol, Andrea and herself. They thought themselves so adult, so superior. They were the clever ones, the intellectuals. Penny crawled inside now to think what dreadful snobs they were. Proles, they called less fortunate mortals. Plebs. Even Jill, who prefaced many of her more outrageous statements with 'Come the revolution'. Come the revolution, all private property would be abolished. Come the revolution, there would be all-night parties every day of the week.

Penny sat with her chin in her hand, looking back over the years. Thank God they weren't to know what lay ahead, those fresh, arrogant, innocent girls. Jill, Carol, Andrea and herself. She knew what had happened to Jill, but what of the others? Where were Carol and Andrea now? Once they had been so close, closer than sisters, and now she did not even know where they lived. Perhaps she would not even recognise them if she passed them in the street. On impulse, she went into the bedroom and pulled a cardboard box out from the cupboards on top of the mirror-fronted wardrobes. Must change those, she thought in passing, as she did every time she looked at them. Gerry, the exhibitionist, had liked to make love with the lights on, and watch himself. He loved himself most of all. But the pain was only fleeting this time. Penny was intent on the distant past.

She heaved the bulging box onto the floor and knelt beside it on the white shag carpet. There it was, all her personal history, bundled away for her old age, or for a generation yet to be born who would see her only as a decrepit, tiresome has-been. At least they would discover that she had been something. She lifted off the layers of playbills and pages from the *Radio* and *TV Times*, publicity photographs and snapshots with names and places written on the back, invitations and programmes, menu cards with dates scribbled on the corners, a fading spray of pressed flowers, a tattered silver horseshoe, letters, stacks of greeting cards . . . and there, almost at the bottom, was the photograph she sought.

Penny sat back on her heels, gazing at it. She had kept this particular snap because it was the only one from that distant summer with all four of them on it. Carol's boyfriend had taken it, the one they called Satisfaction Smith, because of his fabled sexual powers. Absently she sang the song to herself – 'I can't get no satisfaction.' But her thoughts were all with the four ingenuous faces. Oh, they tried so hard to put on a show, to look sophisticated. Carol, her fair hair bleached almost blonde in the sun, pouted at the camera with what she liked to think was her smouldering Julie Christie look. The full pale-lipsticked lips were all right, but the effect was spoilt by the fact that her eyeliner was smudged from swimming. Andrea had on her prim face. Neat, dark and contained, she sat with her legs tucked properly to one side and her hands clasped in her lap, as if trying to pretend that she was wearing rather more clothes. But, Penny noticed with a smile, she had stuck out her chest, making the most of her underdeveloped breasts. And there was Jill, caught in the act of tossing back her mane of hair from her face. It was Jill who had organised the photograph, who had dragooned Satisfaction into taking it and lent him her expensive camera for the purpose. And finally there was Penny herself, striking a histrionic pose and giggling as she did so. A moment later, she remembered, she had toppled over and fallen onto Carol and Andrea, sending them all sprawling down the grassy bank of the reservoir, screaming and laughing while Satisfaction yelled at them for being silly cows.

'David Bailey doesn't have this trouble. His models do as he tells them.'

They laughed a lot that summer, laughed and cried and sang – all those songs. Every one of them seemed to have a deep significance, to have been written especially for them. And then in a few horrifying moments, Jennifer died, and the carefree time died with her.

'I wonder if you remember that summer?' Penny asked of the smooth, fresh faces.

CHAPTER TWO

A Sunday calm hung over Hilltop House. From her oak-fitted kitchen, Andrea could hear only the blurred jangle of her small daughter Sally playing story tapes in her bedroom. The two boys had been delivered at St James', looking unnaturally scrubbed and shiny, for church parade, and her husband Robert was in the lounge with a pot of Earl Grey and the Sunday papers. Sooner or later he would wander in with some nugget of information from the business section, which Andrea would take an interest in, since it was of importance to him. She liked to feel included in his world. For now, though, nobody was making demands on her, so she worked quickly and methodically at preparing the lunch so that it could get on with cooking itself once their guests arrived.

Andrea had mixed feelings about the Hastings. She supposed that Camilla was her closest friend, yet she always made Andrea feel vaguely uncomfortable. Sometimes more than vaguely. It was Camilla, who believed in speaking her mind and looking truth in the face, who had suggested last year that Robert might be having an affair.

'An affair?' Andrea echoed, incredulous. 'Robert? Oh no, it's not that, I'm sure it's not, he isn't the type. Robert's devoted to us all, he would never do a thing like that.'

'Why not?' Camilla asked. 'Other men do.'

'Robert loves me,' Andrea stated, with quiet conviction. Then added, 'He bought me flowers only last week. A beautiful bunch of roses. Roses, at this time of year! Not many men do that after nearly fifteen years of marriage.'

'Not unless they're feeling guilty about something,' Camilla said.

Andrea refused to believe her. Robert was the bedrock of her life, her security, her reason for living. It was unthinkable that he should be unfaithful. Camilla was just envious of her happy marriage. She and Martin were going through a sticky patch. And of course Andrea had been quite right. Robert explained himself later, saying that the long knives had been out at work, that there had even been a danger of his being made redundant at one point, and he had not wanted to worry her about it. It was all right now, though. Two of his contemporaries had gone, and one of the directors, but Robert had managed to keep his head down and survive the shake-up. Andrea held him close, saying that of course she understood, but he should have told her about it. She wanted to share his troubles. That night he had been his old self in bed again, and soon afterwards they got away for a weekend by themselves that had been almost as good as a second honeymoon.

Quietly, Andrea walked across the spacious hall to peep in at the large through lounge. There was Robert, sprawled in his favourite armchair by the patio doors, engrossed in the papers. His thinning hair caught her heart with a stab of tenderness. Darling Robert, he was nearly bald on top now, but she liked it that way. The fifteen years' difference between them made her feel secure. She could not have coped with a dashing husband like Martin Hastings.

Sensing her presence, Robert looked up, smiled.

'Finished? Like a flick through the comic?' He offered the colour supplement.

'No, I'm hardly halfway. I'll have a look at it later.' She did not like to say she had only come to make sure he was still there. It would have sounded so silly. She went back to the kitchen.

Andrea liked traditional Sunday lunches. Roast

leg of lamb with tarragon went into the oven, with a chocolate cake for teatime. Raspberry mousse and hazelnut cheesecake stood ready on the worktop. Andrea busied herself with the vegetables and the watercress soup. Camilla was a slapdash cook, too occupied with her growing practice as a physiotherapist to lavish the same amount of time and thought on a meal that Andrea liked to. The Hastings would not sit down to a lunch like this at home. Perhaps it would deter Camilla from pursuing her latest campaign, that of getting Andrea out of the house. With Sally now at school, Andrea had very scant defence against Camilla's insistence that she should find a job, take up an interest, do voluntary work.

'You're free now, you can start doing something interesting with your life,' Camilla insisted.

'My life is interesting,' Andrea maintained. 'I like being at home. Besides, what would I do? It's all right for you, you can go back to your old job, do as much or as little as you like, fit it in with the family. What would I do? I don't want to go back to being somebody's secretary again, not full-time, and you don't get responsible jobs like that part-time.'

'There are dozens of things you could do,' Camilla told her.

Chopping up the carrots, Andrea reflected that if it had not been for Jill, she too would have had a job she could take up again. She had been all set to train as a teacher until Jill persuaded her that she should aim higher, go to university. But then, if she had done that, she would not have met Robert, so really she had a lot to thank Jill for. Not that Jill had foreseen that, of course, when trying to direct the course of her life. She had loftier paths in mind. Come to think of it, Camilla was a bit like Jill. Funny how she always seemed to find bossy friends.

She brought the potatoes up to the boil, drained

and shook them, stirred the onion sauce, checked the joint. Ten past eleven. Time for a brief sit-down with Robert and the papers before picking up the boys, then changing ready for the Hastings' arrival. She went once more into the lounge, pleased as always by its generous proportions. The front, Tudor-style windows looked out on the gravelled semi-circular driveway to the quiet road, the patio doors at the back gave onto the large garden, Andrea's creation. Decorated in subdued conservative taste, the lounge was exactly what Andrea wanted it to be, a comfortable, peaceful background to her family life.

Taking the colour supplement, Andrea flicked mechanically through the pages, her mind still on the problem of work. She supposed she ought to do something. Practically all women seemed to now. She had postponed the question when the boys went to school by becoming pregnant again, but she could not take that way out again. Robert had said several times lately how nice it was that the children were growing up a bit and not demanding constant attention. She looked at him as he sat frowning at the business section. Darling Robert. It was wonderful to know that he still wanted her company, needed to have her to himself at times. Another baby would spoil that.

Then the photograph caught her eye.

'Oh!' she said out loud, and peered at it, disbelieving.

'Mm?' Robert's attention was half diverted.

'I've just seen – no, it can't be – but it does look like her, and the name, and the age is right— ' Andrea realised she was burbling, and explained, 'It's one of my old schoolfriends, in the magazine. Jill. You know, I've told you about her. The one who organised us all.'

'Really?' Robert sounded politely interested. His

own acquaintances often popped up in the business columns. 'What is she, an actress?'

'No, that was Penny. Jill's an MP, member for Standingleigh East.'

'Really?' Robert repeated, but this time he put down his own paper and looked at her. 'She's done well. Unmarried, I suppose?'

'Oh no, it shows her here with her husband and children. Look.' She pointed the picture out. Robert gave it a casual glance and nodded.

'I expect she has help in the home, and a nanny for the children,' she commented, following the line of thought she was on before seeing the article. 'You couldn't do something like being an MP and be a full-time mother.'

'Husband must be a pretty tolerant chap, letting her spend half her time up at Westminster. Can't say I'd like that.'

'Wouldn't you?' Andrea seized this lifebelt. 'You wouldn't like it if I went back to work, then?'

Robert looked at her in surprise.

'What would you want to do that for? We don't need the extra money.' And then with a touch of suspicion, 'You're not going in for the Women's Lib bit, are you? Independence and separate identity and all that?'

'Oh no,' Andrea hastened to reassure him. 'I'm quite happy as I am. It's just that with Sally at school now I thought I ought to do something else.'

'Plenty for you to do around here,' Robert pointed out. 'There's all that rough ground at the end of the garden. You said you wanted to bring that under cultivation. Soft fruit, wasn't it?'

'Amongst other things.'

Andrea gazed out over the dripping winter garden. Even now, before the bulbs came up, there was plenty of colour out there. She had spent many a happy evening planning plantings so that there was something to please the eye at every season. Yes, there was always work in the garden, and she could start on the rough ground in the spring. But Jill's fearless face in the magazine mocked her. Spend your life digging gardens? Andrea could almost hear her say in that carrying voice of hers. We've got to change the world! And then another point struck her.

'That's funny,' she remarked. 'Jill was very left-wing when we were at school. She was always talking about revolution and changing the world. Now she's a Tory.'

'Obviously seen the light,' Robert said.

'Yes.' Andrea accepted this simple explanation. After all, they always voted Conservative. So did all their friends. She was more occupied with how Jill managed her present life. She certainly did not spend her time cooking and gardening and ferrying kids around—

'Heavens, the boys!' she cried, jumping up. 'Look at the time, they'll be out by now.'

She hurried through the playroom and into the double garage where her new Metro stood waiting obediently for her. At the church, Anthony and Matthew were waiting impatiently, shivering in their Cub and Scout uniforms.

'Come on, Mum, where did you get to?'

Andrea apologised, hurried them into the car.

'Was it a nice service?'

'Putrid.'

'Rubbish. Mum, why do we have to go to church parade? It's all so stupid.'

'It's part of your duty as a Cub.'

'Boring.'

Andrea recalled the infinite boredom of chapel twice every Sunday, plus Sunday school in the afternoon, and yet she never questioned the fact that she had to go. It was just part of life. Her parents' whole existence centred round the chapel, and to a lesser extent, God. Andrea graduated from being a Sunday school pupil at fourteen to being a teacher of the babies' class, and on Tuesday evenings went to the Young People's Bible Class, until that folded for lack of support. Her contemporaries defected to the church youth club, where they played table tennis and danced, the girls all together, to the latest records. The vicar only turned up for a token prayer before chucking-out time, a fact which was ruthlessly taken advantage of by the irreligious who did a quick bunk before he arrived. Andrea's parents refused to let her go at first, but then realised that it was preferable to the local authority youth club where religion was not even given a passing nod. Andrea was still going there once a week, her big night out, when she went into the sixth form and met up with Jill.

'Don't you let your Nanna and Grandad hear you talking like that,' she warned.

The boys groaned. Nanna and Grandad had put them off church for life. There were snorts of suppressed laughter in the back seat. Looking in her rear-view mirror, Andrea could see her sons mouthing at each other. They were probably giving their wicked imitations of their grandparents. She ignored it, pretending she had not noticed. Robert would have sorted them out.

They rounded the corner into their road.

'You must get changed directly we get in,' Andrea said. 'The Hastings are coming to lunch, remember.'

More groans.

'Oh no, Abigail Hastings.'

'Yuk.'

More imitations, out loud this time.

'Well, you don't have to play with her, she'll go off with Sally. And you like Ben.'

'He's all right, I suppose.'

'Bit of a Pranny.'

Matthew put on his Kenny Everett voice.

'Don't strain your brain, have a spak attack.'

Gales of laughter from the back seat.

Andrea drove into the garage, smiling. The boys were awful, of course, but she couldn't help agreeing with them. Her own children were so much nicer than Camilla's. She wondered briefly what Jill's were like. They looked just about the same age as Anthony and Matthew.

By the time the Hastings pulled up in their BMW, Andrea had laid the table and changed into a fawn dress with a brown velvet floppy bow at the collar. Camilla was wearing a bright pink boiler suit adorned with tabs and zips in unlikely places. She was on top form, bursting with energy.

'We've all been swimming at the leisure centre this morning,' she announced. 'You really must all come with us next week, it will tone you up.'

Andrea was relieved. Perhaps she would drop the back to work bit. As they sipped their drinks, Camilla told them all how unfit they were and Martin sat looking at her with adoration. Their marriage was going through one of its idyllic phases. Andrea felt a flow of self-satisfaction. Not for all the world would she trade her own peaceful relationship for the Hastings' dramatic one. Not for her the unsettling peaks and troughs. She was secure in Robert's steady love.

She was sure of acclaim for the meal, as well. The children turned their noses up at the watercress soup, but she expected that. It was not made to impress them. Camilla did try to persuade them that too much red meat was bad for them when the lamb was brought on, but Martin silenced her after one mouthful.

'Wonderful, Andrea,' he declared. 'Quite orgasmic.'

While Camilla was glaring at her husband, Robert got his word in.

'All this fitness business is fine for some, but personally I like to sit down with the papers. Andrea found an old schoolfriend of hers in the magazine this morning. She nearly jumped out of her seat. I thought she'd been shot.'

Andrea explained once more about Jill. Martin and Camilla looked faintly impressed.

'Clever little lot at your school, weren't you?' Martin remarked. 'Isn't another of your friends an actress?'

'Yes, Penny Fairchild. She's quite often on television. I lost touch with her a long time ago, of course.'

They drifted onto the subject of schooldays, and how many of their old friends they had kept up with. Andrea thought of the four of them. Jill and Penny had gone their separate ways after that last summer, Penny to a small rep theatre on the south coast, and Jill, in a last-minute change of plan, not to the London School of Economics that she had set her heart on, but to staider Reading. Carol she still saw something of for a while, especially after the hurried wedding and the baby. But after that their lives had been so different, Carol submerged in nappies in her two-roomed flat, Andrea working in an office in the City, that they had nothing in common. In the end, the friendship simply petered out. Without Jill to direct them, they had no purpose. The last Andrea heard of Carol was through her parents, who were then still running their newsagents shop. Carol had left the baby with them and gone off to London. Andrea was more shocked at that now that she had children of her own than she had been at the time. She could not understand how any woman could walk out on her baby daughter.

Penny's life was easier to follow. A grapevine of

mutual acquaintances brought the news that she had got the longed-for place at drama school after her year as assistant stage manager. After that, Andrea would occasionally spot the familiar face on the television screen of an evening. It was very odd, seeing someone she had once known so well there on the box. People on television were a race apart, larger than life yet less real. It was almost as if Penny had died and now existed on another plane.

'. . . None of my crowd made it to Westminster, though,' Martin was saying. 'Pete Crawford's on the council, and old Andy Rivers is a big noise with the SDP, but then he always was a nutter. He's mellowed a lot since we were kids, though. Used to preach red revolution in the Sixties.'

'So did Jill,' said Andrea, without thinking.

'All students were left-wing then, weren't they?' Robert said. 'All those sit-ins and protest marches.'

'I wasn't,' Martin said smugly. 'I was a Young Conservative.'

Camilla could see the conversation slipping away from her.

'With all these famous friends, Andrea, don't you feel the urge to get out there and do something yourself?'

There it was again. Get out of the house, be someone, achieve something.

'Not really,' she said, knowing that she was inviting another lecture.

The children were becoming restive. Ben Hastings had left all his vegetables, and Andrea's boys, who were always made to eat theirs, were working up to a major protest. Andrea seized upon her duties as hostess with relief, and started clearing the plates. She knew she could rely on Camilla not offering to help. When she came back with the magnificent choice of desserts, plus ice-cream for Ben Hastings who never liked anything, Camilla was still in full flight.

'Now honestly, Robert, don't you think Andrea's wasting her talents? She could do something worthwhile with her time.' With masterly skill, she used the diversion of the food to her own ends. 'Now just look at that gorgeous spread. You could go into cooking for select dinner parties, Andrea.'

'She does,' said Robert. 'For me.'

Andrea shot him a look of gratitude. Darling Robert, always there to defend her.

Camilla was momentarily stopped.

'That wasn't what I meant,' she said.

Andrea busied herself with serving. When the admiration had died down, Camilla returned to the attack.

'Honestly, Andrea, you could use a skill like this. I know lots of people who would pay a bomb to have you prepare a meal for them for special occasions. Now, don't you agree with me, Robert? Andrea could make a going concern out of it.'

'What for?' Robert asked. 'I don't see the point. It would just mean that she would be out every evening cooking other people's dinners when she could be here cooking ours.'

'Oh God, Robert! I just don't *believe* you at times! Keep the little woman in the kitchen.'

'Sounds like a good idea to me,' Martin put in lazily. 'Keep 'em pregnant and beat 'em once a week. You women are getting above yourselves.'

But he smiled as he said it, waiting for the reaction. Camilla on her soapbox was a splendid sight, her shiny blonde hair swinging, a flush on her strong Nordic features. She gave off enough volts to run a power station.

The argument ran for the rest of the meal, mostly between Camilla and the two men. Andrea, when appealed to by either side, tried to make noncommittal noises. When told by Camilla that she could not possibly sit on the fence over such an issue, she gave the children permission to leave the table and retreated to the kitchen again to make coffee.

Was Camilla right, she wondered, as she stacked the dishwasher. Should she be content with being a housewife and mother when people like Jill were Members of Parliament? She was sure Jill would agree, and Penny too. What about Carol? Jill had her all lined up to go to art school, and she was doing her pre-diploma course when she fell pregnant. Was Carol now out there being Somebody? It struck her that it would be very interesting to find out, if she could but trace them all.

CHAPTER THREE

Carol listened for the sound of the car starting up and gave a sigh of relief. The old cow would be out of the way for a good hour. She looked for a moment at the silver cigarette box on the wall unit, thought better of it and went to get one of her own out of her handbag. It didn't do to push your luck too hard. She made herself a cup of tea in the pine kitchen, drawing calming lungfuls of smoke. That was better.

The kitchen, gleaming from Carol's hands, was a picture of imitation cottage cosiness, from the plastic beamed ceiling to the mock patchwork cushions on the chairs. This morning, Mrs Cleve had regarded it with dissatisfaction.

'I think I'll have to have this refitted,' she said. 'The pine look's really outmoded now, isn't it? Never was really me. I saw a lovely one in that place in the High Street yesterday. Rosewood, with white worktops. Nice, it was. Sophisticated. Yes, I think I'll have to get it done, I'm fed up with all this frilly stuff.'

'Looks all right to me,' Carol commented.

'But you don't have to live with it, do you, Mrs Short? It gets on your nerves all day long.'

Shovelling two spoonfuls of sugar into her tea, Carol made a noise of mingled envy and disgust.

'Bloody hell,' she said out loud. 'You should see what I have to live with all day long, mate.'

Ten years ago, the council started renovating its older properties. Carol had seen the ones that had been done. New kitchens, new bathrooms, double glazing, central heating. The lot. But they had run out of money long before they got to Carol's estate, and went in for selling off the houses instead.

'Rosewood,' she minced, in imitation of her employer. 'Sophisticated.'

She picked up the tea, went into the lounge and plumped down on the gold dralon settee.

'I tell you what's getting on my nerves, mate.' she said. 'And that's you. Always bloody moaning. Got it made, you have. Lovely house, bags of money, old man out all day long, kids at school, me to do the housework. You wouldn't find me moaning at a set-up like this.'

The lounge, with its onyx coffee tables and American Shadows carpet, had not yet been cleaned. Mrs Cleve had left Carol to do it while she went to collect some brochures from the kitchen fitters. Carol put her feet up and pulled an overflowing ashtray over to be within easy reach. That was the first thing she had checked when coming to apply for this job. It was bad enough having to slave in someone else's house without being told not to smoke. People were getting so fussy about it now. Stupid, in Carol's view. You had to have some pleasure in life, didn't you? Her grandfather smoked thirty a day and lived to be eighty-three. All this eating beans and going jogging was rubbish, too. Mind you, if exercise classes kept Mrs Cleve out of the way for a couple of mornings a week, that was all right. Mrs Cleve went to the new Health Studio on the corner where Carol's parents' newsagents had once stood. She leapt around in a pink leotard pretending to be Jane Fonda, then had a jacuzzi or a legwax. It was all changed down there now. Redeveloped.

Carol sighed and looked morosely at her body. She needed redeveloping. She wouldn't dare go near a leotard, pink or otherwise. It was all right for people like Mrs Cleve, they could afford to slim. All that salad and stuff cost money. Her daughter Samantha nagged her at times.

'Why don't you do something about yourself, Mum. You look a right mess. You've really let yourself go. Why don't you go and have your hair cut? It looks awful like that, with all the dark roots growing out. I don't know why you went and bleached it in the first place.'

'I like it blonde,' Carol protested feebly. 'I used to have lovely fair hair, shoulder length, with flick-ups.'

'Christ, Mum, save us the "those were the days" bit, will you? I've given up history.'

Samantha wore her hair an inch long all over, slicked back at the sides and standing up on top. Rail-thin, she wore shapeless dungarees and lace-up ankle boots to school, disguising any hint of femininity. When Carol pointed out that she did not look like every man's dream herself, Samantha glared at her with uncomprehending outrage.

'Christ, Mum, you don't want me to be nothing but a sex object, do you? I've got a mind as well, you know.'

Carol couldn't understand her. What was wrong with being a sex object? She wished she was. She hadn't had a man for nearly a year, and it was killing her. And for all her anti-men attitude, Sam didn't mean what she said. She'd been on the Pill for three years now, since she was fifteen. She had gone along to the doctor's and got herself fixed up, without ever a word to her mother. When Carol found an empty packet in the bin and challenged her, Sam shrugged.

'So what's all the fuss? You don't want me to go and get pregnant like you did, do you? I want a life of my own, thank you.'

Carol supposed she was right. If she had not had Sam when she did, everything would have been different. She would have gone to art school and married some decent feller, not ended up in that crummy house with four kids she didn't understand. Well, Carly was all right. She was a sweetie, but then she was only six. Plenty of time for her to get stroppy like the others.

Turning away from solving the insoluble, Carol picked up a couple of magazines from the heap on the floor. The *Woman's Own* she had read already. She turned to the other one, a supplement from one of the posh Sundays. Mrs Cleve only bought it to impress people. Carol knew she preferred the *News of the World*. She flicked moodily through the pages. They were all full of upmarket adverts. Flash cars, more bloody kitchens, exercise bikes. Carol looked at them with resentment. It was all right if you had money, it was all there for the taking. Nice houses, big cars, holidays abroad. Carol had not had a holiday since before Carly was born. The Cleves went to Florida last summer and the Canaries at Christmas. They were talking about a villa in Spain, as an investment.

'I wouldn't mind a caravan at Clacton,' Carol muttered. Anything, just to get away from this dump of a town.

There was a feature on some American artist. Carol passed over it. She had long ago abandoned any interest in the world of art. Then a thing about politicians. She was about to turn that over as well and throw the magazine down, when she saw the photograph. She stared at it, read the caption, looked again.

'Can't be,' she said.

The brass clock under its glass dome tinkled out the hour. Carol jumped.

'Gawd!' she squeaked. She hadn't realised how long she had been sitting down. The old cow would be back in another half-hour, expecting everything to be done. Leaving the magazine open on the settee, Carol lumbered about emptying ashtrays and straightening cushions. She got the vacuum cleaner out, so that she was doing something obviously useful should Mrs Cleve reappear sooner than expected, and ran it round, picking up odd shoes, newspaper and crisp packets as she did so. By working at double speed, she managed to get the lounge clear. A quick flick with the duster and squirt with the Mr Sheen and it smelt as if every surface had been polished. Carol relaxed, and went back to her usual leisurely pace. She was halfway through the Spanish-style dining-room by the time Mrs Cleve did come in with her arms full of shiny brochures.

Full of her new scheme, and lacking anyone else to impress, Mrs Cleve spread them out on the newly polished table.

'There,' she said, pulling first one then another forward for consideration. 'Lovely, aren't they? Really nice. What I'd call quality. What do you think of this blue and white one, Mrs Short? They call that the Georgian look. Or this, the Manhattan.'

'All that black would make the place look like a funeral parlour if you ask me,' Carol commented, unwisely.

Mrs Cleve gave her a pitying look.

'Your trouble is, you've got no eye for interior design, Mrs Short. You can never beat black for elegance, never.'

'What about the rosewood?' Carol asked.

'I don't know about that. I might change my mind. Make us a coffee, will you, Mrs Short? I must have a ciggy and think about this.'

As Carol filled the kettle, her employer called from the lounge.

'Oh Mrs Short, there's a book here you haven't put away.'

Carol said, 'Right,' and added under her breath, 'Can't you do anything for yourself, you lazy cow?' She plugged in and went to pick up the offending magazine. Once again the photograph caught her attention.

'Mrs Jill Lovesey, Member for Standingleigh East.' She wandered back into the dining-room, still studying it.

'We'll have to buy all new equipment to go with it, of course,' Mrs Cleve told her. 'I mean, you can't have new units with old appliances, can you? And the microwave's past it anyway. I want one of those ones that browns as well.'

'Yes,' said Carol. 'About this magazine. I was wondering if I could take it home.'

'What? Oh, yes, yes, if you like.' Mrs Cleve was busy comparing decorative trims.

'It's just that there's a piece in here about an old friend of mine,' Carol persisted. 'It's quite a long bit, with a picture as well, and I wanted to read it. Look.'

She put the article on top of the Georgian and the Manhattan, pointing at the picture of Jill. Jill's house was bigger and posher than the Cleves'. It was wide, with Tudory windows and lots of bays and gables in brownish brick and tiles. Jill, looking elegant and confident, stood on the gravel driveway with her husband, kids and a couple of horses.

'I was at school with her. Great buddies, we were. Says here that she's an MP.'

'Really? Well I never. I thought you was local, Mrs Short. Always lived round here.' Mrs Cleve, unable to dispute the article itself, searched for ways to disprove Carol's story.

'I have. Well, mostly, anyway. Jill went to college, then I suppose she moved to wherever it is her husband lives.' She paused before playing her trump card. 'We were both at school together, though. Northfield High.' Her employer, Carol knew, had gone to the secondary modern. It was all different now, of course, all the kids went to comprehensives. But back in those days, the eleven plus ruled supreme. Whatever had happened to her since, Carol had started out as a success, a grammar-school girl.

'Really?' Mrs Cleve repeated. 'Very nice. Funny how things turn out, isn't it? That kettle boiling yet?'

Carol took the hint and made two cups. She knew she was pushing it. It wouldn't be wise to needle the old cow too much, since she knew Carol was on the Social and not declaring her extra earnings. But just for once Carol wanted to get one over on her. All those hours of cleaning the Cleves' wealth of possessions, clearing up their children's mess, scouring out their mucky bathrooms and most of all listening to Mrs Cleve rabbiting on about what they were going to buy next had finally stuck in her throat. She sat down and retrieved the magazine from where Mrs Cleve had pushed it aside.

'Of course, Jill was always interested in politics

and that,' she said. 'Her dad was on the council, Mr Somers. You must have heard of him. I think he's an alderman or something now.'

'Oh yes.' Mrs Cleve shuffled the brochures about again. 'This is nice. Fumed oak. Now isn't that classy? Like one of those stately homes.'

'I thought you'd gone off the country look,' Carol remarked. 'Yes, it is funny how things turn out, isn't it? I haven't seen Jill for years and years, not since we were kids, yet we used to be inseparable. There were four of us, me and Jill, and Penny – she's an actress, you often see her on the telly – and Andrea.' Carol paused. What was Andrea? The last Carol had heard of her, she was working in an office in town. She never did have a definite role in the group. Inventing swiftly, she said, 'She's one of these liberated businesswomen, you know, seat on the board and all that sort of thing. Wouldn't suit me, but she was always very efficient. Got every bit of homework done before time, and all lovely and neat, and read all the background books as well as the set ones.'

That was all true. Andrea did work twice as hard as the rest of them, but she rarely got high marks. She lacked Penny's imagination, Jill's sheer intellectual power. Carol, of course, scraped by, but then she was only doing English Lit. as an extra. What she was really interested in was art.

'Yes. Very nice.' Mrs Cleve had switched off. 'I think I might have tile worktops this time. Italian. They are the best, aren't they?'

'Awful to clean,' said Carol. 'All the gunge gets stuck in the grouting.'

Mrs Cleve gave a tight smile.

'Yes, tiles would be nice.'

'We all met up in the sixth form,' Carol elaborated. 'We knew each other before, of course, but we were in different classes. It was when we all started on English Literature A level that we palled up. All that Shakespeare and Milton. Penny was terrific at it. She acted out all the parts. When she did it, I could understand what it was all about. It never looked the same on the page, I couldn't make head nor tail of some of it. But you should have heard her being Cleopatra, it brought it all to life, like they were real people.'

This was true, too. Carol and Andrea, struggling with Shakespearian English, would never have reached the character beneath it if it had not been for Penny. In Carol's sitting-room above the shop, or Jill's spacious bedroom, or even on the banks of the reservoir, Penny would become Antony or Cleopatra, Charmian or even Enobarbus, while the others read the supporting parts.

Carol gave a sigh. Everything was so easy then. All they ever worried about was the next essay, and whether a proper boutique was really going to open in the High Street, and who was going out with whom. Life was one long party. That was why Carol had stayed on to the sixth. She could have left at sixteen and fallen into a job. Work was there for the asking, columns and columns of vacancies every day in the papers. But there was no pressure at home to contribute to the family budget, and Carol rather liked the idea of two more years with all her least favourite subjects cut out. Art came easily to her, she was something of a star. Her paintings and drawings were always represented at the schools exhibition at the local gallery. A couple of years in the sixth doing what she was good at appealed far more to her than catching the commuter train into London each morning. Beyond that she did not think. Careers advice at Northfield High was limited in the extreme. It was Jill who decided that she ought to use her talent, to go to the art department at the local college of technology and then apply for proper art school. The Slade, Jill suggested. She always went for the top. And Carol, seeing the chance of infinitely prolonging the dashing-off of masterpieces in between boyfriends, readily agreed.

'Mrs Short? You with me?'

Carol started. She had let her attention wander so much that she had not even made a pretence of listening to the continuing indecision over the new kitchen.

'What?'

Mrs Cleve was glaring at her. Carol had failed to fulfil her role. She was not patently sick with envy and admiration. Half the pleasure had been taken out of her employer's morning. What was the point of having the builders wrecking the place if there was nobody to gloat over?

'Have you finished in here, Mrs Short? I can still see some dust on the glass.'

Carol shrugged.

'Really? I was so interested in your kitchen I never noticed.' Slowly, she got up and took the coffee cups out.

Jill didn't grub around in other people's houses, she thought as she flicked a duster over the collection of coloured glass animals. Jill didn't grub around in her own house, by the look of her. She had some mug like Carol to do it for her. At least she had style, unlike the Cleves. That house in the picture looked lovely. The Cleves were common, common and vulgar. With money like theirs, Carol could have created something really tasteful. Her own home was far from that, for she had given up long ago. What could you do when there was never enough money to pay the electricity, let alone buy new furniture? And anyway, there were always kids around. When they stopped being sick all over the place they used it as an adventure playground. Paul and Rory were almost over the Star Wars stage now, but they still occasionally used the settee as a vaulting horse. When they weren't doing that they lay around with their feet on the arms, moaning about not having a video. Carol gave the glittery bar a desultory wipe. Jill would have a video, and a television in every room, too, so there would be no rows about what they were going to watch. Come to that, her kids probably went to boarding school, and when they were home there would be all those lessons to go to. Ballet, piano, squash – if you had money, you pay someone to look after your kids almost all the time.

Jill was always the one with the most money. Her old man was rolling in it. They had a colour television when they first came out. Carol thought of that big posh house out on the Heights, and Jill striding through it with her long mane swinging behind her.

'A monument to capitalist oppression! Three families could live in here. Come the revolution, each shall be rehoused according to his wants.'

Or was it 'according to his needs'? Carol never really listened to Jill's political theories. It was being part of her group that mattered. Gradually, the four of them had become the leaders of Northfield High sixth form. The In Crowd. Carol smiled as the song came back to her. 'I'm in with the in crowd, I go where the in crowd goes.' And Carol had been the one with the looks, the one the other girls copied. Those were the days. During school time there was only a limited amount you could do – shorten your skirt, wear a button-down shirt instead of a regulation blouse, heave your books around in a daisy-printed carrier bag. But out of school there was no stopping Carol. The white lips and the black eyeliner, the over-the-knee boots and the op-art dress. For when she came to think about it, Carol realised that she had more to spend on herself then than Jill. Busy with the shop morning, noon and night,

Carol's parents handed out pocket money by the fistful, whereas Jill's believed in making her account for every penny she spent. It was Carol who bought all the latest records for them to dance to, she even bought some especially for Jill, the protest singers, the Bob Dylans and the Pete Seegers, the clear soaring notes of Joan Baez.

Carol sighed. Everything had gone down and down since then. While Jill was now a rich man's wife instead of a rich man's daughter, Carol was cleaning the Cleves' vulgar knick-knacks. And it was all Jill's fault. If it hadn't been for Jennifer's drowning, she would never have gone and got herself pregnant. That had been the beginning of the end. She had let herself be pushed into a quick wedding with John. Satisfaction Smith, indeed! That was just about all he cared about. He only agreed to marry her because his shocked parents leaned on him to Do The Proper Thing. A right disaster that was, from start to messy finish. Carol dragged her mind away. Yes, it was all Jill's fault, and she walked out of it scot-free. It wasn't fair. Some people had all the breaks, while Carol had nothing but unreliable men and uncontrollable kids.

Penny had done all right. Carol had seen her on the television. She probably went out on the town every night with a different man. Actors, producers, that sort of thing. Yes, Jill and Penny had got to where they wanted. What about Andrea? Somehow, Carol could not see her in the role she had mapped out for Mrs Cleve's benefit. Andrea had most likely married some nice Semi-Detached Suburban Mr James and spent her time at coffee mornings. She might even have gone back to God.

'There you are, Mrs Short. Do try to be on time Thursday, won't you? You know it's my day at the salon.'

Carol took the dog-eared notes and stuffed them into her handbag.

'Ta,' she muttered. Her thoughts were still on the past. She went back into the dining-room and picked up the magazine. 'Do you mind if I have this? I didn't have time to read it. About my friend, you know.'

Mrs Cleve hesitated, then shrugged.

'Yes, all right, if you like. It's Sunday's, after all.'

'Thanks,' Carol said, and let herself out. She would have a proper look at that article this evening.

CHAPTER FOUR

Every time she walked in the door, Jill still experienced that lift of excitement. Even now that she was familiar with the House, knew the other members, had made a corner for herself, she had never become blasé about it. She was no longer surprised to see the nation's leaders as real people, passing her in the corridor or drinking in the bar, but she had not lost the feeling of being at the centre of power. This was where the decisions were made that affected the lives of fifty million people, and she was part of it. However tired she was, however fraught with the demands of family and constituency, just to breathe the air of the House was a shot in the arm, as invigorating and just as addictive.

Even her present job, wading through the drifts of correspondence that accumulated each week, was worth the slog. You never knew when something of real interest was going to come up, and she had long ago accepted the fact that to get anywhere you had to cope with the hard work and the tedium if you wanted the fascination and the glory. And Jill wanted it. Winning a backbench seat was just the beginning. She had a long way to go yet.

She put aside the report she was reading and looked at her secretary, just a yard away in the cramped little office that she shared with two other members. They were all jammed into the space that would be given to one secretary in her husband's firm, but this only fuelled Jill's need to succeed. After the next election, she intended being in a position that warranted better working conditions.

'Right then, what's the postman brought, Anna?' she asked.

The younger woman touched each neat pile in turn.

'All these about the parking in the High Street, usual arguments. A lot about the rumours of the closure of Parsons, all against. The nuclear ones, for and against. A petition and a counter-petition about that suspended teacher— '

It was all fairly routine. Jill gave general outlines of answers, knowing that Anna could fill in the details. After that there were the more unusual ones, some of which Jill dictated answers to, others that had to be put in the tray for further research. They went on to the invitations and the requests for appearances, the fetes, the bazaars, the prize-givings. Anna got out the diary and they fitted in as many as possible, starting with the ones relating to the local party.

'Must keep the Faithful happy, especially if their rates are going up next year,' Jill said.

'There's an invitation to speak at a seminar on job creation,' Anna said, handing her the letter, 'but it's on the same day as the Round Table dinner.'

'Damn.'

Jill scanned the letter. It was just the sort of thing she was interested in, just the right platform to spread the word. Every aspiring MP has a specialist interest, and hers was the wide and desperately important one of revitalising the economy. Not for Jill the traditional woman's areas of welfare and education, though naturally she had views on those as well. Jill had views on everything.

'I can't miss the dinner,' she said. 'I'd have to get off my deathbed for that, if necessary.'

She owed so much to Mark. He was unfailing in his support and encouragement, took over a great many of her responsibilities with the children and very rarely protested about her being away so much. The Round Table dinner meant a great deal to him, and she was going to be there with him, come what may. The one thing she wanted to avoid at all costs was his becoming known as Mr Jill Lovesey.

But the seminar was very tempting.

'I know,' she said. 'Write to them and suggest they might like me to speak in the morning rather than the afternoon, and book me a train and cars to and from, and I could still be home in time for a four o'clock hair appointment.'

'Right.' Anna made a note of it. 'That's it, then, except for this personal one.' She handed an unopened envelope to Jill.

The names jumped off the page at her. Carol, Penny and the signature at the bottom, Andrea. The stone keep she had built around herself shook ominously. Mrs Jill Lovesey, MP, wife, mother, ex-town councillor, the scourge of red tape and committees, was once again a resentful, rebellious teenager, living in the inexorable shadow of her wonderful elder sister. She concentrated on the three names, using them to hold off Jennifer's ghost.

It had been her first deliberate gathering of forces, that little gang in the sixth form. She had always been a natural leader, but not until then had she set out to draw people who might be useful about her, people who would enhance her status, who would help in the unending battle against Jennifer's huge superiority.

Carol was the one with the looks. It was the fair hair that first caught Jill's attention, so like Jennifer's, thick and shiny with the fashionable flick-ups. Carol could transform even their drab school uniform into an outfit of some allure. Other girls tried to copy her, but without Carol's flair, Carol's languid prettiness, their attempts just looked silly. Jill could see her clearly, lounging against the washbasins with their sludge of red Lifebuoy soap, adjusting the forbidden mascara on her long eyelashes.

'They've got these fabulous earrings in Daisy's, enormous hoops in transparent plastic. I'm going to buy some to go with my Quant dress.'

Carol was a fount of worldly wisdom. With a whole shopful of magazines at her disposal, she knew everything that was going on in the world of pop and fashion. She was also, even when they first got to know each other in the lower sixth, rumoured to know more about sex than anyone else. Jill was not sure whether to believe that or not when she deliberately sat in the seat next to Carol's for the first English lesson. She was shrewd enough to realise that it might be just that Carol simply looked as if she knew about it and did not bother to deny the whispers. True or false, it certainly added to Carol's stature. Jill set about cultivating her.

It was easy enough. Most of Carol's friends had left after the fifth form and gone to jobs in the City or the smaller local offices. She was flattered by the attention of a girl as clever and positive as Jill and fell in happily with Jill's suggestions of things to do after school. If there was one thing Carol liked, it was being entertained. Left to her own devices at home, she became bored very easily.

Before the month was out, Jill discovered another huge asset in Carol. She was allowed to keep open house.

'Sure,' she would say easily, when a venue was needed for any event from a poetry reading to a protest meeting. 'Come to my place, my Mum won't mind.'

And she didn't. The sitting-room above the shop might be filled with smoke and bodies and the thump of music, and Carol's mum would simply stick her head round the door and smile at them all with bemused goodwill.

'All right, dears?' she would ask. 'That's nice. There's plenty more Coca-Cola downstairs if you want it.'

And they would smile and thank her like the well-brought-up children they were underneath, and omit to tell her that they were drinking cider, or Red Ruby sherry, or vodka and lime. They all adored Carol's mum, and despised her a little for not seeing through them, and abused her hospitality for two whole years.

Jill smiled, remembering the parties, the candles in bottles, the marvellous optimistic songs they danced to, the gritty, gloomy ones they sat in the dark and listened to. While couples entwined in shadowy corners, Jill and the other intense ones would agree passionately that their parents' generation had got it all wrong and that they, the young and clear-sighted, were going to sweep away the old, rotten order and replace it with a new age of equality.

Yet we did not see ourselves as equal, Jill mused. We may have read *Animal Farm* and burned with indignation over the wickedness of the pigs, but we were the biggest pigs of all. We certainly considered ourselves more equal than others, we knew we were the top ten per cent, the ones with the brains. We would change the world, and the plebs would have to go along with us.

Her parents had been shocked and horrified at the change in their other, unconsidered daughter. Her father had literally shaken with anger at seeing the six-foot high poster of Lenin in Jill's bedroom. For once, she had their full attention. With malicious glee, she wielded this new weapon she had found, ploughing doggedly through *Das Kapital* to discover handy pieces of rhetoric to quote at them. But their discomfort was a poor substitute for their love and admiration.

'Why can't you be more like Jennifer?' they demanded.

So Jill turned more and more to her new friends, who thought her brilliant and original, and whose own talents blossomed under her attention.

Penny certainly had talent, and she needed Jill's encouragement to use it. Unlike Jill, she suffered from too much parental pushing. That dreadful little council house, Jill recalled, and that disgusting malingerer of a father. Nowadays it was more difficult to separate the scroungers from the genuinely needy. Even Jill was prepared to admit that many people were unemployed through no fault of their own. But then it was different. Penny's father simply did not want to work. Come the revolution, Jill muttered darkly, each will have to work according to his abilities, and Penny's mother will not have to struggle to support them all on her earnings as a machinist.

But Penny's mother, admirable though she was, could not be allowed to stand in Penny's way. She was not to be permitted to force her daughter into medicine if Penny's whole heart was given to the stage. And besides, having the school's star actress as a friend was as big an advantage as having the trend-setter and sex expert. Jill set about boosting Penny's confidence in her abilities and supporting her in her stand against her mother's well-meaning ambitions for a career as a doctor.

'It's *your* future, you must do what *you* want,' Jill insisted. 'You can't lie down under the tyranny of the old. Look what a mess they've made of the world, what right have they to dictate to us?'

Jill arranged play and poetry readings, and Penny reduced them all to tears of ravishing desolation with portrayals of love lost and betrayed. They larked about on the way back to Carol's from school, performing ham versions of the balcony scene from *Romeo and Juliet* with Penny as Juliet on the footbridge over the main road, revelling in the disapproving glances of staid passers-by.

It was Penny with whom Jill had the most in common of the four, and who came the closest to challenging her position as leader of the group. Penny, under the influence of Red Ruby, invented the game of Flying Home, when they abandoned all pretence of being adult and tried to go the entire way from a party they had gatecrashed, and got bored with, to Jill's house without touching the ground. Shrieking and giggling, they balanced along garden walls, leapt across gaps from gatepost to gatepost, traversed driveways by scrambling over the boots of cars.

'Look at me!' Penny cried, standing on one leg on a rickety fence. 'I'm the fairy on the Christmas tree and I'm going to fly away!'

Springing across a path to the neighbouring roughstone wall she misjudged the distance, lost her footing and nearly fell, saved only by clinging to a convenient holly tree.

'I'm being murdered!' she screamed, fighting her way out of the prickles.

A window banged open, a middle-aged man glared out at them.

'Get off my wall before you damage my dahlias, you young hooligans!'

'Your wall? *Your* wall?' Jill taunted. 'All property is theft!'

Laughing hysterically, they slipped and scrambled on their way, Andrea trailing miserably in the rear, begging them to come down.

'Come on, Andy Pandy,' Jill ordered. 'If you don't join in, we'll all go to your house instead, and then what would your mummy say?'

With a threat like that hanging over her, Andrea had to comply.

Andrea was an irresistible challenge to Jill. Looking at the neat signature at the end of the letter, she saw her again as she had been in that first term in the lower sixth. Unlike the others, Andrea had been in Jill's fifth form class, but Jill had never taken any notice of her. Indeed, she was so self-effacing that very few people took any notice of her. She was the sort of girl whom teachers did not know the name of at the end of a whole year, quiet, obedient, always giving in work on time and yet never distinguishing herself with brilliant marks. She was part of the God squad, trotting along every Friday to Christian Union squashes, which would normally have been quite enough to put Jill off her. But on one particular day, Jill's thoughts were far away from the Milton they were supposed to be reading. A letter had arrived that morning from Jennifer, the first since she had gone up to Cambridge on her scholarship. Her voice trembling with love and pride, Jill's mother read it out aloud over the breakfast table, retailing the details of people Jennifer had met, lectures she had attended, societies she was going to join.

'"Lady Isobel Marchand, but we all call her

Izzy," ' her mother repeated, dwelling on the names since the academic details meant nothing to her. 'The best families still go to Oxbridge, of course.'

'It's who you know that counts, our Jennifer knows that,' her father said with approval.

Jill pushed her plate away, her usually good appetite gone. Jennifer, Jennifer, always Jennifer. If anything, it was worse now that she was away from home. Her parents spent their time wondering what she was doing and imagining the new heights of glory to which she was climbing. Whatever Jill did, however much she achieved, she would never be as clever, as beautiful, as talented as Jennifer.

And then, at school, there was Andrea, less clever, less beautiful, less talented than Jill. An attraction even stronger than those of Carol and Penny. As they walked out of the classroom at the end of the lesson, Jill struck up a conversation and was warmed by Andrea's evident surprise. She did not expect to be spoken to by as dashing a person as Jill Somers. From that day, Jill decided to take her over.

The others were a great help in corrupting Andrea. Carol in particular gave copious advice on dress and make-up and boys, and fixed her up with blind dates. Penny was useful when it came to inventing stories to be fed to Andrea's parents. While the four of them went to the folk club at a disreputable pub, or climbed over the fence of the outdoor swimming pool with a group of boys for a midnight dip, or split into pairs for a hitch-hiking race to Oxford, Andrea's mother and father waited calmly at home, thinking their quiet little daughter was helping friends with their homework, or taking part in a youth club charity knit-in. A fragment of time ran in Jill's mind, like a clip from an old movie. They were squeezed into a telephone box, Carol practically wetting herself trying not to laugh, Jill frantically keeping an agonised Andrea quiet and Penny with a handkerchief over the mouthpiece pretending to be some adult as she spoke to Andrea's mother. What awful deed they were about to perpetrate, and who Penny was supposed to be, Jill could not recall, but she could almost hear the tone of Penny's voice.

Oh yes, she was clever, was Penny, Jill mused. Of her three supports, Penny was the only one who had come anywhere near fulfilling Jill's plans for them. She was not the acclaimed classical actress that Jill had decided upon, she had not become the mainstay of the Royal Shakespeare Company or the National Theatre, but she was doing well enough. Jill always made a point of watching her television parts, and went twice to each of the West End productions she had been in. She had never tried to contact her, though. Penny belonged to the past, along with Carol and Andrea, the past that had died on that stormy summer day with Jennifer.

Jill rubbed a hand over her face, trying to erase the memories – escaping from that dreadful lunch party, sailing alone with black hatred in her heart, cajoling Jennifer into coming out with her – then she shook her head. She gripped the top of the heavy desk. This was reality, this was now. She was a mature woman, with responsibilities. She was a successful woman, and set to rise to great heights. But you will never beat Jennifer, said a small voice in her brain. Jennifer is for ever the might-have-been. Even if you get to Number Ten, Jennifer might have achieved more.

'Are you all right, Mrs Lovesey?' Anna's concerned voice broke into her thoughts.

'Yes— yes—' Jill focused again on the letter, trying to extract the sense from it. 'Quite all right. Don't worry.'

A reunion lunch, Andrea was offering. A chance

to catch up with each other. Recapture those happy days at Northfield High.

Happy! Jill thought. But then she considered it. Yes, she had been happy for much of the time, certainly when she was with the others. It was the total irresponsibility of those times that made them so desirable. They had nobody to consider but themselves, their ambitions, their pleasures. But there was no going back, it was silly and dangerous to try. She took up a pen and swiftly wrote a polite refusal.

CHAPTER FIVE

Andrea was having not second, but third and fourth thoughts about the wisdom of the reunion lunch by the time the day came around. She went about the preparations with her usual neat efficiency. The actual feeding and entertaining side of it did not worry her, for she was used to coping with guests that Robert brought home. Complete strangers generally, important clients and often foreigners, away from home and needing some cosseting to lull them into signing important agreements. But friends she had not seen for nearly half a lifetime? What had started as an interesting project now seemed doomed to disaster. It had been Jill's refusal that put her off. Without Jill, the meeting rather lost its point.

It had been fun tracking the other two down. Penny, as she had expected, was now living in a flat in northwest London. A surprised and warmingly eager letter came back from her, expressing the same curiosity about what had happened to them all that Andrea had felt. Penny was not going to be a problem. She would have plenty to talk about. Andrea looked forward to lots of interesting little anecdotes that could be relayed on to friends at coffee mornings and dinner parties.

Carol she had been amazed to find was still living in Brackstead. Not only was she still in the town, but only two roads away from Penny's old house. Andrea found it odd that she had never run into Carol in the High Street or at the new Sainsbury's where she always seemed to see somebody she knew. All this time, they had been only a few miles apart.

There was the sound of a car on the gravel driveway. Andrea's stomach lurched with nerves. Carol or Penny? She had been so much in awe of them both when they were at school. They were bolder, brighter, more talented, they made her feel dull and inadequate. But, she told herself, Carol was now living on the London Road estate. She drew confidence from her gracious home, and went to answer the door.

It was Penny. Older, slimmer, with startling pink streaks in her hair, but definitely Penny.

'Andrea!' She stepped inside, kissed Andrea's cheek, stood back to look at her. 'You haven't changed a bit, you really haven't. I'd have known you anywhere. How are you? Marvellous idea to get us all together again. I saw that article about Jill as well, and I wondered where you'd all gone to, but it didn't occur to me to try to find out. Thank you,' as Andrea took her jacket, and looking round her, 'Nice place you've got here. Loads of space. Have you been here long?'

'Four years. We bought it new. It's our third house,' Andrea explained, leading the way into the sitting-room.

'It's lovely,' Penny said, accepting a drink. 'The others are coming, I take it?'

'Jill isn't, unfortunately. She's too tied up with work, she says.' She saw Penny's brief look of disappointment, and hurried on, 'But Carol's coming. Just fancy, she's living just round the corner from your old place, in Haslemere Road.'

'Poor Carol. I was glad to get away from that dump, I can tell you.'

There was no trace of the girl in the expertly recycled jumble sale clothes about Penny now. In her red silk shirt, multicoloured handmade sweater, full red suede skirt and navy calf-length boots, she made a vibrant splash of colour in Andrea's quiet room. She might have stepped out of the television set.

'It seems quite odd, seeing you there,' Andrea said. 'I've often seen you in plays and things, and it was you, but not you, if you see what I mean.'

'Ah, who is the real me?' Penny asked with a wry laugh. 'I don't know myself at times. At the moment I'm in the process of becoming a neurotic virgin who'll sell secrets to the Reds, given the right encouragement.' She grinned at Andrea's stupefied expression. 'My new part,' she explained, 'rehearsals start next week. Do you mind if I prowl around? I get twitchy after driving, especially now the car's on the blink. Couldn't get it into second at all. I'll have it fixed once we start rehearsing. Are these your kids?' She picked up a framed studio photograph of the three children and studied it.

'Yes,' all Andrea's love and pride was in her voice, 'that was taken just before Christmas. Anthony's the eldest, then Matthew, then Sally – she's my baby.'

'Nice kids. The younger two look like you.'

'Yes. Anthony takes after his father. He's the clever one.' The good hostess in her stopped before launching into a long description of her offspring. 'What about you? Do you have children?'

'One, Justin, he's thirteen. God knows who he takes after. He looks like me.' She put the photograph down, paced about the room, turned to smile at Andrea. 'I'm so nervous,' she admitted disarmingly, 'isn't it ridiculous? To be afraid of seeing people who used to be your closest friends. I wanted to know what had happened to you all, but driving over here I wondered if it was really such a good idea. I mean – it's like visiting a place where you were once very happy. It never looks the same when you go back under different circumstances.'

She was right, Andrea realised. That was just how she had felt, but she had not known how to express it.

'Perhaps I shouldn't have got us all together again,' she said. It was going to be a disaster. That was what came of having too much time on her hands.

'Oh no, don't say that,' Penny swooped towards her and took her hands. 'I was wrong. About you, anyway. Just look at you! You're just as you should be – lovely house, lovely children, lovely husband too, if you've stuck it out for fifteen years. And you really don't look any different. It's amazing.'

But was that a good thing, Andrea wondered. Surely she should have changed? Jill would have expected it.

'I wonder what Carol's been up to?' Penny mused.

'She was always up to something,' Andrea said.

They smiled at each other, remembering, and for the first time Andrea caught a little of how it used to be, the understanding, the confidences. This was not a bright exotic stranger, but her friend Penny.

The doorbell rang.

'Dead on cue,' said Penny.

Carol was a shock. It was no wonder that Andrea had not seen her about the town. If she had passed her pushing a trolley round Sainsbury's, she would not have recognised her. She pushed her face into a smile of welcome.

'Hello Carol, so good of you to come. Do come in.'

The overweight woman in the grubby fake fur coat stepped inside.

'Nice of you to ask.'

Under the cover of settling her guest, Andrea took in the new Carol. A tight black skirt and limp frilly blouse emerged from under the coat. The makeup was still as skilfully applied, but it needed to be. A recent cut and style could not quite disguise the dark roots of her once fair hair. Ageing tart, was Andrea's instant assessment, and directly afterwards a stab of guilt. What a thing to think of a friend! Making amends, she took Carol's arm.

'Penny's here already, she's dying to see you. Through here.'

She supposed that it was Penny's acting training that came to her aid. She certainly did not appear to move a muscle in surprise. Carol was less circumspect.

'Blimey, Pen, you look fantastic. I thought only kids could get away with hair like that.'

Penny laughed and ran a hand over the carefully-wild locks.

'It's all got to come out soon. I've got to look neat and uptight. They'll probably put me in a pleated skirt and Marks jumper.'

Several of her skirts, Andrea thought, were pleated. And she nearly always bought her jumpers at Marks. Was she uptight? Penny probably thought so. They all used to. She gave Carol the large gin and tonic she asked for. Seeking safe ground, she returned to children.

'Penny was just telling me about her son. Your daughter must be almost grown up now, surely?'

'Sam?' Carol took a long gulp of gin. She sat uncomfortably on the edge of her chair with her large knees pressed together. 'Yeah, nearly eighteen. Doesn't seem possible, does it. Goes her own way now, but then don't they all?'

'We did,' Penny pointed out. 'Or at least, Jill made us.'

'Yeah, Jill. Old bossy boots. You can just see her in Parliament, can't you? Is she coming?'

'No,' Andrea admitted. 'She's too busy. She sends her regards to us all, and asks to be remembered.'

'Who could ever forget?' Carol asked.

There was a brief silence. They all sipped their drinks. Andrea looked at her two guests and her misgivings about the meeting all seemed horribly justified. Without Jill there to hold them together and direct them, they had no common purpose, no meeting ground.

'We're lucky to have you here, if you're starting rehearsals next week,' she said brightly to Penny. 'I suppose you don't get much time off?'

'You're telling me. We do six days' rehearsal, two days in the studio and one day off for each episode. It's killing, especially as we're recording at Pebble Mill this time, so it's up early and drag off to bloody Birmingham every few days. Then there will be some location work, which can be marvellous or hellish, depending on whether the chemistry's right.'

'Where are you going?' Andrea asked.

'Well, it's supposed to be East Germany for some of the scenes, but we won't be setting foot outside this country. Then some of it is on an executive development in Berkshire, some on an industrial estate, and some in London. No swanning about in

Bermuda, you see. But it's not so much where you are that matters, although that does help. I've had an absolutely ghastly time in the Dordogne and a terrific one on the North Yorkshire moors in winter. It all depends what the company's like.'

'But you love doing it? Acting?'

'Yes I do. I love it. It's a drug. I'm really bloody to live with when I'm not working, I suffer withdrawal symptoms.'

'It all sounds very exciting,' Andrea commented. She felt duller than ever. What had she done since they went their separate ways? Produced three children.

'It does from the outside.' Penny was saying. 'But you would not believe the waiting about.'

'You get to meet some tasty men, though?' Carol asked.

Trust Carol, Andrea thought. Maybe she had not changed, underneath.

'Ah well, men.' Penny gave a wry smile. 'I never was the expert in that field, remember, Carol. What I need is our old vetting committee. I don't think I'm a very good judge of character. Maybe if I paraded the next new one in front of you three, I'd stand a better chance. Remember how you all put me off that Rick? I hated you all for a week, but you were absolutely right, he was a nasty little bastard, and I had to admit it in the end. There weren't that many that passed the test, were there? We were very fussy in those days. Jill wasn't at all keen on old Satisfaction Smith, was she? He wasn't intelligent enough to get her approval.'

'Him? Right dead loss, he was,' Carol took another swig of gin. 'We were too young, weren't we? We didn't know what life was about. I gave him the boot soon enough. You can't ruin your whole life over one mistake you made when you were a kid, can you?'

'Too true,' Penny agreed. 'Did you marry again? I don't even know what your name is now.'

'Short,' Carol told her. 'Yeah, he was all right, was Keith. But you know how it is, I got bored. He looked after me OK. You know, nice house, two cars, holidays, all that. Had a couple of kids, boys. He was all right with them, too. But – well – you get fed up with all that security bit, don't you? So I gave him the boot, too.'

Did you get fed up with security, Andrea wondered. She never had. She loved it. She liked to know exactly where she was, and to be certain that it was going to stay that way. That was what was so wonderful about Robert. He felt exactly the same about it.

'So you've got two boys and a girl?' she asked.

'Two girls,' Carol told her. 'There's Carly as well, she's the little one.'

'You married a third time, then?' Andrea asked, trying to keep the disapproval out of her voice.

'No, not that one. I'm not that daft. Stay free, that's what I say.'

Penny laughed. She, Andrea noticed, took it all without a blink.

But then people in the theatrical profession tended to switch partners fairly often, so she would be used to that sort of attitude.

'Do you realise,' Penny remarked, 'that you have had as many husbands and children as Andy and me put together, Carol? That's quite an achievement.'

'Yeah, I suppose so.' Carol began to relax a little. She sat back in her seat, crossed her legs, accepted the refill that Andrea offered.

Andrea listened in silence as Carol, encouraged by Penny, chattered about her various men friends. There was quite a list. An airline pilot, an Arab sheik – 'Or at least he said he was, but who's to know? He was rich enough' – an antique dealer, the owner of a haulage company. All of them seemed to suffer the same fate. Carol got bored with them, packed them in, gave them the boot. Where did she meet them all, Andrea wondered. How did she fit all this romance in with bringing up four children? She waited for a pause in the flow of tales and suggested eating, directing her guests to two of the bathrooms.

It was with the food that Andrea gained her little chance to shine, as usual. The salmon mousse, the gougère with salads and baked potatoes, the fruit compote all met with great appreciation, especially from Penny, who seemed to know something about food.

'It's only a matter of practice, really,' she said modestly, and on Penny's asking, described the amount of entertaining she did.

'That must be really difficult, producing an impressive meal for a bunch of strangers at a few hours' notice,' Penny said. 'I'd hate to have to do that.'

'I did at first, but I know what I'm doing now,' Andrea told her.

'Do you have to do much of the Company Wife bit?' Penny wanted to know.

Carol listened with growing envy. It was a different world, the sort of thing that she only read about, in glossy magazines at the Cleves'. Andrea's whole set-up was enough to make her sick. The lovely house, all expensive and polished-looking as if a kid never even breathed in it, the double garage, the elegant table setting with the matching lace-edged cloth and napkins, the bone china and the antique-look cutlery, Carol wanted them all, and knew they were way beyond her reach. And there was plain, mousy old Andy Pandy, sitting so calmly in the middle of it all. How on earth had she managed to get the man that provided all this, and hang on to him, too? It wasn't fair.

'And you do all the garden as well?' Penny was

saying. 'By yourself? God, I wouldn't know where to start. I don't know a weed from a daffodil. I had to do this scene once where I was waiting in a garden and someone came and gave me some bad news. The director said, "Crush that – whatever – slowly in your hands." Well, I didn't know which one he meant, and I picked this flower and it stung. My hands hurt for a week. Of course, I'd got the wrong one.'

She had known that Penny was successful, but still it was mortifying to see her looking so fantastic when it used to be she, Carol, who set all the trends. She looked at the frills on the cream satin blouse with distaste. She should have bought something new to wear as well, but the trip to the hairdresser's had cleaned her out. She cursed herself silently. After all, she could have ordered something off a catalogue. She started. The other two, she realised, were talking to her.

'. . . Carol? Did you ever take up art again? What are you doing now?'

No way could she admit to cleaning for Mrs Cleve. Not with Penny and Andrea both sitting there looking so bloody pleased with themselves. The chaos at the Cleves' rose briefly before her eyes. The kitchen project had been temporarily shelved. The lounge was being redecorated instead.

'Oh, I'm into interior design,' she lied brightly. 'You should see this place I'm working on now. They want it all Hollywood style, like something out of Dallas. It's not my taste at all, but you've got to give the customers what they want, haven't you? And they're over the moon about it. They keep saying how terrific it's going to look.'

They were impressed, she could see. And what did it matter? They were never going to find out.

'How interesting,' Penny said. 'You go and talk to clients, do you, and find out what they want, then draw up a scheme?'

'Yeah, that's about it,' Carol agreed.

'So you are doing some art work, even though you didn't make it to the Slade? That's great. Do they always know what they want, or do you get a completely free hand sometimes?'

'Sometimes.' Caught now, Carol elaborated recklessly. 'I got a terrific job a while ago, doing up this penthouse flat for this businessman. Lovely place, all glass, you know, with views for miles. I did it all dark and sophisticated. Masculine. He didn't have a clue what he wanted, he just let me get on with it, so I really let myself go, and when it was done he threw this fantastic party to show all his friends. Champagne, caviar, the lot, just to launch his flat.'

Andrea was looking at her with saucer eyes.

'You're all so talented,' she said. 'It must be marvellous to see something you've created come into being. Do you do all the work yourself? All the painting and papering and so on?'

'Oh no, I've a couple of men doing the graft,' Carol told her. She thought of the two working at the Cleves', a gloomy middle-aged bloke and a daft kid on the YOP scheme. Neither of them the least use as talent. 'Sid's in charge. He's a real old-fashioned craftsman. Knows the lot, but not exactly lively company, if you know what I mean. Reliable, though. If you tell Sid to do something, you can leave him to get on with it and know he won't make a mess of it behind your back. Kevin's a wally. We've got him on the Youth Opportunities lark, but I think he'll have to go when his time's up.'

'So you're an employer.' Andrea sounded full of admiration. 'How do you cope with VAT and national insurance and all that sort of thing?'

'It's OK when you know how,' Carol said airily. She almost believed herself now. Andrea's posh house and Penny's glamorous life no longer rankled so badly.

'What interesting lives you all lead,' Andrea said sadly.

Carol sat back in her seat. A warm glow of satisfaction, gin and moselle spread through her, restoring her flagging self-esteem. She had not felt so good for ages.

'Yes, it's certainly been interesting,' she agreed. Two husbands, four kids and an assortment of boyfriends had meant variety, which was more than could be said for Andy's staid old set-up. All right, so she was down at the moment. She would bounce back. Someone would turn up, they always did. She smoothed a lock of hair, feeling its newly blowdried crispness. She had always been the one with the looks.

' . . . only the other day that it needed doing. We do use it quite a lot, and it hasn't been decorated for about five years. I wonder – would you be interested in taking it on?'

Carol's wandering attention jolted back to Andrea.

'What?'

'Our guest bedroom,' Andrea repeated patiently. 'Do you think you could do it for us?'

Panic paralysed her brain. She gaped helplessly at Andrea.

'I— er— ' she faltered. Oh God, what now? 'I – I've got a lot on at the moment,' she improvised. 'I don't know whether I could fit you in.'

'Oh.' Andrea looked disappointed. 'Never mind. I don't mind waiting. Come as soon as you've finished everything else. I'd really like to have you plan it for us, and I'm sure Robert would too. It's very important that his clients feel comfortable when they stay here. You will come as soon as you've done the jobs you're on, won't you?'

She just could not back down in front of the pair of them. Consigning the inevitable moment of truth to some comfortably vague time in the future, Carol magnanimously agreed.

'Yeah, sure. Be a pleasure. Thanks, Andy.'

Penny was leaning forward, her expression full of questions. Any minute now, Carol foresaw with horrible certainty, she was going to ask something that Carol could not answer. She had to stop her, and quickly.

'Pity old Jill couldn't make it,' she remarked, choosing the one subject they could all discuss endlessly. 'It's not the same without her, is it?'

'She must lead a very busy life,' Penny said. 'I think she probably genuinely couldn't fit this in.'

Andrea looked at her in surprise.

'Do you think she might have made that an excuse, then?'

'Well, yes. After all, we know all about her past, don't we? She might not want to be reminded of all that. Look at how she's changed: Conservative MP, husband the big boss-man, kids probably at private schools. She's everything she used to rebel against.'

'Oh. I hadn't thought of it like that.' Andrea sounded doubtful. 'I didn't think she had changed at all, from what you could tell from that article. She's still organising people's lives. That was what she enjoyed doing most, making speeches and deciding what was best for everyone. She's doing that now, surely, but on a larger scale?'

'But she's part of the system,' Penny argued. 'She always hated the system. I don't mean all that "come the revolution" bit. I would have expected her to grow out of that. After all, we don't go in for hanging people from lamp posts in this country, do we? But to join the very party that her parents are in, to support everything they represent, that really does surprise me. I would have thought she'd have become a Labour MP, if she went into parliament, or a trade union leader, or an activist for militant tendency. But definitely not a true blue.'

'That would have been very embarrassing for her husband though, wouldn't it?' Andrea pointed out. 'I mean, he runs an engineering company, doesn't he? I'm sure Robert wouldn't be pleased if I did something like that.'

'I can't see Jill letting her old man get in her way if she wanted to do something,' Carol said. 'She never let anything stop her, did she? I bet old what's-his-name – Mark – has to walk two paces behind her, like Denis Thatcher.'

They all laughed. Andrea's good food and generous wine were working well, but more than that, they had found a common meeting-ground after the polite probing into each other's progress. They felt something of the old closeness, a taste of the intimacy that they had all missed in the intervening years. Elbows on the table, they leaned forward like the eager conspirators they used to be.

'Of course,' Carol said, 'you know why she wouldn't come today?'

'Why?' Andrea asked.

Carol's face took on a knowing look.

'It's obvious. Like Pen said, we know too much about her past. We're the only ones who really know what happened that day at the reservoir.'

'You mean – when Jennifer drowned?' Andrea's voice was hushed.

'Do we?' said Penny.

'Of course,' Carol repeated. 'We're the ones who know the truth.'

They were both staring back at her, Andrea bewildered, Penny guarded.

'Which is?' Penny prompted.

'She hated Jennifer, didn't she? Jennifer was her parents' favourite, Jill never got a look-in. Even at school, she was known as Jennifer's younger sister, the one who didn't get to be head girl. So, that day it was too much – she pushed her.'

'Carol!' Andrea gave a squeal of shock. 'Of course she didn't, she tried to save her, you know she did.'

'Rubbish. That's just what she said. She wouldn't admit to it, would she? But she didn't try to save her at all, she held her under.'

'I don't believe it,' Andrea stated. 'I know she was jealous of Jennifer, but she wouldn't have— have— '

'Murdered her?' Carol supplied, with relish.

'Don't! No, she wouldn't, it's horrible. You don't think she did it, do you, Pen?'

Penny shook her head slowly, considering.

'I don't know. I didn't know at the time, and I still don't now. She could have done, she was quite capable of it. She was – is – a ruthless character, and as Carol says, she did hate Jennifer. But kill her own sister? I don't know. Perhaps not even Jill could do that, when it came to the point.'

'But of course she didn't!' Andrea cried. 'How can you even think it? Jill wouldn't do something as dreadful as that. I know she was very forceful, but to kill someone – it's a horrible idea!'

'No, it isn't,' Carol argued. 'There are several people I've wanted to kill, only I didn't have the guts to do it. Jill did.'

'It's not a question of guts, it's a question of morals,' Andrea said. She was so incensed that she did not stop to realise that she was stepping out of her usual background role. Even in her absence, Jill was stirring them up as she used to do. 'It's wrong to do murder, it's wicked, it's a crime, and Jill would not have done it.'

'Now, if she were here, we could ask her,' Penny said. 'I think you're right, Carol. Maybe she is afraid of meeting us again. I thought it was just because of the way in which she's changed her views, but she'd enjoy arguing about that. She'd have us all voting for her by the end of the afternoon. So it's not that. Even after all this time, she doesn't want to go over the Jennifer business again.'

'Who would?' Andrea asked, shuddering. 'It must be a terrible thing to have to live with.'

'All the same, I did think she might be curious to see what had become of us three,' Penny mused. 'She did change all of our lives, didn't she? None of us would be who we are now if it wasn't for her.'

'Yeah, she's got a lot to answer for,' Carol said, her voice laden with significance.

Penny looked at her in surprise. Despite appearances, Carol seemed to have got herself sorted out pretty well. Even if this decorating business was not quite what she said it was – and Penny had her doubts about it – Carol's personal life sounded as if it was blooming. Maybe she wasn't still married to old Satisfaction Smith, but then who would want to be? She had a variety of rich boyfriends, and Carol always liked that. She certainly never had any trouble in meeting someone suitable. Andrea, too. Penny studied her covertly. Andrea was as happy as a pig in clover with this Robert guy. She envied them. They had each found what they wanted. In comparison, her love life was a string of disasters. But she couldn't blame that on Jill.

'I'm very grateful to her,' she said. 'I would never have made a doctor. Even if I had got into medical school, I would never have stayed the course. Jill gave me the courage to stick out for what I wanted to do. What I'm good at, too. Acting's the only thing I am good at, and without her help I might never have broken loose and made a career of it.'

'I wouldn't have met Robert if she hadn't made me apply for university,' Andrea said. 'I know I didn't get in, but because of that I went to work in the City, and that's where we met. And I might not have had the courage to stand up to my parents about marrying him, either. They didn't altogether approve of him, what with him being older than me and everything. If I hadn't known Jill in the sixth form, I would still have been right under their thumbs.'

'Well, I'm not the least bit grateful to her,' Carol stated. 'If it hadn't been for her, I would never have got pregnant, and that certainly changed my life, and not for the better, neither.'

CHAPTER SIX

They emerged from the police station on that warm summer's evening, four frightened girls, shaken by their first brush with real tragedy. Jill was whisked away by her shocked parents; Penny's mother appeared, ready to engage in battle with anyone from the Chief Constable downwards who might do the slightest hurt to her daughter; Andrea's parents, anxious and suspicious, walked off with their chick between them, questioning poor Andrea far more sharply than the sympathetic police had done. Through some mix-up, Carol's parents had not arrived.

'It's all right,' Carol said. 'They'll be outside, honest.'

She just wanted to get away from the cold tiles and the harsh strip lights, the questions and the uniforms. She was confused and scared. It had all happened so quickly that she no longer knew what she had seen and what she hadn't. She desperately needed some comfort, someone to convince her that everything was going to be fine again. She hesitated in the doorway, expecting to see her mother or father hurrying down the road, but there was nobody there. Instead, kicking the litter about under the sycamore trees, she saw John Satisfaction Smith. He looked up hopefully as she walked down the steps.

'Johnny!' She broke into a run, flung herself into his arms and burst into tears.

'Come on, sweetie, it's OK, don't cry— ' Johnny held her, patting her shaking shoulders ineffectually. He glanced uneasily at the red brick police station. 'Look, let's get away from here, huh? This place gives me the creeps.'

Carol gave a muffled consent, and they set off towards the High Street. It was a depressing place in the glare of the low evening sun, dirty and gritty after the long day, the shops shut and dust and litter stirring in the wind. At the far end, Carol's parents' newsagents would still be open, ready to catch any trickle of passing trade. She found she could not face it, not yet, not another round of shocked faces and questions.

'I don't want to go home,' she croaked, her voice hoarse with sobbing.

'OK, that's all right, we'll go somewhere else.' As confused as they all were in this new and frightening situation, Johnny strove to think of the right gesture, the appropriate word. 'We'll go somewhere quiet, eh? Away from people. What about the park?'

He took Carol's mumbled reply as agreement, and steered her down a side road redolent with memories of happy times. Often they had walked down here together, arms round each other, laughing and talking in in-jokes and innuendoes, neither quite mentioning what they both knew was to come. The park was full of hideaways behind the bushes, and in the summer it was warm and dry and infinitely more inviting than the back of a car or a risky settee. This evening, though, no thought of repeating those hours of pleasure crossed Johnny's mind. It was simply the only place he could think of where they could sit and not be interrupted.

They went in through a side gate, Carol's tears subsiding into the odd hiccuping sob, past the playground where a gang of rowdy fourteen-year-olds were fooling around on the children's swings, past the cricket pavilion behind which the bushes were already full of whispers and the odd giggle, through to the rose garden where couples did not often come. The formal beds and thorny plants did not make for good cover. They sat down on a bench, and Carol pressed against Johnny's whip-thin body, rubbing her head against his shoulder. He was warm and alive, and she needed to feel that life.

'I can't believe it,' she said. 'I can't believe it's happened. It isn't true, not really,'

Accidents happened to other people. You saw it on the television and read about it in the newspapers, you even heard about it occasionally from customers in the shop, but it never touched you. Death only took the old, the infirm, it had nothing to do with the young and beautiful, not with someone you had known and touched and spoken to.

Johnny mumbled some reply, kissing the top of her head. She shivered and nestled even closer, half aware of the thud of his heart beneath her ear, pulling her mind away from the huge fact that she did not want to face. Jennifer was alive and now she was dead. They would never see her again.

'She liked my sunglasses,' she said. 'She asked to try them. She wanted to know where I'd got them so she could buy some, and now she w-won't— '

Now she would never need sunglasses again. They had wrapped up her cold, sodden body and taken it away to the hospital. Carol started to shake, remembering the terrible inert look of the lifeless limbs, the flop of the head with its trails of wet blonde hair. It hadn't happened, it couldn't have happened. But now, away from the panic and people trying to give artificial respiration and the kiss of life, the ambulance men and the police and the questions, now that it was quiet and the light was beginning to fade, she knew that it had happened, that Jennifer, beautiful, brilliant and poised, would never more walk on the banks of the reservoir with the sun making a halo of her hair.

'Don't think about it,' Johnny told her. 'It won't do any good. It won't bring her back.'

'No,' Carol agreed. That was true. Nothing would bring her back. She remembered the brush of Jennifer's fingers as she took the sunglasses, the pearl pink of her nail varnish against the tan of her skin. So alive, talking of the Conservative Club dance next week. 'Daddy wants us both to go with them. He's promised us a new dress each. I shall choose something utterly fabulous and keep it for the May Ball next year. You can't imagine how romantic it is.'

Carol had been flattered by her attention. Even she, the most copied girl in the school, felt slightly inadequate beside Jennifer's charm. And now it was all gone. Vaguely through her distress, she felt Johnny's arms round her, his hand at her waist, caressing, and she clutched at the advice he offered – don't think about it. It was too vast, too terrifying to face now. She turned away from the void and accepted the comfort nearest at hand, pulling his head down to kiss him with fevered intensity. The old magic began to work, smothering her fear with its demands.

She led him, fired by the need to escape from the events of the day, and also by the odd reluctance she sensed in him. She had never known Johnny to hold back before. Baffled and frustrated, she guided his hands, caressed his body, wanting to know that they were both alive.

Across the park, a bell sounded, warning that the

gates were about to be locked. Johnny eased away from her, started to zip up his jeans.

'Got to get you home,' he muttered.

'No!' Carol was horrified. They had hardly started.

'But your parents— ' he protested, 'the police, they'll have rung them, they'll be waiting— '

'Let them' said Carol. She looked at the rose garden with distaste. Another couple, younger than themselves, had come in and were sitting on a bench at the other end. 'Come on, it's no good here, let's go to our place in the bushes.'

And because he did not know what else to do for her, Johnny agreed. Everything was turned on its head today. He, with his reputation to maintain, had never before urged that a girl should go home to her parents. Always it had been the other way round. Not for nothing had he gained his nickname. But right now he felt far from being the famous Satisfaction Smith. The whole situation was too much for him. He hardly knew Jennifer, regarding her as a creature as far removed from his orbit as a star on a distant concert stage. Jill he did not much care for, disliking her all-too-obvious mental superiority and resenting her hold over Carol. But he did care about what the accident had done to Carol.

Big sexy Carol, about whom he did not need to boast. Just being seen with her was evidence of his pulling power. Envious friends asked about her, avid for details, but he dismissed them with lordly disdain. 'You couldn't handle it, kid. Leave it to the men.'

But what to do with her now? It had been bad enough when she was crying. He had tried to console her in the way that his mother used to comfort falls and disappointments, but he had known that it was not enough to support the shock of death. He wanted to rid himself of the emotional burden, hand her over to her parents, but a new, demanding Carol had emerged, one whom he would have delighted in under different circumstances. Following close behind her as they pushed their way through the laurels, he put a hand out to touch the buttocks only just covered by her brief mini skirt, and the strange new sense of responsibility faded. What did another half-hour matter, after all? It was what she wanted, she insisted. And he would take her straight back home afterwards.

There was a layer of dead leaves under the bushes, and in a dry space between them Carol and Johnny had added a heap of hay from when some long grass had been cut in the park. It was the perfect hideaway, used as a den by children during the day and taken over by their big brothers and sisters in the evening. Through the carefree summer, Carol had spent many an hour of pleasure there.

She flung herself on to the hay, smiling provocatively at Johnny as he stood looking down at her. As he still hesitated, she pulled her t-shirt off and tossed it aside, undid her bra and let it slide off, and, still holding his eyes, lay back and raised her arms above her head. No nineteen-year-old could resist an invitation like that, let alone one with the appetite of Satisfaction Smith.

'Oh Carol,' he groaned, dropping to his knees, stretching out beside her. He cupped her firm young breasts and she shivered with pleasure. 'God, but you're beautiful. The most beautiful tits in the world.'

She was acting entirely on instinct, not thinking at all. She just wanted to get as far away from the events of the afternoon as possible, and that meant being part of the life force. She scrabbled at the buttons of his shirt, tugged at his belt, needing the feel of his warm skin against hers, sighed with delight at the weight of his hard young body. Already the nightmare was receding, leaving nothing but the here and now, the two of them enjoying each other. With eagerness still tinged with desperation, Carol used every trick of pleasing that she knew, rushing towards the point when she would forget everything in the plunge into the vortex. She lay panting, waiting as Johnny groped for his jeans, ransacked the pockets.

'Oh no!' His face twisted in anguish, he went through every one again, searching feverishly. 'Oh no, I can't have – oh Jeez, Carol, I haven't got any rubbers with me!'

He thumped the ground with his fist, raging at himself.

'It doesn't matter.' Carol reached across, pulled him down. 'What the hell, we could be dead tomorrow.'

'But Carol— '

'It doesn't matter,' she repeated, and rolled on top of him. 'Come on. Now.' She cried out as he rose to meet her, and at last left the outside world behind as she closed around him.

It was just as they were drifting into satiated sleep that Johnny kissed her gently on the soft skin of her neck.

'I love you.'

She ran a hand lazily down his back.

'I love you, too.'

At that moment, they both meant it.

The glow of it helped her through the rest of the evening as she fielded the shocked exclamations and questions of her parents. But then there was the next day to face, and after the fuss had died down, the slow realisation that nothing was going to be quite the same again. Life went on, yes. Life always does. But the careless fun of it had gone. Jill was subdued and withdrawn. She unaccountably decided not to take up her place at the London School of Economics and chose Reading instead. Their little group ceased to be the centre of social life and though others sometimes invited them to parties, Jill and Andrea refused to go and Penny and Carol found that it was not the same without them. They still met, and talked, and made plans for the future, but the conviction had disappeared along with the sparkle. Carol turned to Johnny for light relief.

As the four of them parted company, Andrea starting her secretarial course, Penny going off to the south coast theatre, Jill departing to Reading, Carol found that the way her relationship with Johnny worked had reversed. Instead of him waiting for when she had a free evening to go out with him, she was left kicking her heels until he happened not to have anything on with his friends. There were boys at the art department of the college, of course, but somehow she didn't fancy any of them. The less she saw of Johnny, the more she wanted to be with him.

And then there was the gnawing worry about the possibility of her being pregnant. Carol was no fool, she had read all the magazine articles about it. One missed period, she knew, could be put down to strain and anxiety. What with Jennifer's death, her friends leaving, and starting art college, that was quite enough to account for the odd behaviour of her insides. But was it enough for it to happen twice? She needed someone to talk to. She just might have confided in her mother, if a suitable moment had ever presented itself, but they never seemed to be alone together for long enough for the right atmosphere to develop. It was no good telling Johnny until she was sure. She knew instinctively that he would just brush her fears aside unless she had actual medical proof. What she needed was her friends, the old intimate evenings when they sat discussing everything from lipsticks to civil rights. They would have sorted something out, she was sure. So she did the next best thing. She wrote a long and rather incoherent letter to Jill.

Back came a reply that was the old Jill to the last full stop.

'Stop dithering about and find out one way or the other,' she commanded. 'You might well be worrying about nothing. You don't have to go to your family doctor, try another one, they can't refuse to see you. Or go up to London.' There were the addresses, Marie Stopes, the Brook Advisory Centre. Jill had found out with her usual efficiency, and what was more, she expected the information to be acted upon. Carol was to see someone at once, and to tell Jill as soon she knew.

'And for God's sake,' she went on, 'if you are pregnant, don't go marrying that twit. He's not good enough for you. Nobody can make you. Go to a mother and baby home if you must, but better still have an abortion. It can be done. It costs, but get him to help you pay. It's his responsibility as well, remember.'

The headmistress tone dropped with the conclusion, and became the voice of a friend.

'Please, please write to me and tell me what the results are, and what you're going to do. I'll come down if you want me to, but please let me know, I shall worry about you,

Love, Jill.'

Carol read the letter through quickly, rejected any idea of doing something constructive about her problem and shoved it under a pile of magazines. Ten minutes later, she fished it out again, studied it closely, thought about it for the rest of the day and halfway through the night. The next day, she phoned one of the numbers Jill had given her.

The result of the pregnancy test was positive. For once, her mother happened to be there when she received the news. Carol, when she could stop crying, blurted out the reason for it, and from then on there was nothing that Jill could do to stop the course of events.

Carol's father blew his top.

'That oversexed little bastard! How dare he lay a finger on my daughter? If I get my hands on him, so help me I'll kill him!'

Her mother tried to reason with him.

'They didn't mean to do it, Geoff, they just got sort of carried away. It's very difficult being a young person nowadays, you know, what with the Bomb and all that. They're all insecure.'

'Insecure! I'll give 'em insecure. They don't know they're born. Good God, Joan, we were the insecure ones. When we were their age there was a war on.'

'But it was that poor girl getting drowned, Geoff. It sort of upset them, like.'

'That's the excuse, is it? Oh, wonderful. Listen, I saw my mates shot to pieces right by my side, but I didn't go round getting nice girls in the family way. No, he's got to be taught a lesson, and right now. He's not getting away with it.'

Nothing Carol or Joan could say would change his mind. He stormed out of the house, leaving his daughter in an agonised state of suspense. She still had not said a word about it to Johnny. What on earth was he going to say when confronted with it?

The Smiths, a quiet couple who had no idea what their son got up to behind their backs, were equally appalled, though they apportioned the blame rather differently. Carol, with her blatantly alluring looks, had never struck them as being a Nice Girl. But on one point, all four parents were in perfect accord: John and Carol must get married.

'Why didn't you tell me?' Johnny asked reproachfully, when at last they were allowed some time alone. 'We could have done something, fixed something up.'

But it was too late now, they were both caught up in the hurry of the hasty wedding and the setting up of a home. They even quite liked the fuss. Carol and her mum went shopping for clothes and household goods, presents began to arrive from relatives. Johnny found that it enhanced his status no end when it became known that he had fathered a child. Carol left the college, since there did not seem much point in carrying on with a course that she was not going to finish. Instead, she got a job in the office of a small clothing factory, which she settled into fairly happily. She did not much like the manager, but the other girls were all right, and anyway it was not for long. The bump was already beginning to show.

They found a flat in the older part of town, near the railway station. It was two rooms and what was described as a kitchenette on the first floor of a Victorian house. The bathroom they had to share with the other occupants, but the rent was only five pounds a week.

'It's a bit dingy,' Carol said doubtfully, wrinkling her nose at the smell of damp.

'Soon see to that,' Johnny told her, and bought two large cans of white emulsion.

He was rather taken with the idea of a place of his own. His parents' house, with its floral prints and polished surfaces, severely cramped his style. His pad was going to be the Latest. It certainly looked a whole lot brighter once he had painted everything white. With the money that their parents gave them, they bought a bed, a chrome and glass dining set and a low sofa cut from a wedge of foam. They imported the wedding presents and their own possessions and the flat began to look like home. They were enchanted with it, playing at keeping house like a couple of kids.

'Be great for parties,' Johnny said. 'We can have some real rave-ups here. All-nighters.'

'Fabulous,' Carol agreed. She felt no twinge of apprehension. Never having had anything to do with a baby, she could not imagine it changing her life that much, and far from feeling ill, the pregnancy made her bloom. She saw a happy continuation of her school life, with friends dropping in at all hours and not even the very light restrictions of her parents imposed upon her. No irritating homework to intrude on the fun, either. Now that the trauma of discovering she was pregnant and telling everyone was over, she was coming to like the idea more and more. After all, she had not taken to the art college, and she did love Johnny and enjoyed being with him. He was a good laugh.

The wedding was fixed for the beginning of December. Carol's parents, ashamed of the hurried affair, insisted that it be a small occasion. Only the closest relatives and a few friends were invited, with a buffet in a rather staid pub afterwards. Carol and Johnny did not mind very much. Neither of them were particularly fond of any of their relations, and they had been allowed to ask their best friends. Carol was looking forward to seeing the gang again. She felt vastly superior. She was going to be a wife and a mother, she had a place of her own.

On the day before, she received a letter from Jill, written from a hospital. With a wrench of foreboding, she scanned it, frowning as she tried to follow the sense of the words. The style was most unlike Jill's, rambling disjointedly from one subject to another. But one theme cropped up again and again, explaining the whole. 'They've put me under the Trick Cyclist. It's ridiculous, there's nothing wrong with me'. The world seemed to shift slightly on its axis. Jill, capable, managing Jill who always knew exactly what everybody should do, in a mental hospital? Carol could not believe it. It was as unthinkable as one of her parents being certified. Things like that did not happen to the props of your life. With relief, she latched on to the last paragraph, where the real Jill showed through again.

'I'm saner than you. What are you doing, marrying that idiot? I told you not to. But if you must, good luck anyway, and keep up the painting. Don't let all that talent go to waste. Promise me.

Love, Jill.'

She must be all right really, Carol comforted herself. Just strain, or something. The result of all that business about Jennifer. Jill would soon be out, organising the world again. But she was desperately disappointed. She had not realised until then just how much she was depending on having the group around her as moral support on her wedding day.

Then in the evening, the second blow fell. Penny phoned from a call box, her voice distant and crackly.

'Carol? Darling, how are you? Look, I'm terribly sorry, I don't know how to tell you this, but I can't make it for tomorrow— '

Carol gave a cry of dismay. Penny as well! They were all deserting her.

'Oh Carol, I *am* sorry. I was all set to come, I even started packing, but the female lead's gone down with flu and I've been given the chance to step in. It's like a fairy tale, Carol, my big break and all that. You do see that I have to do it, don't you?'

'Yes,' Carol agreed sadly. Penny sounded so far away, so full of her own new life. Already they had grown apart. Last summer, Penny would have dropped even an opportunity like this one in order to come to her best friend's wedding. But perhaps they were not best friends any longer. Penny had other friends now, people in the theatre. Tears burned in Carol's eyes.

'Carol? Are you still there? I'll be thinking of you all day, really I will. What are you wearing? Is it going to be the whole long white dress and veil bit?'

'No,' Carol told her, speaking with difficulty through a tight throat. 'No, I've got a short blue dress and jacket, and a hat.'

'A hat? How romantic! With a floppy brim and flowers?'

'Yes, something like that.'

'And are – oh damn!' The pips sounded. 'Look, I've no more change. I hope it all goes wonderfully tomorrow – best of luck for the future and all that – 'bye!'

' 'Bye, Penny,' Carol answered, but the line had already gone dead.

She stood looking at the receiver for a few moments, then slowly put it down. She felt lost. No Jill, no Penny. Andrea would come, but she had never been so close to her. They had left her, just when she needed them most. Two big tears welled up and rolled down her face.

After that, Carol could not regain the feeling of excitement. The whole affair seemed tacky and second-rate. The registry office was cold, the registrar sounded bored, the relations all looked disapproving, either staring pointedly at Carol's stomach or just as pointedly avoiding it, Johnny's friends grinned and muttered smutty remarks to each other, both mothers cried. The short ceremony was not nearly short enough for Carol. For the first time in her pregnancy, she felt queasy.

Outside, people were throwing confetti. The photographs had to be taken very quickly as it had started to rain. The reception was dreadful. The Smiths and the Fosters virtually ignored each other, the speeches were met with chill politeness. The atmosphere spread to the younger ones, who lapsed into uneasy quiet.

Carol nibbled at a dried egg sandwich and an ageing sausage roll, and looked at Johnny. There was a growing expression of horror in his face. The realisation of what he had done was just beginning to dawn on him. He caught Carol's eye and smiled wanly.

'How soon can we get away from here?' he asked.

'Right after we've cut the cake,' Carol said.

Their escape marked the break-up of the occasion. With insincere thanks to Carol's parents, the guests went their separate ways.

In their white-painted nest, the newlyweds got stoned out of their minds on Merrydown cider, so much so that they could not even manage to make love on their legally blessed double bed.

It was fun at first. They were both earning, and though they now had to keep themselves, there was still enough left over to go out and enjoy themselves. And it was wonderful having nobody to answer to. As Johnny had predicted, they held some wild parties and made themselves very unpopular with the neighbours. Carol invited Andrea, but after the first one, she made excuses not to turn up. Some of the girls from the factory came, but mostly it was Johnny's friends. They brought their own drink and turned the record player up full blast. Once, two of them fell down the stairs and they had to call an ambulance. The neighbours complained to the police. Johnny laughed.

The spring came around, and Carol grew bigger and bigger. Her mother bought a carrycot and transporter. Johnny's mother, not to be outdone, knitted a layette and bought two dozen of the best quality nappies. Despite the hard little heels pummelling her under the ribs, Carol still could not quite believe that she was about to produce a real baby. She took up smoking. Now that she had left work, she was bored sitting round in the little flat. She did think about getting out her paints, but somehow it was all too much effort. At the beginning of May, Samantha was born.

'Is that ours?' Johnny gazed at the small pink head with its fluff of fair hair with something near to wonder. 'Isn't it little?'

'You can pick her up if you like,' Carol said. 'She won't bite.'

'Can I?' He sounded doubtful. Greatly daring, he eased his hands round the tiny body. Samantha screwed up her face and hiccupped into an ear-splitting yell. Her father quickly put her down. 'Perhaps not,' he said.

Carol's mum needed no coaxing.

'Come to Nanna, then,' she crooned, cradling her first grandchild. It took more than Samantha's screams to put her off. 'That's right, then, have a good cry, exercise those little lungs. Who looks just like her mummy, then?'

Carol smiled distantly at all her visitors, and thanked them for the cards and the flowers, and watched the nurses as they deftly changed and washed the baby. She spent a lot of time just looking at Samantha, trying to take in the huge fact that she was now a mother. She had made this odd little creature that snuffled and burped and screamed. She knew it was hers, she had stitches to prove it that pulled every time she sat down, but the nurses seemed to be more in charge of it than she was. They handed out the bottles at feeding time, and took the babies away at night to the nursery so that the mothers could get their sleep. It was almost like being back at school again. She did not have to make any decisions, just rest and do her exercises when she was told. The ten days slipped away, and Johnny arrived with a bag of clothes and a car he had borrowed from the garage where he worked. They were going home, a family.

CHAPTER SEVEN

Samantha was a screamer.

'Three-month colic,' the health visitor said. 'She'll grow out of it, dear. Of course, if you had breast-fed her— '

Gritty-eyed and aching in every bone from lack of sleep, Carol snapped that it was too late now to tell her that, and anyway, she didn't want to breast-feed. She wasn't a cow, thank you very much. The health visitor pursed her lips and left.

'Ah, come to Nanna then,' Carol's mum soothed, cuddling the red-faced bundle of fury to her cheek. 'There, that's all she wants, a nice little love with her Nanna. What's all this about you crying all the time, then? Babies are supposed to cry, aren't they? That's right, you have a nice yell.'

But Samantha's Nanna did not have to listen to her having a nice yell for what felt like twenty hours out of the twenty-four.

'You spoil her,' Johnny's mother said. 'Don't keep picking her up. If you pick her up every time she cries, then of course she'll cry. When is her next feed due?'

'I don't know,' Carol admitted. 'I gave her one in the night, and another about seven and another about tennish but she didn't have much of that— '

'No wonder she's crying! You've got no routine. Babies must have a routine. If you feed her every four hours, ten o'clock, two o'clock and six o'clock, then she'll soon get to know when to wake up and when to go to sleep. Now, don't give her anything else till two o'clock this afternoon.'

In desperation, Carol tried it for a couple of days, watching the hands of the clock creep round to the appointed hour while Samantha worked herself up into paroxysms of angry hunger. She was a big, greedy baby and needed plenty of milk to fuel her crying. Carol soon gave up the Routine. At least when she was feeding, Samantha was quiet. The motion of the pram helped a little. Carol tramped up and down the High Street, round and round the park, stopping to doze a while when the baby finally dropped off for a brief sleep. Often she passed the place where Samantha had been conceived. It seemed like another life.

Johnny, after his first flush of pride in being a father, soon became fed up with it all.

'Can't you shut that bloody kid up?' he demanded, as Samantha drowned out the sound from the radio.

'She's your bloody kid as well!' Carol shouted. 'You shut her up. It's all right for you, you're out at work. I'm stuck with her all day and all night.'

'Yeah, that's right, I'm out at work earning enough to keep you and her,' Johnny retorted. 'All you got to do is look after three rooms and a baby, and still there's no tea when I get in. I'm bloody starving.'

'Cut yourself a sandwich, then. What's the matter with you? Can't you even spread some butter?'

'I don't want a sandwich, I want my tea. My mum always – Oh for Chrissakes, Carol, do something about that baby, I can't hear myself think!'

'You can't hear yourself think! What do you think I feel like, then?'

She stormed into the kitchen to warm up yet another bottle. Discarded ones littered the sink, along with the unwashed coffee mugs and the remains of Carol's lunch. A bucket of nappies stood soaking in the corner. She had nothing in the place for tea, she realised. Somehow, she had forgotton to get to the shops. Thinking ahead even as far as the next meal was becoming too much of an effort. Bottle in hand, she went back to scoop up Samantha, and in the ensuing moments of peace, she turned beseeching eyes on Johnny.

'Go up the chippy for us will you, love? I just don't feel up to cooking.'

Once, she could have got anything out of him with that look and that coaxing voice. He would have done murder for her, just for the promise in her eyes. Now he looked at her with distaste. Her hair was unkempt, her face haggard. Her clothes smelt faintly of sick. It was not love, but hunger that drove him to agree.

'OK,' he said, sighing.

Afterwards, he went out to the pub with his friends.

It was a pattern that repeated itself more and more. Unable to stand Samantha's crying and Carol's complaints and short temper, Johnny stayed out. Carol was lonely. None of her friends had babies. Andrea came to see her sometimes, but they had nothing in common any more. Her mother, as usual, was far too busy with the shop to listen properly to her problems and Johnny's mother did nothing but lecture her on baby care. Sometimes she chatted to people in shops or at the launderette, but there was nobody to really talk to.

Money was becoming tight. There was only Johnny's income now, and with him out most evenings pretending to be single and carefree still, it did not go very far. Carol missed the generous flow of pocket money from her parents. No longer could she fritter away pounds on clothes and make-up, nor buy each hit record as it came into the shops. Her mother still doled out the profits of her unending labour, but now it was Samantha who enjoyed the benefits. She was the best dressed baby in town, and endowed with a menagerie of fluffy toys and pretty dolls. Carol leafed through the back numbers of magazines from the shop and sighed. Only a year ago, all the excitement depicted in the glossy pages had been hers for the taking. It was all out there, ready for when she left school and emerged into a world just waiting for her, her looks and her talent. Now it was an unattainable dream. There was nothing to look forward to, just life going on and on in the tiny flat with a screaming baby and a dissatisfied husband. Even sex was no longer the same. It was not that she had gone off it, precisely. She was just too exhausted and dispirited to enjoy it. Her lack of reaction was yet another cause for argument.

'Oh so you're tired, are you?' Johnny asked, heavily sarcastic. 'Amazing. I suppose you've got a headache as well?'

'As a matter of fact, I have,' Carol told him. 'Anyone would have a headache having to listen to that brat of yours screaming all day long.'

'Don't go blaming me for that.' There was real threat in Johnny's voice now. 'You would insist on having it that night. Bit different from now, eh? You were panting for it then. And now look where it's got me. Stuck here with you and her when all my mates are out living it up.'

'*You're* stuck! What about me? You go out to work, you go out in the evenings. You've still got mates. I haven't. I don't see anyone except you, and a fat lot of good you are.'

'What do you mean by that?' He loomed over her, menacing.

Carol glared at him in the half light.

'You're boring,' she said, challenging him to make something of it. And even as he gathered breath to shout back, she realised the truth in what she had said. He was boring. She had heard all his jokes, all his anecdotes, she knew just what he would say to any given situation. The only interests they shared were pop music and going out and enjoying themselves. If she hadn't married him, she would have ditched him months ago. He was all right as a boyfriend for a few brief summer weeks, but not at all right for her as a life partner. The argument dragged miserably on, ending inconclusively with them lying sleepless back to back, not touching. It was to be repeated with monotonous regularity.

The summer passed drearily, a world removed from the last carefree one. Once, Carol walked out as far as the reservoir, and stood gazing at the bright sails of the dinghies, the groups of laughing young people. It was as if she were looking through a sheet of one-way glass. They did not notice her, a down-at-heel woman pushing a pram, they were a different race, brash and confident. They were what she had been, only a year ago. She did not go back again.

She ran into Andrea in the High Street. She looked neat and well groomed in a linen-type skirt and flowery blouse. She was wearing tights, even though the weather was quite hot, and white shoes, and on her arm a matching white handbag. She made Carol feel scruffy.

Andrea glanced into the pram, where Samantha stared stonily back at her.

'Hasn't she grown?' she said, just like Carol's aunts used to. 'Does she still cry a lot?'

'Not so much,' Carol admitted. 'She sleeps a lot better at night, too. How's the job? Still liking it?'

'Oh yes, very much. I'm in the agency department now, they're very nice people.'

There was an uneasy pause. Neither of them wanted to bore the other with the details of their lives.

'Have you heard from the others?' Carol asked. 'I thought Jill might be home for the holidays, but I haven't seen her.'

'She's been sent off to America for the summer,' Andrea told her. She lowered her voice, leaned nearer. 'I think she's still a little – well – not quite right. Her parents probably thought it was better for her to be away from here for a while.'

Carol gaped at her.

'Jill? Still off her nut? I thought – well, it's just not like her, is it?'

Andrea looked faintly disapproving.

'You did know she's been ill?'

'Yes, yes of course. She wrote to me just before the wedding. But I thought it was just strain or something. I thought she'd got over it ages ago.'

'Didn't you write to her?'

Carol hadn't. She hadn't wanted to bring down yet another of Jill's lectures on her head.

'What about Pen?' she asked, to change the subject.

'She's still at the theatre. I wrote to her several times, and gave her your address, but I only got a postcard back. Has she written to you?'

'No,' Carol said. She had still not quite forgiven Penny for not coming to the wedding. So Andrea had not heard from her, either.

'She seems to be having a whale of a time,' Andrea said. 'I suppose she's too busy to keep up with us stay-at-homes.'

'Yes,' Carol sighed. She looked at Samantha, who gave a gummy smile. Sometimes, almost against her wishes, she felt a surge of protective love towards the baby. She looked so sweet, lying there with her big blue eyes and her peaches-and-cream skin, like a real live doll. But Jill was in America, Penny was having fun on the south coast, even Andrea had a job she enjoyed and people to talk to and money for new clothes. The charms of Johnny, the flat and Samantha in her most adorable mood seemed threadbare by comparison.

'How's Johnny?' Andrea asked brightly, as if enquiring after a chronically sick patient.

'He's OK.' Carol could stand it no longer, being

patronised by this girl whom she used to feel so superior to. 'I've got to go. It's nearly time for her feed.'

Once the weather turned, the little flat seemed smaller than ever. Fed up with Carol's complaints of boredom, Johnny bought a second-hand television to keep her company in the evenings. Carol had it on most of the time, schools broadcasts, religious programmes, children's TV, it did not matter. At least it was a human voice talking to her. Samantha could now move around the floor and sit up by herself. The place was continually awash with her toys, but at least she was a great deal happier now that she could get about and amuse herself. Carol made one or two friends nearby with babies of a similar age, with whom she would spend afternoons drinking coffee and talking about husbands and children. But still she felt that she was in a dark tunnel, groping her way towards a dim, uncertain light that was a long, long way away.

Then, after Christmas, it happened. Samantha was teething. It was back to the broken nights and the rows and the noise. In desperation one evening, Carol put the screaming baby into her almost outgrown carrycot and transporter and pushed her round the streets to get her off to sleep. It was a clear, bright night and the pavements were slippery with frost. Carol shivered in her thin coat and hurried along, her heels tap-tapping in the quiet. From out of a lighted window came the sound of the latest Stones hit, and the song went round and round Carol's head as she walked – Goodbye, Ruby Tuesday, Who could hang a name on you – ? The wailing in the pram ceased, but still she marched on, engrossed in her own thoughts. She was Ruby Tuesday, she ought to be free, but they had tied her down and caged her until she had almost forgotten what she was.

Her feet and legs were beginning to ache, her gloveless hands were white on the metal pram handle, but she hardly noticed. She was thinking of how it ought to be, of sharing a place with a group of girls and going out every night and meeting lots of different men. She remembered the thrill of the chase, the heady knowledge that someone she fancied felt the same way, the elaborate game of bluff and counter-bluff. And the evenings of going out with a girlfriend just to see what talent was about, not knowing who you would end up with or where you would go, the prospect of enjoyment, the spice of possible danger, the notion that maybe this was the night, the fateful moment when the one great love of your life might arrive. The freedom.

She found herself in the street where Johnny's favourite pub stood, and paused outside the bright windows of the public bar. A thick fug of smoke and beer drifted out, along with the thud of the jukebox and the babble of voices. Carol stood on tiptoe, stretching above the old-fashioned frosting on the glass to peer in.

She felt no surprise. She had known it all along, really. He was not just drinking with his mates, he was in a small mixed group with his arm hanging loosely round the shoulders of a girl with dark back-combed hair. As she watched, he leaned nearer to say something just to the girl, and they both laughed. Carol clenched her teeth on a turmoil of murderous jealousy. She wanted to jump up and down, to scream with rage, to tear the nasty nest of hair off the girl's head in handfuls.

With vengeance in her heart, she wrenched open the outer door of the pub, and was just about to go into the public bar when she caught sight of herself in a tarnished mirror. The image brought her up short. She looked dreadful. Vanity crushed even the need to confront her cheating husband.

She stared at the distraught, puffy-eyed face. She could not go in there looking like that. The girl, all made-up and wearing the latest dress, would look at her as if she were something the cat had brought in. She, Carol, the trendsetter of Northfield High, would be made to feel like yesterday's news. She turned, bolted out, nearly collided with the pram.

'It's not fair, it's not fair,' she muttered as she marched back up the street, half blinded by tears. That was what hurt the most, not that the girl was with Johnny, but that she was there at all, out having fun while Carol was stuck in night after night with nothing but Samantha and the television. Determination hardened within her. She was not going to be left out any longer. Two could play at that game. But Samantha? She looked at the baby, sleeping so peacefully now, her thumb stuck in her mouth. She couldn't leave Samantha. She was trapped.

Sluggishly, her brain began to work. Given a real problem to solve, she found herself thinking constructively for the first time in months. The answers popped up. Her mother could look after the baby. She was always going on about Samantha being her darling little person, so she would be given the chance to spend some time with her granddaughter. Then she would need money, and she must make herself look presentable. No point in going out looking like she did now. With purpose in her step, Carol made for home.

It was already half-past ten. She nearly gave up the idea, since it was far too late to go anywhere locally. The pubs would be turning out any minute, there were never any dances on a Thursday and the coffee bars weren't that lively mid-week. But again the answer came into her head, daring and enticing: why stay here? Why not go to London?

'London,' she said out loud, scrabbling in

drawers for make-up and clothes, and the name sounded like a charm. London was where it was at. She would go there. Just for a night. She would come back tomorrow.

Moving faster than she had done in an age, she changed, laid on the eyeliner, threw a few essentials into one carrier bag for herself, another for Samantha. She was out of the door again in twenty minutes flat, heading for the High Street.

The parents were in bed.

'Carol!' her father, in his dressing-gown, stared at her in disbelief. 'What the blazes are you doing here at this time of night?'

Carol pushed the pram over the doorstep, held out the bag.

'Sorry Dad, but it's an emergency. I've got to go up to town straight away.'

'But what— ?'

'No time to explain. It's a matter of life and death.' She pressed the bag into his hands, stepped back. 'I'll be back tomorrow. Thanks ever so, 'Bye!'

And she was free. Closing her mind to thoughts of how Samantha might react when she woke up to find she was not at home, Carol headed for the main road. She already had it worked out. The last up train had left, and anyway she only had half a week's housekeeping in her purse. Two pounds seventeen and sixpence wasn't going to go very far, so she would have to use her thumb. She felt a thrill of excitement mixed with fear. She had never hitched by herself before, and certainly not this late at night.

'Always go in pairs,' Jill had stipulated. 'It's asking for trouble otherwise.'

But tonight she could not believe that anything dreadful would happen to her. She had come out of the tunnel. She was young, she was pretty, she was on the loose. The whole world was before her, just waiting with all its wonderful chances. Bounding with energy, swinging her bag, she strode along the streets to the main road, high on the sheer joy of being herself.

She found a good pitch by the side of the road, with plenty of space for drivers to see her, a pull-in for them to stop. The oncoming headlights dazzled her and a chill wind curled round her bare thighs. Bubbles of exhilaration gathered in her stomach, burst in her head. Who would pick her up? A lorry driver? A motorist? What would would he be like? She had met a real mixed bunch on her travels in the past, concerned middle-aged couples who bought her meals, salesmen bored by the road, even a chauffeur taking the family's third best Rolls to the Continent for the summer. She fixed a hopeful smile on her face, stuck out her thumb.

A lorry thundered past, too fast to stop, a couple of cars, then a large van tooted and pulled into the lay-by. Carol couldn't believe her luck. She had never got a lift so quickly before. Picking up her bag, she ran to the van, arriving just as the driver opened the door for her. She had a confused impression in the darkness of a pudgy man in his thirties. There was a flash of a gold on his left hand. He smiled.

'Where to, darling?'

'London.'

The smile broadened.

'Hop in.'

CHAPTER EIGHT

Penny had had her fill of London, and of so-called freedom.

'I'm getting old,' she said to the bathroom mirror, anxiously examining the lines on her face. Laughter lines, they were kindly called these days, not crow's-feet. But the effect was the same. Ageing. It was all part and parcel of the longing for security that had been growing in her recently, particularly since the lunch with the girls. Andrea's set-up, the reliable husband, the gentle round of suburban entertaining, the school run, seemed infinitely desirable compared with the chaos of her life.

With practised care, she applied make-up, moisturiser, foundation, toners and blushers, powder. That was a bit better. At least she felt dressed. She climbed into a jumpsuit and went to look at Justin. He was still asleep, sprawled untidily with his feet and arms sticking out from under the crumpled duvet.

'Juss?'

He stirred and focused blearily on her.

'Come on, love, get up, I've got to go in a minute.'

A grunt, and he turned over.

'Justin, get up, you'll be late for school.'

'Not got to go in till later.'

'What do you mean? Of course you've got to go in.'

He glared at her.

'Haven't. Nothing on till ten.'

Penny was nonplussed. Were they allowed to start later at his age? He was only in the third year, surely he was supposed to be there for registration?

'Are you sure?' she asked.

''Course I'm sure,' he growled, and pulled the duvet over his head, signalling the end of the conversation.

She knew she ought to go in to it more fully. Something was wrong. But she had to be at the studios on time and the traffic was foul at this hour. Briefly, she thought of Andrea, delivering her boys to the school gate each morning. No problems for her, wondering what they were getting up to behind her back.

'Well, mind you do get there by ten,' she said to the lump in the bed.

No reply.

It was a bad start to a bad day. The chemistry was all wrong in the new production, the two leading men were at each other's throats and the air was twanging with petty rivalries. Penny tried to keep her head down and not take sides, but it was almost impossible not to be drawn in. The director was run ragged trying to keep things going smoothly, and took it out on his unfortunate production assistant, who was looking increasingly haggard as the days went on. They were all professionals, and did not let the personal differences affect their performances, but the working atmosphere was dreadful. Penny thought longingly of little series that had never been reviewed and failed to feature in the ratings, but which had been a pleasure to work on, the company mucking in like the proverbial big happy family and living in each other's pockets after work as well as during the day. If only she had someone sympathetic to listen to her in the evenings, it would be a lot more bearable, but as it was there was only the increasingly difficult battle with Justin.

'Pen, darling, these bitches are driving me crazy.' Graham, one of the supporting actors, sat down beside her in the canteen. 'You're the only sane person round here. Isn't Peter just too much? It's all because of Marcia, you know. If she didn't stamp on his poor little ego all the time, we wouldn't have all this trouble.'

Penny sighed. Graham was the biggest bitch of all.

'I couldn't give a monkey's,' she said.

But there was no putting him off. He treated her to his view of the complex situation all through what was meant to be a break. Penny poked at her wilting salad and tried to switch off in her head.

'Sweetie, I just knew you felt the same as me.' Graham gave her a peck on the cheek. 'Look, why don't you and I go out this evening? There's this fantastic little Mexican place I know where you don't see a frigging actor from one week's end to the next.'

Penny put all her considerable projection into one really freezing look.

'Keep it for your boyfriends, sweetie. Your wife happens to be a friend of mine.'

Graham flounced off.

One more little black cloud in the sky, Penny thought. Why was she only ever propositioned by married men these days?

Justin was not in when she got home. Telling herself that he had probably gone round to a friend's and would phone her soon, she rummaged around in the freezer for something to eat. She had just stuck a couple of shepherd's pies in the oven when the telephone warbled. Dead on cue, she thought with disproportionate pleasure. Justin was thoughtful really, he knew she liked to know where he was.

'Mum?'

'Hello, darling.'

'I'm round at Dad's. I thought I'd stay the night.'

Penny's heart twisted in terrible foreboding. It was happening, he was leaving.

'But Juss— ' the cry was torn from her before she could control her voice, act the calm and sensible mother.

There was a muttering at the other end of the

line, then a hurried 'Dad wants to speak to you,' from Justin.

'Penny? Now don't go getting into a state. Justin happened to call in and it seemed the best thing to do. After all, you are going to Birmingham tomorrow, aren't you?'

If there was one thing guaranteed to send Penny into a 'state' it was Mike telling her not to get into one.

'You're exploiting my weak point, Mike. Just because I'm going to be away for one night, there's no need to start stretching the time to the night before. You can't make a case for neglect on those grounds.'

Mike sounded weary.

'I'm not doing anything of the sort. It simply seemed the easiest thing to do, since he's going to be here tomorrow anyway. Be reasonable, Penny.'

Part of her was reasonable, could see the sense of the idea, hated the continual scenes over nothing. But the rest of her had had a stressful day and was frightened of losing her son.

'You won't take Justin away from me this way. If you do this again, I'll make other arrangements for him next time I go to Birmingham.'

She could hear herself being emotional and irrational, knew that short of demanding that Justin came home immediately she could not win, knew also that she was casting herself as the villain of the piece, but she could not help it. She could picture them there in the cramped little house, Mike looking fraught, Justin hunted, the children subdued, and wonderful Wendy soothing them all and putting them together again. She was only binding them closer.

'Penny— '

'All right, all right, keep him this once. But I warn you, you'll not take my son away from me. You try, and I'll move, to the other end of the country if need be, and then you'll only see him for holidays.'

As she knew would happen, Mike agreed with her, saying anything just to stop the threats. It was not Mike who was the problem, it was Justin himself. Mike would not dare make a move to get custody unless Justin persuaded him.

She rang off, shaking, and burst into tears.

The kitchen filled with the smell of a dinner that nobody was going to eat. Penny went into the living-room and turned on the television. The flat felt hollow with emptiness. The phone rang again.

'Is that Penny? It's Carol here.'

For a moment, she could not place the voice. She knew several Carols.

'Carol Foster, as was,' the caller said, with a nervous laugh.

'Oh – Carol!' She felt a great wave of gratitude. Darling Carol, from the happy uncomplicated past. 'How lovely to hear from you. How are you?'

'Fine, fine. And you?'

'Great, thanks.' She didn't want to let on, she was afraid she might weep down the telephone line. 'To what do I owe the pleasure?'

'What? Oh – I just thought I'd call you,' Carol said vaguely. 'It was nice at Andrea's, wasn't it? I mean – seeing each other again?'

She waffled on for a while, remarking on Andrea's family, Jill's absence. Penny's jerking nerves calmed a little. It was so soothing to have an undemanding chat.

Then Carol's voice changed, becoming halting, embarrassed.

'Look – er – there was something I wanted to ask you about. Stupid, really. I mean – well, it was all of you being so successful and all that. The thing is – you know I said I was doing this interior decorating thing?'

'Yes?' Penny recalled having her doubts about it at the time.

'Well – Andrea wants her guest bedroom done up and – well – you see I don't— ' she faltered into silence.

'Your business isn't quite what you told her?' Penny guessed.

'No, not really. Not at all, in fact. I just – well, the thing is, what am I going to do? She's leaning on me to go round and have a look. I don't know what to say.'

'Say?' Penny repeated stupidly. She found it difficult to focus on someone else's problem. 'Well— ' What would she do in the circumstances? Certainly not back down in front of Andrea. No way. 'Say you'll do it,' she decided. 'That's what I always do. If someone offers me a part, I take it, and worry about whether I can manage it afterwards. The hardest ones are always the best in the end, they bring out things in you that you never knew you had.'

'Ye-es,' Carol sounded unsure.

'After all,' Penny told her, warming to her theme, 'you were always the one with the artistic talent. You could do a super job on Andrea's guest bedroom.'

There was a laugh at the other end of the line.

'Yeah, perhaps I could. You've sold it to me. Thanks, Pen, you're a real friend.'

A real friend. Help, advice and a good laugh always available. Those were the days. On impulse, she said,

'Look, Carol, why don't you come up to town for the day? Can you get away? I've a day off Friday, could you make it?'

'Well— ' Penny could almost hear the calculations going on in Carol's head, and knew the difficulties of what she was asking. It was bad enough arranging for one child to be minded, let alone four. Three, rather, as Samantha was old enough to look after herself. 'OK, why not? I mean, great, I'd really like that. Thanks, Pen.'

'Ring me when you know what train you're getting, and I'll meet you at the station.'

When Penny finally put the phone down, the loneliness had receded. She hugged herself, smiling. Carol always got so much out of life. A day with her would make her see things with new eyes. It was something to look forward to after the recording. She made herself a coffee and a sandwich and sat in the living-room with the television burbling unheard in the background, wondering about the sudden end of their friendship. It was not surprising that they should grow apart. The sheer physical distance between them would have seen to that. But why had she cut herself off so completely? Life with the theatre company had been so totally different from everything she had known before that she had needed a safety strap to hold on to, a connection with her former self, and yet she had deliberately turned her back on it, answering Andrea's copious letters with a brief postcard, not going to Carol's wedding, ignoring Jill altogether. That was it, of course. Jill. She was afraid to keep up with any of them in case she got drawn into the mystery surrounding Jill and Jennifer again. If she had to, she would swear black was white to get Jill out of trouble, but she much preferred to leave it all behind her.

That was not the way a friend should behave, she knew. She had long felt guilty about it. She should have answered Andrea, have shared a little of her new life with her, since she so genuinely wanted to know how she was faring. She should never have told that terrible lie to Carol about not being able to go to the wedding. Stepping into a part, indeed!

Wonderful, fairytale things like that did happen sometimes, had even happened to her, but not then. She simply had not felt up to meeting the others again. And Jill. Most of all she should have given some support to Jill, should have written to her if not actually visited her. After all, she had known about the nervous breakdown. Andrea had told her.

Did she do it? she wondered, recalling the conversation at the lunch. Andrea did not think so for a minute, a second. Carol believed she had but condoned it. And she, Penny, did not know. That was why she had broken all contact with Jill, she told herself, because she did not want to know. If Jill had confessed to her, she would not have been able to admire her any more, so she had run away.

It was not as simple as all that. That was far too neat, like a textbook on psychology. But the result, Penny thought ruefully, was that she had been running away from relationships ever since. On impulse, she went to the telephone again. She would phone Jill.

After three false starts, she was becoming annoyed. Andrea, she thought, would have got through by now. All that secretarial experience helped no end in dealing with switchboards and personal assistants. At the fourth try she was connected with an answering machine. A voice – Jill's? – told her that Mrs Lovesey was attending a sitting. For a moment, Penny thought it had said 'sit-in' and a vision of the old, long-haired Jill chanting and waving a banner rose in her mind. Then sense prevailed and she realised that the Member for Standingleigh East was doing her bit. Frustrated, she left a message, asking Jill to contact her. There was still, she told herself, the day with Carol to look forward to.

It more than lived up to her hopes. Away from the constraint of having to behave well in Andrea's polite middle-class home, Carol was her old self, out on the town.

'Oh, I am glad you suggested this,' she declared, drinking in the rush and the crowds. 'I haven't had a day's shopping for ages. Where shall we go? Show me where you get your clothes.'

Always ready to share her delight in fashion, Penny took her to her favourite shops. Carol exclaimed and sighed, pulling garments out and holding them against herself, asking for Penny's opinion, but always looking at the price tag and putting them regretfully back. Penny watched her with sympathy. How well she knew how it felt to be forever window shopping, never buying. She restrained herself from buying two or three things she fancied. It seemed tactless in the face of Carol's lack of funds. She almost suggested that Carol use a Visa card, then realised that she might not have one. Life without plastic money! She looked at Carol, considering a particularly gorgeous wool skirt and shirt in blues and browns with longing in her face.

'Try it on,' she urged. 'I'll try this, it's just the colour I was looking for.'

A transformed Carol gazed at herself in the changing-room mirror.

'It's beautiful,' she sighed.

Penny agreed, suppressing an unworthy twinge of envy. Even with all the weight she had put on, Carol fashionably dressed retained a great deal of what she had possessed in abundance as a girl. It wasn't just prettiness, Penny realised, it was sheer sex appeal, something that men recognised instantly. No wonder there had been all the boyfriends in her life.

With great reluctance, Carol started to change back into her old things, the cheaply-made skirt, the skimpy acrylic jumper. Penny's heart was wrung. Clothes were her comfort and consolation in the bad times, her flags of triumph in the good. Not to be able to buy them was purgatory. And here was Carol evidently without a decent stitch to her name. She hung the outfit over her arm.

'Let me buy it for you,' she begged. 'It's absolutely you, you just must have it.'

Carol flushed, looked embarrassed, mumbled a refusal.

'No, please let me. Remember all those things you used to give me? You were always so generous. I owe you an awful lot of favours, I really do. Besides,' she laughed, turning it into a joke, 'I'm in the money at the moment. Work guaranteed for weeks! If you don't help me spend it on something sensible I might be tempted to pay the rates.'

A little more persuasion, and Carol agreed. She watched, slightly stunned, while Penny signed for an amount that was rather more than twice what Carol paid for food every week, and they emerged from the shop laughing. When they stopped for lunch, Carol disappeared into the loo and put her new clothes on. Penny noticed men's eyes following her as she came back to their table. Carol was glowing with all her old confidence.

'Have you told Andrea that you'll do her room for her?' Penny asked.

'Yes. I must be mad. It's all your fault.'

'Rubbish. You can do it, I know you can.'

'You sound like Jill.'

Penny gave a wry smile.

'God, I hope not. But you have to admit that Jill did try to bring the best out in us, and that can't be bad. Anyway, how far have you got with the planning?'

Carol admitted that she had hardly started. She had looked in some magazines and played about with some colours.

'I'm so out of practice,' she said gloomily.

'We could look at some interior design places this afternoon, then perhaps you'd get some ideas,' Penny suggested. 'Not that you want anything too extreme for Andrea. Strictly middle-of-the-road for her, I would think.'

'Nothing to upset the clients,' Carol agreed.

'No penthouse flat stuff,' Penny laughed. 'Did you make all that up on the spur of the moment? It was very convincing.'

Carol grinned.

'Not bad, was it? Andy swallowed it whole.'

'Draw her up a nice gentle design and she'll not suspect a thing. She might even put some more custom your way.'

By the end of the afternoon, they were both exhausted, but Carol was feeling a lot more confident about pretending to be a designer. Back at Penny's flat, they played around with all the brochures they had picked up, making outrageous suggestions for Andrea's room and trying to get Justin involved. He shrugged it off without interest, bolted his meal and informed Penny that he had been asked round to his friend's for the night.

'Which friend?' Penny asked, immediately suspicious.

'Des. *You* know. He's got this video out and it's got to go back tomorrow. *Children of The Vortex*. Brill. Can I? Thanks, Mum.'

'What about his mother, does she know you're coming?' Penny asked his retreating back.

''Course.'

Knowing she was not going to get much more out of him, Penny phoned Des' mother to check. A woman with a washed-out voice answered. Yes, Des had said something about it and yes, it was all right if Justin stayed. Penny thanked her and put the phone down, relieved. It was all above board, Justin was not lying. Most of all, he was not going to Mike and Wendy's.

After a further wrangle over whether Justin should go by bike or have Penny run him round, which thought seemed to cause him agonies of embarrassment, he finally departed. Carol watched it all with sympathy.

'Drive you round the bend, don't they?' she said. 'Kids?'

Penny sat down and held her head in her hands.

'It's these continual battles that get me down. I don't like checking up on him all the time. I don't like being so suspicious, but I have to. I must know where he is, mustn't I? He's only thirteen, I can't let him roam around without any idea of what he's up to.'

Carol shrugged.

'They go their own way these days, don't they?'

'But he's only thirteen,' Penny repeated. 'He's hardly more than a child.' She looked at Carol. 'How do you cope? You've got four of them, I don't seem to be able to control one.'

'Dunno, really. I used to belt 'em, but they're getting a bit big for that now, the boys. They're always in for their meals, I know that much.'

Penny could not understand how she could be so relaxed about it.

'Don't you worry about them?'

'Yes.' Carol appeared to consider the matter. 'But it's no use mollycoddling them, is it? They've got to learn to look after themselves or else the other boys are going to get them, aren't they? And they've never got into trouble. I mean, there are some right toughs on our estate. Well, you know that. It wasn't choice when you lived there and it's got a lot worse since. You should hear the language! I don't let them talk like that in the house, and I don't stand for cheek. But otherwise, what can you do? You can't keep them in all the time, can you?'

'No, I know. I don't expect Justin to be in all the time. He's got a right to his friends, but— ' She hesitated. It had been so long since she had had anyone to whom she could confide her real worries about Justin, and Carol would understand, really understand, since she was in the same position herself, with an ex-husband in the background somewhere. The need to bring her fears into the open was overwhelming. 'It's Mike,' she admitted, 'his father. I'm so afraid of losing Justin to him. He's got it all going for him – nice steady job, nice reliable wife there at home all day to look after the children, nice cosy family atmosphere. And look at me! Wicked working mother flying around all hours getting on with her career. I don't sound like an ideal parent, do I?'

'You're not the only single mother in the world,' Carol pointed out. 'So he's being difficult. All kids are difficult. Look at us lot. It's not because you're on your own, it's because he's the age he is.'

Penny sighed.

'You could be right, but how can you ever prove it? It stands to reason that it must be better for a boy to live with two parents, whatever the feminists say.'

'But Mike's new wife isn't Justin's mother. If he went to them, he'd still only be with one parent.'

'I know, I know, but she's such a bloody wonderful earth-mother figure. All home-made bread and breast-feeding.'

Carol made a face.

'Yuk.'

Penny caught her eye and found herself smiling.

'Yes, she is completely yuk. I can't bear the woman. She's perfect for Mike, of course, she mothers him along with all the rest. But Justin— '

'Justin's gone out for the night and my little horrors are all being looked after. *And* I'm wearing this gorgeous outfit. So what are we waiting for?' Carol got up, stubbed out her cigarette and headed for the bathroom. 'I'm going to repair my face.'

Penny, all set for a soul-searching session, found that there was no stopping Carol when it came to the pursuit of pleasure. She appeared newly made-up and raring to go.

'Come on,' she told Penny, 'sitting there tearing your heart out won't get you anywhere. It'll all come out in the wash. How about you and me going out and picking up a couple of fellas?'

Penny gave in.

'You're incorrigible, Carol.'

Carol laughed.

'That's me, baby. Let's go for it.'

CHAPTER NINE

The wine bar was full of media people, and hangers-on who wanted to be noticed by media people. It was just the place for Carol, Penny decided, since there was sure to be somebody she knew there whom she could introduce Carol to, and if it was somebody with a name, all the better. Carol needed some glitz injected into her life.

'Great, just great,' Carol breathed, as they plunged into the chattering heat, faces glowing after the chill outside.

She gazed round, briefly taking in the grey, black and silver decor before focusing on the faces. With a squeal, she clutched Penny's arm.

'Look!' she hissed, signalling frantically towards a group by the bar. 'Isn't that the man in the Jaguar ad?'

Penny looked.

'Oh yes, so it is. Married, with five kids.' She distracted Carol's disappointment by pointing out a film producer and a couple of voices from Capital Radio. Then she noticed Graham. Fortunately, he had his back to her. 'God, not him,' she muttered, and steered Carol round a partition. 'You get the drinks,' she said. 'There's someone over there I don't want to meet. I'm working with him at the moment and he's a complete pain. I can do without seeing him in the evenings as well.'

Carol was only too willing to oblige. Married or not, she wanted to take a closer look at the Jaguar man. She went off in the direction of the bar. Penny sat at one of the chrome and lacquer tables, as indifferent to her surroundings as Carol was fascinated. She liked this place when she was in a sociable mood, it was lively and sophisticated and she could depend upon meeting amusing people and hearing all the latest gossip. This evening, though, she was haunted by the problem of Justin. How did Carol manage to be so off-hand? Bringing up four children on her own was a horrendously daunting task. As she had admitted to Carol, she found coping with one beyond her at times. Perhaps, though, the very numbers explained it. With just one, all your energy was concentrated. With four, you had to spread it around. But all the same—

'Excuse me— '

Unwelcome, the voice broke into her thoughts. She looked up coldly at a man a few years younger than herself who smiled back, confident, friendly. He gestured at the spare seat opposite her.

'May I?'

She felt oddly breathless. The worries that only

seconds ago had possessed her mind were wiped out, as if they had never been.

'I— ' her voice came out strangely. She swallowed, tried again. 'I'm waiting for a friend.'

'I know, but she's tied up at the bar at the moment.'

Without further invitation, he sat down. Normally, Penny would have been outraged by such cavalier behaviour. She could not stand men who assumed that you were just waiting for the gift of their company. Now, she stared at him, bewildered by the sense of recognition. She was sure that she did not know him, and yet there was something about him— Another life? She wondered, and even as she mocked herself for thinking anything so corny, the idea appealed immensely.

Unaware of the effect he was having, the newcomer introduced himself.

'Duncan Randall. It's Penny Fairchild, isn't it? I saw you in *Grant's Folly*, you were terrific. All that suppressed emotion. Very powerful.'

'Thanks,' Penny said, surprised. It was over two years since that play folded, and the part had been one of the most challenging ones she had taken. It was warming to know that someone remembered it. The cynical part of her that always stayed aloof during exchanges like these, that told her that this was only a line, was having great difficulty in making itself heard. 'I loved playing Louise, she was such a complex character.'

'You ought to do Ibsen, that would really give you something to get your teeth into.'

Penny forced a laugh.

'That'll be the day.'

How did he manage to put his finger on her dearest ambition? It was unnerving.

'I mean it, I can just see you in *A Doll's House*, or *Ghosts*. *Ghosts* is long overdue for a revival.'

'*Hedda Gabler*?' Penny questioned, unbelieving.

'Why not? Don't undersell yourself. Look, can I get you a drink? I think your friend is going to be quite a while. She's got herself embroiled with Russ Wetherby and his gang.'

'Oh God.' Penny leaned forward and peered round the black and silver partition. There was Carol, perched on a bar stool with drink in hand, surrounded by three admiring men. She was in her element. Penny smiled, recognizing the old Carol in full flow. It was good to see her friend back in action again.

'See what I mean? What will it be?'

She watched him covertly as he went to order, suddenly loath to let him out of her sight. He had the slim, fit look of a man who kept himself in good condition. She liked the easy grace with which he moved. How old was he? Thirty? Less? It didn't matter. He half-turned and she sat back, not wanting him to catch her looking. Duncan Randall. Nice name, pleasing sound to it. Lovely smiling eyes with a crinkle at the corners. Firm mouth. Careful, she warned herself, recognising the old excitement, but it was already too late. When he arrived back with the drinks her stomach tied itself in knots.

They talked for a while about plays and theatres, discovering similar tastes, arguing passionately over the role of the National. Penny bought the next round, not caring now whether Graham saw her or not. Even he could not spoil her evening. She grinned and winked at Carol, who waved her fingers in reply. *Nice work*, the message ran between them, *have fun*! She realised that she had not yet discovered what Duncan did for a living. They had been so busy discussing her world that they had not got on to his. That in itself was virtually unique. Most men, after a cursory enquiry into your career, launched out on an undiluted ego trip, expecting you to listen with admiration to the recital of their triumphs and disasters.

She meant to ask him about it when she sat down again, but somehow they got on to television, and standards of production and direction, and the lack of really good parts for women. Duncan thought the situation had improved over recent years, and quoted examples, many of them roles Penny had really wanted and not got. Penny told him that it was still grossly biased towards men and came up with examples of her own. He seemed to know exactly what he was talking about, to have a fair amount of inside information, but she became so engrossed in the discussion that she did not get round to finding out what his interest in the business was. Acquaintances greeted her occasionally, but she hardly gave them more than a passing wave. Carol she nearly forgot about. The noisy bar was merely a background buzz to the two of them, and what they were saying, and the electric charge that was building between them. He could feel it as well, she could tell, just from the way his eyes dwelt on her. All the while they were talking, they were also communicating on quite a different level.

'But what about this thing you're working on at the moment, what is it? *Traitors*. There are some good female parts in that, surely?'

'Some,' Penny agreed, 'but not enough. Still too many stereotypes.'

'Yours is quite an interesting one.'

'Ye-es. I'm finding her terribly hard going, though.'

'That must be partly the fault of the production. It's not what you might call the happiest of teams, is it?'

With a steel-tipped shaft of premonition, she saw it coming. Something in his tone of voice, some shade of change in his expression gave it away. She nearly cried out with the pain and the disappointment. She might have known, she should have seen it, nothing this good ever happened to her. Holding onto a shadow of hope, she attacked immediately, unable to live with the doubt.

'And which muck-raking tabloid wants to know, might I ask? The *Sun*?'

At least he did not try to laugh it off with a glib joke and a handful of flattery. He even looked ashamed, though to Penny, mistaking it for chagrin at being found out, that was no consolation. There was a tense silence. Duncan ducked his head, made a deprecating gesture.

'The *Mirror*,' he admitted.

Penny felt betrayed and humiliated. She had been completely taken in by this clever charmer. Masking the hurt as best she could, she turned her arctic look on him.

'If you want the full dose of dirt, I suggest you go and talk to Graham Law. He's sitting over that way. I'm sure he'll be delighted to play.'

Duncan reached out to cover her hand with his.

'Look, I know it looks bad— ' he began.

'Too true it does, sweetie,' Penny retorted, snatching her hand away.

'I didn't come over here just to pump you about the production— '

'Really?' Penny gave him a smile of chilling disbelief.

'Really. I've already— '

'Thanks, but I don't think I want to listen to any more.' Penny gathered up her coat and bag, stood up. 'Goodbye.'

'Penny— '

She walked off without looking back. She was good at exits. He was not to know that inside she was aching to turn around, to listen to any explanation he could offer, to believe in the magic she thought she had sensed.

Carol was still holding court.

'I'm off,' Penny told her. 'If you want to crash out at my place, do. Any hour. I don't mind answering the door.'

'Oh— right— ' Carol's glance flickered from Penny's face to where she had been sitting and back again. She slid off her stool. 'Coming to the little girls' room?' she asked.

Penny hugged her briefly, grateful for the proffered sympathetic ear. But she was acutely conscious of Duncan's still being in the bar, and wanted to go while the going was good.

'No thanks, love. See you soon, eh? Don't forget— there's a spare bed if you need it.'

In the taxi home, she wondered if she had done the right thing.

The first person she saw when she arrived at the studios the next morning was Graham. The mere association with the evening before made her insides lurch uncontrollably.

'Oh God,' she said to herself, trying to make a joke of it. 'Morning sickness.'

'Hello, Penny darling. As luscious as ever, I see. How do you do it so early in the day? My wife looks like something the cat brought in until she's had her second gin.'

Penny glared at him. She had no energy for answering him in kind, which she knew was the best defence against him.

'Oh sod off, Graham.'

Graham tutted.

'You were hand in glove with that nice boy from the *Mirror* last night, weren't you? Thought I'd have to throw a bucket of water over the pair of you at one point.'

So he had seen her. Penny struggled to control the irrational temper that settled just below the surface. If she snapped now, she knew she would end up bursting into tears, which would give Graham endless ammunition.

'I told him he'd do better to talk to you. You're the one who knows what everyone's up to.'

'Oh, I'd already had a nice little chat, darling. *I* passed him on to *you*.'

'Well, thanks a bundle, Graham. That was just what I needed on my day off.'

Graham looked hurt.

'I was doing you a favour, darling. You know what they say about publicity. We need something to give this production a kick up the knickers.'

Penny's need to know got the better of her. She had to find out about Duncan, even if it meant asking Graham.

'Who is he, anyway?' she said, in her most off-hand manner. 'Duncan What's-his-name? I've never heard of him before.'

Nothing escaped Graham. He gave a knowing grin.

'Interested, are you? He's the hottest thing on three legs, sweetie. Got the push from LWT and now he's wowing them in Fleet Street. I'm amazed you haven't run into him before. Be careful though, Penny dear. He flits from flower to flower, does our Duncan. Just like a pretty butterfly.'

Penny didn't know whether to be pleased or disappointed when someone called Graham away. She spent the rest of the day, when not performing, hiding in corners hunched over her lines. But the words blurred and faded before her eyes. However much she told herself that Duncan Randall was an underhand little bastard, she could not keep the sound of his voice, the expression of his narrow face out of her head. She just had to see him again.

She had hardly got in the door that evening when the phone rang. With a surge of hope, Penny pounced on it before Justin had got out of his seat in front of the television. But it was only Carol. She was so disappointed she hardly heard what Carol was saying. When she pulled herself together she gathered that it was just a bread-and-butter call. Carol had had a terrific day, and night. Perhaps they could do it again sometime?

'Yes, yes,' Penny agreed absently. 'Any time. Just call me.'

After burbling on a while longer about Andrea and the dreaded guest room, Carol rang off.

Penny tried to apply herself to being a good mother. She asked after Justin's day and got the usual monosyllabic replies, tried to find out what he would like to eat and was told 'anything' and finally gave up and fished around in the freezer for something easy.

'Oh, by the way— ' Justin appeared in the kitchen doorway, holding a long narrow box. 'I forgot. This came.'

Her heart thudding in her throat, Penny took it from him. Through the cellophane window she could see the single red rose, and a card, tantalisingly folded with the message inside. She tore off the ribbon and lifted the lid. The note read simply 'Sorry'.

The phone rang again twenty minutes later, just when she was shoving the beefburgers and oven chips in front of Justin. She forced herself to let it ring three times before picking it up.

'Hallo? Penny?'

His voice sent shivers through her. It took all of her acting ability not to let it show.

'Yes.'

'Duncan Randall.'

'Oh yes?'

There was a slight pause. He was evidently taken in by her cool tone. She almost ruined it all by telling him how wonderful it was simply to hear him again. Her hand shook as she held the receiver.

'I hope my apology has arrived?'

'Yes,' she said again, then allowing herself to unbend a little, 'Thank you. I love roses.'

'Am I forgiven?'

Oh yes, yes she wanted to say.

'That depends,' she told him.

'Look, will you give me a chance to explain? Have dinner with me. Are you free tonight?'

'I'm sorry,' this time she did not have to make up a put-off line. 'I can't, my son's at home this evening.'

Duncan was in the middle of suggesting babysitting agencies when Justin called from the kitchen.

'It's all right, Mum. I asked Des round. He wants to try my new computer tape.'

'Oh. Right.' She broke in on Duncan. 'It's OK, he says he's fixed up. But I can't stay late, I've got to work in the morning.'

She should have held out a little longer, she knew. She had made it far too easy for him. If he had gone to the trouble of sending a rose, he would have tried again even if she had given a definite 'no' this time. But she needed to see him too badly to play the game to its fullest.

Next came the agonising dithering over what to wear. Cool and understated? Cheerful and lively? Glitzy? Sophisticated elegance? The pile of garments on Penny's bed grew with her indecision. The hands on the clock crept round. She took a shower, made up, started hanging everything back in the wardrobes again, and finally plumped for a glorious peacock brocade Crolla jacket over turquoise silk baggies.

'Right,' she said, nodding to her many reflections. 'That's it. Knock him between the eyes.'

But she nearly took it all off again. Only the doorbell stopped her. Justin's friend Des gaped at her as she went to answer the door.

'Bloody 'ell,' he muttered to Justin. 'That your mum?'

Duncan's reaction was far more gratifying.

'Wow.' His expression as he took in the full impact was frankly admiring. 'Perhaps I should have tried for a table at Langan's.'

'You haven't?' Penny was appalled.

'No,' he promised. 'Nowhere so public. Strictly and absolutely off-duty tonight. No beautiful people, no pushy trendies. Do you like Japanese food?'

'Never tried it,' Penny admitted.

'Now's the time to start. I've found one where the waiters do speak English, and treat you like treasured guests.'

It was just as he said. They were the only westerners amongst a clientele of homesick Japanese businessmen. Kneeling at a low table between painted paper screens, they were served with plates of exquisite food arranged like works of art. Penny was floating in pink cloud land. She hardly felt the discomfort of her cramped knees. The flower-shaped morsels were wasted on her. The magic she had sensed yesterday was there again, multiplied a hundredfold.

Duncan was quick to offer explanations.

'I really didn't come over to you to dig around the problems with *Traitors*,' he told her. 'I admit I was working on it, it will be in tomorrow's edition, but I got everything I wanted from Graham Law. Just as you said, he gave me enough copy for a week. But I spoke to him first. He pointed you out to me, but I had no intention of using you to elaborate on what he had been telling me.'

The normal, cynical Penny would have taken this with a large sprinkling of salt. This evening, she swallowed it whole.

'He mentioned he sent you over,' she said. 'I didn't think he'd seen me. I was trying to avoid him.'

'I'm glad he did see you,' Duncan smiled into her eyes. 'He may be the biggest pain south of Watford but he's justified his existence now.'

Dancing inside, Penny agreed.

'It's only by chance I was there. My friend wanted to go out, and it seemed a good place to take her to see people.'

'The fates were conspiring with me,' Duncan joked, but with a serious undertone.

Tonight, Penny could believe it. It was about time they gave her a break. Only a small pessimistic corner of her mind warned that this was too good to be true.

'Who is your friend, anyway?' Duncan was asking. 'She seemed to be getting down to it with Russ and company yesterday.'

Penny felt a surge of irrational jealousy. Why did he want to know? Was it Carol he was really interested in?

'She's an old schoolfriend of mine. We hadn't seen each other for years.'

They drifted on to school and early days, and Penny's fears subsided when she learnt that she had Carol to thank for Duncan's knowing where she lived. He had cornered her in the wine bar and charmed Penny's address out of her. They discovered remarkably similar backgrounds. Duncan also had an ambitious mother, a widow who strove to keep up appearances at all costs and squeezed out her last penny to give her son a good start in life.

'She thought the end of the world had come when they went comprehensive in our area,' Duncan said. 'A raving Tory is my ma. No way was she having her nicely brought-up little lad mixing with the working classes, so do you know what she did? She sold our house, which was a shrine to my father, moved into a flat and sent me to the local private school. It was a rubbish place, of course. The only boys who went there were those without the brains to go to decent public schools, but to my mother's way of thinking, it was the door to a better life.'

Penny knew instantly just what his childhood had been like, for it was a slightly upmarket version of her own.

'My mother would have done that, if necessary.' she said. 'Though thank God it wasn't. She was hard-put as it was with myself, my brother and my father to keep. My father was a hopeless case, she abandoned all ambitions for him soon after I was born, but my brother and I, and me especially, she wanted the earth for us.'

Ducan nodded, recognising the situation.

'She didn't go out scrubbing floors?'

'Not quite as corny as that. She was a machinist, and that was in the days when decent pay for women was a distant dream.'

'And does she lap up every tiniest thing you do, now? Mine has every single word I have ever written pasted into files, even though she would never voluntarily read anything other than *The Times*. "Page Three is the opiate of the masses," I keep telling her. "If the proles keep taking the tabloids they won't have time to revolt." '

Penny laughed, enchanted.

'That takes me back. Another of my schoolfriends was always bashing on about the revolution, and yet she always spoke of proles. She had the greatest contempt for the masses really. We were all the most ghastly elitists. Were you?'

'I was the most conceited little swine that ever existed. My mother worshipped the ground I trod on, and because I was stuck in amongst all these thickos who'd failed their CE I thought I was brilliant. It came as a nasty shock to me when I went to university to find I was very average.'

But he wasn't very average, Penny thought, drinking him in across the low table. The thick, swept-back hair, the intense eyes, the lines running from the nose to the sensuous mouth with its lazy smile were all mouth-wateringly attractive. And behind that self-deprecating charm she could sense a mind like a knife, which frightened her. She would not want him as an enemy.

'I only caught the tail end of the Sixties,' Duncan was saying. 'It must have been a wonderful time.'

'It was,' Penny said, trying not to show how his remark jolted her. He was years younger that her. He must usually go out with girls in their twenties. He was just being kind to her, an ageing divorcee. With difficulty, she carried on, 'You only needed an ounce of talent and a dash of luck to get exactly where you wanted. We were all completely irresponsible. It was glorious.'

'But it takes more than an ounce of talent to stay the course,' Duncan pointed out. 'Plenty of the big names burnt themselves out.'

If he was just being nice to her, it was irresistible. When she looked at herself in the mirror in the loo a face bright with happiness glowed back at her, a girl's face, eager with anticipation. She ran her hands over a body kept trim with fibre and aerobics. Nobody would know that she was nearly thirty-seven. 'Oh God,' she prayed, 'let Justin be asleep.' She ran a comb through her hair, applied more lipstick, practically skipped through the door.

As they hit the cold outside they drew together as naturally as breathing.

'I think I could get to like the Japanese way of life,' Penny said, as she pressed against him.

'I think I could get to like you, if you would only let me.'

Let you! She thought, Oh yes, please.

'Am I so unapproachable?' she asked.

'No, not unapproachable, more – elusive. You're holding a great deal back.'

He was giving her the right line to take on a plate, she knew. Keep him guessing, don't give too much away at once. On top of that, the professional in her wanted enough physical and emotional energy left for another gruelling day at the studios tomorrow. But she could not play the game and hold him off, she was too afraid he might just take it at face value and never appear again. London was full of beautiful, desirable girls ten, fifteen years younger than herself. When they reached his car, it was only the thought of Justin alone in the flat that made her refuse an invitation to his Dockland apartment.

'I might just be able to find a nice mug of cocoa at my place, though,' she offered.

He ran a hand down her silk-covered leg.

'Make that Ovaltine, and you're on.'

As the green Morgan growled its way along the wet streets, even the arctic draughts whipping through the gaps in the hood could not chill the fire inside her. She huddled down in the bucket seat and watched the lights sweeping across his profile, stern as he concentrated on the lunatic late evening traffic. He looked down at her as they stopped at a junction, and his face softened.

'You look frozen. I'm sorry, I should have warned you that this is a sheepskin and fur boots vehicle.'

She was thrilled by his concern. Most men would have just bored on about power and acceleration.

'It's sure got character,' she said.

'It has that,' he agreed, holding her eyes.

Of its own accord, it seemed, her hand slid over his knee. She could have eaten him alive, right there. There was a frantic chorus of horns behind them as the lights changed. Duncan swore under his breath.

As they drew up outside her block, Penny felt anticipation tighten.

Their feet tapped hollow on the polished vinyl floor of the corridor. Faintly from behind the doors they could hear the droning of televisions. Duncan stood close behind her as she fitted the key into the lock, his hands on her shoulders. She could feel his breath on the back of her neck.

The door opened soundlessly, and as it did so, a blood-stopping scream ripped out of the lounge. With a yelp of fear, Penny leapt across the hall and burst through the inner door. White-faced with guilt and shock, Justin's and Des' faces reared up over the back of the sofa, whilst on the television screen there flickered the image of a man with a chainsaw and a manic leer slowly approaching a woman tied naked and spreadeagled on a bed.

'Justin!' Penny stood frozen with horror. It was too appalling to take in, let alone do anything. The boys stared back at her, fear and defiance mixed now in their faces.

Duncan strode across the room, flicked the off-switch and ejected the video.

'Degrading filth,' he spat.

The boys transferred their gaze to him, warily

recognising raw anger. Penny was shaking, her voice near to tears.

'Oh Justin, how could you?' she wailed.

Her son shrugged.

'Everyone watches them,' he declared sullenly.

'That's no reason for you to do the same,' Duncan told him. 'How old are you?'

'Thirteen.'

'And you've got school tomorrow, and it's now nearly midnight. You ought to have been in bed at least two hours ago. You – ' he turned to Des '– are you staying the night?'

Des glared at his feet.

'Dunno.'

'What do you mean, you don't know? Of course you must know. Is your mother expecting you home?'

'Dunno.'

'Well, if you can't make up your own mind, I'll do it for you. You are going home, now. What's more, I'll take you and make sure you get there.'

Cunning lit in Des' eyes.

'My mum says I'm not to take lifts from strange men.'

'Cut the cheek, sonny, and fetch your coat.'

Reluctantly, Des obeyed.

Penny gaped at him in amazement. For someone with no children of his own, he was fantastic at handling them. She had never got more than a grunt of acknowledgement out of Des, let alone managed to compel him to do anything. Justin's head was swivelling from Duncan to herself like a spectator at a tennis match, not quite believing this whirlwind that had broken up his evening's entertainment. Then Duncan started on him.

'And you, Justin isn't it? You can apologise to your mother.'

Penny caught her breath. Justin was never

spoken to in that way. For a tense moment, Justin scowled mutinously at Duncan. Penny could not bear the strain. She was just about to say that it did not matter, to fly to Justin's defence, when he cracked.

'Sorry, Mum,' he muttered.

'Right, now go to bed, and I don't want to hear of your making any more trouble for your mother. Understand?'

'Yeah, yeah.'

'Good.'

Sulking with every line of his body, Justin left the room. He passed Des on the way out and the two boys exchanged looks of disgust.

Penny found her voice at last.

'I'm terribly sorry about this – I had no idea— '

Duncan squeezed her arm briefly.

'Of course you didn't.'

'It was a marvellous evening —'

'Wonderful. We must do it again some time.'

Inhibited by Des' sullen presence, Penny could say no more. When they had gone, she collapsed on the sofa. She was too shattered even to cry. The whole thing was blown. She would never see him again. Just for a few magic hours, she had got it right, had lived with every fibre of her being. Now he was gone, leaving behind a great howling gap that sucked her in like a black hole.

CHAPTER TEN

The voice on the answering tape haunted Jill. To have Penny suddenly talk to her like that, out of the blue, had shaken her to the core. She felt that the past was reaching out to her. First the letter from Andrea, now this. She cursed herself for agreeing to the interview with the Sunday paper. That was what had started all this off. She rubbed the message off the tape and tried to forget about it, but still it came back, threatening her. Her rational side knew that Penny was only acting out of friendly curiosity, simply wanting to find out what had happened to her after all these years, but still she could not suppress the suspicion that there was more to it than that. They were trying to get at her, Andrea and Penny. Before long, Carol would join in as well.

She rubbed her hands over her face. It was ridiculous. She must not let these ideas take root. She must hold on to reality. For always there was the terrifying memory of when everything had slipped and blurred, when she had not seemed to be speaking the same language as the rest of the world and all the safe points in her life disintegrated around her. Never, never would she let that happen to her again. She picked up a report that had to be read.

So much to do, letters, sittings, committees, constituency work. She often wondered how some Members managed to combine it all with other jobs – nice fat briefs and directorships. With all the enthusiasm of a newcomer, she still threw herself into everything, had not yet learnt what was and was not essential. The silent flat, the distant growl of traffic, the facts on the printed pages to be absorbed gradually soothed her mental agitation. Work had always helped, had kept her sane and given her a goal. At university, when all essays had been written and seminars and tutorials prepared for, there were always speeches to be written for debates and committees of various societies to be attended. Anything, so long as it might just advance her in some way. She had such an impossible example to pursue.

Looking up, her eyes went automatically to the photograph of her husband standing on the small table beside her armchair. Darling Mark, the cornerstone of her life. Without him, she would not have been able to pick herself up and put herself together again so successfully. She was not going to let one letter, one phone message, eat away at that. She felt an overwhelming need to see him again, to feel his arms around her, to hear his calm, measured voice. Just one more day, she told herself, then it would be the weekend, and they could be together again. Perhaps she would skip off tomorrow's sitting and go home early, be there waiting for him when he came in from work. She allowed herself a small fantasy, imagining his surprise and delight at finding her there. They would have drinks in front of the log fire in the drawing room, touch briefly and enticingly as they changed for dinner, enjoy a family meal catching up with what they and the children had been doing for the past week and then, when Robin and Emily were safely in their rooms, go early to bed and finish what they had started in the dressing-room.

It was a tempting daydream, so tempting that it nearly overrode the ambition that drove her. What was one day, after all? She was there a good deal more than many of her fellow back-benchers. But not all of them had their eyes on a minister's portfolio as Jill did. She turned her attention back to the report.

The phone rang.

'Hello, darling. How are you?'

It was her mother. As usual, Jill experienced the childish need to impress.

'Fine, Mummy. Busy, of course.'

'Oh I know, dear, I do understand.'

Jill was quite convinced that she did not, but let it pass.

'And Mark and the children, dear? Are they all right?'

This she took to be a veiled thrust at her for not being at home caring for them.

'Positively bursting with health, Mummy dear. Emmy's starring in the school play next week. She's quite the little prima donna.'

'The pet!'

Jill expected a query next as to whether she was going to be able to find time to watch her daughter perform, and was all geared up to lie about it, but it soon became apparent that the questions were mere form. Her mother had more pressing matters on her mind.

'Jilly darling, I don't want to worry you, and I know what a busy person you are, but it's Daddy— '

Just as her mother had wished, Jill felt an immediate spurt of anxiety.

'What about him? Is he ill?'

'Well he isn't too grand, darling. They're doing tests on him.'

'You mean he's in hospital?'

'Yes, at the General. But he won't stay there, of course. If there's anything to be done, he'll go up to town. I shall insist.'

Jill knew where her duty lay. With sinking resignation, she said,

'I'll come down and visit. Which ward is he in?'

'Oh darling, would you? He would be so pleased. But if you can't fit it in— '

Just as her mother knew she would, Jill insisted that nothing was more important than seeing her sick father, even though she was very nearly certain that the tests would reveal nothing whatsoever wrong with him. He had just been to one too many convivial dinner, that was all. As she put the phone down, she said goodbye to the cosy Friday and a good part of Saturday. Her own needs, her own family would have to take second place again, for would not Jennifer have rushed to her father's side? She picked up her diary and began to rearrange her weekend.

The road through the suburbs was choked with Saturday traffic. Jill tapped her long nails against the steering wheel with impatience and stared through the hypnotic sweep of the windscreen wipers. The shoppers were out in force, heading for the supermarkets, the DIY stores, the cheap furniture warehouses. They dithered or cut each other up at traffic lights, turned without signalling and had rows over which way to go, while in the back seats their children ate crisps and fought. The whole of London seemed to be suffering from end-of-winter gloom. Jill thought with longing of her orderly home, of Mark, of the time she should have been spending with him. Minutes ticked by and piled into nearly an hour. It had never taken her so long to do the journey before. With relief she saw the grimy sign for Brackstead and turned into the familiar road for home.

The place had not changed in essentials. Only the details were different, the home improvements, the number of cars. The acres of red-tiled semis, the council estates of dirty yellow brick, the high street – that now had an Eighties look, but Jill could not judge how much was still there, as it had been pedestrianised and her car was directed round a system of one-way streets that took her past the park. She gripped the wheel tighter as she remembered the heated adolescent gropings. However much she had scorned the Victorian ideals of chastity in theory, when it came to the point she was tense and frightened. After one particularly close escape she had vetoed any suggestion of going to the park after dark. It had taken Mark to patiently break down the barriers and show her what sex was about.

The hospital stood between the Thirties houses and the newer estates that ran out, Jill recalled, to the latest groups of executive properties where Andrea now lived. She quelled the irrational sense of threat and concentrated on finding a parking place. Duty first, then it was onto the motorway and home as fast as the outside lane could allow. Impeccably groomed as always, outwardly confident, even slightly formidable in her stride and stance, she made her way along the polished corridors to the private wing. A nurse conducted her to her father's room.

She had to contain her shock. He looked grey. His large face, once pink and shiny with good living, seemed to have deflated, and his imposing body to have shrunk inside the blue monogrammed pyjamas. Just for a moment, his gaze was uncomprehending. The nurse bustled forward.

'Visitor for you, Mr Somers. Let's get you comfortable, shall we?' She rearranged the pillows on his backrest, found his glasses and handed them to him. 'There we are. Bell's just by the bed here if you need anything, Mrs Lovesey.'

'Hello, Daddy.'

She found her voice, forced a smile into it, produced her gift of his favourite Glenfiddich.

'What on earth are you doing in here? Are you allowed this stuff or shall I give it to Mummy to keep for you?'

'Jill – this is a pleasure – yes, put it in the locker there. I refuse to be dictated to by a lot of girls a third my age.'

His voice was a little weaker but he was, to her relief, still the same person. And then, as the visit progressed, too much the same person. His illness gave him the excuse, if he needed it, to be even more wrapped up in his own affairs than usual. Once he had answered all Jill's enquiries into his present condition with minute detail, he launched into an account of the latest local political manoeuvrings. Jill's mind glazed as she tried to follow the ins and outs of what this and that person had said and done.

'Of course,' she remarked, breaking in on the flow at last, 'all that will have to be rethought when this new bill is passed.'

'Oh— yes— well— '

Had he honestly forgotten that she was playing this game at national level? Did he notice what she was doing at all?

'I can't see that it will make any difference down here,' he said, recovering with the ease of long practice. 'It's a matter of personality, not policy.'

She tried to put her point of view, but he was not listening. Over the years, he had become more and more blinkered. The world outside Brackstead hardly existed. But would it have been different if Jennifer had survived? Would he have followed her career? Of course he would.

'It's clear there's nothing too wrong with you, Daddy,' she told him. 'You'd better hurry up and get out of here. The council will fall apart if you lie around in bed for too long.'

'That's right.' He took her words at face value. 'They don't see that it's not the SDP they've got to worry about, it's the Watch Committee that needs sorting out.'

Jill leaned forward, kissed his dry forehead, stood up.

'I'll tell Mummy you're mending then, shall I?'

'You do that, Jill. And tell her to get some decent food in, too. None of this high-fibre rubbish. A man has to keep his strength up, you know.'

Jill promised, smiled, took her leave. On her way out, she buttonholed the sister, and tried to get some straight answers out of her. From the details of the tests she extracted the one that struck a note of fear – a biopsy of the colon.

'Merely routine,' the sister assured her. 'We have to cover everything. Both Mr and Mrs Somers will be informed when the results come through.'

Beyond that, there was no drawing her. She agreed that Mr Somers did not look well, but that was the reason he was here, wasn't it? Once they had found out what the trouble was, they would set about making him better. Jill had to be content with that. She drove thoughtfully out to where her parents still lived, on the Heights.

The house, built to last in the Thirties, stood solid as ever with its round bays, leaded lights and decorative red shingles. A sea of daffodils as bright as Wordsworth's spread under the shrubs and halfway across the front lawn, but failed to have the same magical effect on Jill's spirits. She parked neatly in front of the garage that looked more like a stable, and scrunched across the gravel driveway to ring the doorbell.

'Jilly darling!'

In a waft of Chanel No.5, they exchanged pecks on the cheek.

'Come and sit down, darling, and I'll bring in some coffee.' Mrs Somers took Jill's jacket, ushered her into the lounge, disappeared into the kitchen. The gloomy day and the evergreens growing close to the windows outside made the room dim, but even in the poor light there was a dull gleam on the silverware, a point of colour from the meticulous arrangement of spring flowers and catkins. Jill hated the place. Try as she might to avoid it, her eyes were drawn compulsively towards the polished mahogany bookcase opposite the fireplace. Here Jennifer's achievements reposed, frozen forever in time. The cups for music and ballet, the O- and A-level certificates with their A grades, the tennis shield, the little pair of ballet shoes cast in silver. And the photographs, three-year-old Jennifer in a mass of blonde curls and a party dress, five-year-old Jennifer in long plaits sitting at the piano, Jennifer lovely still even in adolescence holding her tennis racquet and a cup, Jennifer the young woman, beautiful in a high-waisted ball gown at the Conservative dinner and dance. Jill shivered. It only needed a branch of guttering candles to turn it into a shrine.

'Here we are.'

Jill sipped at the coffee, though she would have preferred a stiff drink. She needed something to steady her jumpy imagination. She tried to concentrate on answering her mother's questions about the children, for at least she did take some interest in Jill's offspring.

'And when is Emily taking her Grade Four?'

'In the summer, probably. Her teacher isn't quite sure whether she'll be ready.'

'I see. Yes, well, it's no good pushing her beyond her ability, is it?'

The nerves all down Jill's spine twitched, for behind her on the bookcase was the certificate that proclaimed Jennifer to have passed Grade Four piano exam by the time she was two years younger than Emily was now.

'And what about Robin? Still enjoying his football?'

'Loving it. The school team's playing this morning, as a matter of fact.'

As a reminder of what she had given up to be a

dutiful daughter, it was an abject failure. Her mother picked it up and turned it round.

'Yes, well you must miss a lot of their little triumphs, mustn't you? Working as hard as you do. And how is his progress at school? Are you expecting a good report this term?'

'Robin's a real trier,' Jill stated, with complete truth. What she did not add was that the trying did not get him very far. There was some doubt as to whether he would manage to scrape through his Common Entrance, but she was not going to expose poor Robin to his grandmother's disappointment, not until it was absolutely necessary. Maybe, with the extra coaching, he would make it after all. She talked on for a while, trying to impress her mother with the names of public schools they had considered for Robin. But Mrs Somers' eyes kept straying to the clock.

'I mustn't keep you, Jilly. Poor Mark will be feeling neglected. Men don't like that, do they?'

Jill took the hint. Passing through the hall, she glanced through the open door of the kitchen to see dishes of food lined up and covered with clingfilm.

'Guests to lunch, Mummy?'

Mrs Somers did have the grace to look uncomfortable.

'Just my golf ladies, dear.'

Before she could stop herself, Jill gave a mirthless smile.

'Then I'd better hurry along, hadn't I? You don't want me under your feet when they arrive.'

'Don't be silly, dear,' her mother reproved, and handed her her jacket. Just as Jill was stepping out of the door, she added, 'Oh, by the way, I saw that friend of yours the other day in Sainsbury's. What's her name? Andrea. She asked after you.'

Jill's voice came out a little high, but on the whole she thought she disguised the jolt quite well.

'Really? Well I never. I haven't seen her for

years. Now, you will let me know the moment the results of Daddy's tests come through, won't you?'

Another kiss, their lips barely brushing each other's cheeks, and she was free. She backed out of the driveway with a splattering of gravel, and accelerated up the road.

'M-way here we come,' she said out loud, and sought a suitably cheerful cassette to slot into the deck. She would not let them upset her. She was a grown-up woman now, she no longer needed her parents' approval. It did not matter if they still measured her against an impossible standard. That was their loss, not hers. She turned into the dual carriageway and the Sierra surged forward, eager to leave Brackstead and all its bitter memories behind.

Five minutes later she had slowed to a crawl. Ahead were blue lights flashing and the wail of a siren as an ambulance left for the hospital. The police were already redirecting the traffic. Slowly, the lanes filtered together and into a side road. Round the back streets they went, until Jill realised with sudden dreadful certainty where they were being diverted to. The road past the reservoir. She wanted to stop, to pull off, but her body did not seem to be obeying her brain. Like a train unable to leave its track she kept with the stream of cars, onto the concrete road, past the high grassy bank, and there it was, gleaming steel grey and moody in the drizzly gloom. The rage and frustration swept over her, raw as it had been all those years ago. Nothing she did measured up to Jennifer's standard, however hard she tried, she would never be as brilliant, as talented, as beautiful – except that she could swim better.

The bows of the dinghy ran gently onto the shore, scarlet sails flapping.

'Coming, Jen? It's fabulous out there today. Going like a bird.'

Her voice sounded cheerful, carefree. Nobody

would have suspected the black hatred behind it. She was as good an actress as Penny when driven to it.

'I don't know, it's a bit squally— '

'Oh come on, Jen. It's great. Really exciting.'

Jennifer with her blonde hair blown across her face, brown and slender in white shorts and suntop. She smiled, agreed.

'OK, I'll just get a life jacket.'

'But you'll have to go all the way back to the clubhouse. Oh come on, Jen, they're such a drag. I'm not wearing one.'

The dinghy rocked beneath her as the waves broke against the shore. Jill cajoled, Jennifer gave in, because she wanted to be nice to her, because Jill's A-level results had not been as good as she had hoped, because she was well aware of the distinction their parents made between them and wanted to do something to make up for it. And Jill knew she was trying to be kind, and hated her all the more for it. Jennifer stepped in with one foot, pushed off with the other, sat down and hauled in the foresheet. Jill braced herself against the tilt of the boat, the force of the wind in the mainsail, and steered out from the shore, tacking into the middle of the reservoir, where the dark ruffles on the water warned of sudden sharp gusts blowing up under the scudding clouds. The little boat lifted and fell with the waves, and sent back shining bursts of spray. Jennifer gasped and turned her laughing face to Jill.

'You're right, it's fabulous!'

Ahead of them, the dancing water became dark and angry.

CHAPTER ELEVEN

It was during her second year at university that Jill began to make a name for herself. Other people might have complaints about the system, or good ideas for meetings or debates, but it took someone like Jill to make the jump from words to action. The buzz got about: if you want something organised, ask Jill Somers. She found herself co-opted onto committees, both of well-established societies and mushroom pressure groups. It was Jill who was one of the main moving forces behind the large contingent that joined the anti-Vietnam war demos. Plenty of students felt strongly enough to want to join in. Jill and her group made sure it was a concerted effort.

They were heady days. The passion and the violence both drew and repelled her. She was afraid of the unleashed strength of the mob, but irresistibly attracted by it. She could submerge her own aggression in that of the crowd and feel no guilt. For days afterwards she would ride high on the after effects. No images of grey water would haunt her. But then came the withdrawal symptoms.

The day Mark first sought her out was about a week after the Grosvenor Square riots.

She sat for fully a minute pretending she was not there. She could not face answering the knock on the door of her room, going through the motions of normal conversation. If she did not answer, whoever it was would go away. Another knock. She felt hunted, trapped. She sat without moving a muscle, scarcely breathing.

Footsteps in the corridor outside.

'This is Jill Somers' room, isn't it?' A man's voice just feet away on the other side of the door.

'Oh yes. She is in. I haven't seen her go out,

anyway.' Her friend Kate's cheerful betrayal. Happy, uncomplicated Kate, who never thought deeply about anything. The handle turned and her smiling face appeared round the door.

'There you are, Jill. Are you in a coma or something? There's a really dishy man waiting out here for you. If you don't do something about him, I will.'

A laugh and a joke with the unseen stranger, then Kate went off and the owner of the voice came in.

'Jill Somers? I'm Mark Lovesey.'

Something in his quiet formality made her get off the bed and shake the hand he was holding out. He was rather older than the usual run of students, and conservatively dressed in a tweed jacket and brown trousers, a shirt and even a tie. He looked at her with faint puzzlement.

'I have got the right person, I hope? You are the Jill Somers who is on the Peace Committee?'

For the first time in days, Jill considered what she looked like. She had managed to make herself get dressed, but her hair was unkempt and her face haggard with great dark circles under the eyes. She had been too afraid to sleep, knowing that Jennifer was waiting just below the surface to drag her down. She had to stay conscious to keep in control. Now she found herself wishing she had taken a shower this morning and dragged a comb across her head.

'That's right,' she said. Did the words sound slurred? Her mouth felt numb. She spoke carefully, trying to string together a coherent sentence. 'What brings you here?'

He did not answer immediately. He appeared to be considering the next move. Much later, he told Jill that he almost left at that juncture, since she had so obviously hit rock bottom, but was fascinated by the contradiction before him. The decisive woman of action or this broken creature? They could not both be the same person.

Jill waited dumbly, unaware that she was at the turning point of her life, doing nothing to influence events, she who always prided herself on being captain of her own destiny.

With the quiet authority that Jill was to come to know and appreciate, Mark took charge.

'I'll make us some coffee, shall I?' he offered. 'Where are the things? In this cupboard?'

It was his competence that attracted her at first. He could make coffee or cut through an emotional muddle with practical suggestions and a soothing lack of fuss. He was the type that Jill and her friends affected to look down upon, not an arts student like them, but an engineer, and even worse, a potential capitalist. He had spent two years working on the floor of his father's firm before coming to college and had scant respect for the high-flown ideals of the majority of the students. He knew something of the realities of life. And he was a Conservative. That was what brought him to Jill in the first place. He wanted her to speak at one of the Conservative Club meetings, to put the Peace Committee's view. When she had got herself together, Jill agreed.

'You were excellent,' he said, at the end of the evening. 'I still don't agree with you, but you make a very good case.'

'Thanks,' Jill said, 'but I haven't given up yet. You'll see things my way in the end, I promise you.'

She was speaking off the top of her head, for she could read more than admiration for her performance on the platform in his eyes. For the first time since Jennifer's death it gave her a thrill of pleasure. Up till now, any hint of a chat-up had sent her running for cover. She did not want any close relationships, she did not even have a special girlfriend, she felt safest dealing with issues and ideas rather than with people. But Mark was different. She found she was glad that she was looking good. Being in the public eye always brought out the best in her, and now, after a stimulating evening arguing for a cause she was utterly committed to, she knew that she was at her most attractive. So although she was not yet ready to trust her instincts entirely, she did at least dare to accept his invitation to dinner.

After that, there was the usual pattern of dances, drinks, trips to the theatre. Slowly and patiently, Mark wound himself into the fabric of her life.

'Are you coming to the sit-in?' people asked her. 'We need someone to organise this protest group.' Or arrange a meeting, or speak in a debate. But Jill was not as available as she used to be. Sometimes she amazed them by refusing.

'What's the matter with you?' they asked, dismayed. 'Are you going soft? Have you joined the other side?'

Kate understood.

'He's just right for you,' she said. 'He's solid. He has integrity.'

The word surprised Jill, but when she thought about it, she discovered that it was true. Almost without her realising it, Mark had taken over from all the causes and crusades. She still believed in them, but they were no longer her reason for living. She refused several tempting invitations in order to help him study for his finals. Then the end of term rushed upon them, and with it the prospect of parting. Jill looked ahead to a summer at Brackstead and beyond that another year at college without Mark by her side, and was horrified. She could not face it. Without him there, all the meaning went out of life.

They went to the end of term Formal Ball. Jill spent the last of her grant on a high-waisted dress of pale green satin and had her hair set in curls on top of her head. She looked magnificent, but there was despair in her heart. This was the end. Tomorrow they went down.

She drank too much and danced to everything, the strict-tempo trio, the trad jazz band, the local pop groups and the big attraction of the evening, Manfred Mann. She danced with everyone who asked her, letting the music and the excitement take her over, trying to numb her brain. But at about three in the morning Mark extricated her from the arms of a drunken sociologist and walked her outside. It was a still, warm night, the air heavy with the scent of roses. Jill clung onto his arm and stumbled in her high-heeled sandals. Behind them the music throbbed and the frantic party rolled on.

'Enjoying it?' Mark asked.

'No,' Jill admitted, and burst into tears. Once she had started, she couldn't stop. With the strain of exams behind her and the future without him ahead, crying was a wonderful luxury, made all the more poignant by his holding her. She lost all sense of time and place.

'Jill.' From far away she heard his voice. 'Jill, stop it.'

The cold water hit her face, startling her back to her senses. She was standing by an ornamental pond, and Mark was shaking her. She stared at him, still racked with sobs, but calmer.

'That's better.'

He did not seem unduly worried by her performance. In fact, if she had been in a fit state to notice it, Jill would have thought he looked rather pleased with himself. He had interpreted the reason for her tears correctly, and was exultant. Until now, he had not been sure of her.

'Listen,' he said. 'I've got to go home for a couple of weeks at least, but after that I'm taking a holiday. I thought I might go to Greece. Do you fancy coming with me?'

She gazed at him, hardly daring to believe what

she had heard. It was too good to be true. All at once, the world was a wonderful place, the future a bright shining adventure. If he had offered the slums of Calcutta she still would have been delighted, but Greece – it was heaven.

'Do I?' she breathed. 'Just try me.'

It was a magical time, three weeks of hot sun, white temples, retsina and olive groves. By the end of it, Jill was a new person, relaxed, assured, at peace with herself. The ghosts no longer seemed relevant. She was a woman now, not a haunted girl. Mark was a considerate lover, though not very original, but Jill, with nobody to compare him with, knew only that he undammed the pent-up emotion in her, and showed her a side of herself that she never knew existed. She was completely happy, for the first time in her life.

They decided that she must stay at college and complete her degree. The year would soon pass, they assured each other. Mark formally asked Jill's father for his daughter's hand.

Jill's parents were delighted with Mark. He was everything a prospective son-in-law should be. Jill, having been briefed not to mention the Peace Committee, made an equally good impression on Mark's mother and father. They were married the following summer.

Imperceptibly, Jill's set opinions began to change. Away from the extremist activities of her university friends, she had to admit that life was not all black and white. The Vietnam war was certainly a clearcut case. Anyone with a sense of fitness and an ounce of compassion must see that the Americans had to be stopped. But when it came to the more everyday issues, things were not quite so clear. Also, it was amazing how different the view was from the other side of the fence. Mark's father owned a precision engineering firm employing five hundred people. Mark, having served his time on the shop floor and gained his degree, was now part of the management team. Listening to him talking about production problems and orders lost through sloppy workmanship, Jill shifted towards the boss' camp. And having changed her mind, being Jill, she gave her allegiance wholeheartedly to the other side.

'What do you mean, nepotism?' she argued, when challenged by an aggressive shop steward over the job she did in the company offices. 'If I've got a stake in this outfit, I'm going to work all the harder, aren't I? And that's going to benefit everyone, including you.'

By the time Robin was born, she was not only a member of the Young Conservatives, but on the committee.

Mark was jubilant. Marrying Jill had been the one gamble in his carefully planned life, and it had worked out just as he had hoped. He had an intelligent, supportive wife of whom he was inordinately proud, and now he had a son as well. It needed only a daughter in a couple of years' time to complete the picture. What he did not anticipate was the severe case of post-natal depression that Jill was afflicted with after the birth. The vital woman he had been so happy with melted away before his eyes, leaving the sunken, apathetic creature he had first met that day he came to see her at the hall of residence. Mark could not understand it. Why was Jill not as delighted with their new son as he was? One thing was clear, something had to be done about it. He knew all about Jill's mental problems and was not going to let her slide down into the state she had been in after Jennifer's death. It did not take him long to find just the right solution.

'Darling?' He came in one evening from the Conservative Club to find her staring uncomprehendingly at the television.

'What?'

Jill tried to focus her attention on him. She did not like feeling this way, but somehow it required just too much effort to pull herself out of it. She felt some of his warmth pass to her as he sat down beside her on the sofa and took her hand.

'I've just been talking to the selection committee.'

He paused, expecting an answer.

'Oh yes?' Was her voice slurred? She tried to form the words properly, for even moving the muscles of her face was difficult.

'Yes. They're trying to find a suitable candidate for Milldown ward in the council elections. They think it could just go to us this time. Those new houses have been built since last time, and they're all occupied by young marrieds and couples with babies. They could just swing the vote if we had someone young and dynamic to represent us.'

Jill entirely failed to catch his drift.

'I expect you're right,' she said dully.

Mark took her other hand, trying to impress what he was saying upon her.

'I suggested your name to them.'

Just at that moment, only Mark could have considered her to be the right person for the job. Young she might be, dynamic she certainly was not. But Mark remembered the girl who made speeches on behalf of the Peace Committee. He knew she could do it.

'Me?'

The idea was ludicrous. It was as if he had presented her with Everest and told her to climb it.

'Yes, you. You're the ideal candidate. You're terrific at speaking in public, you're well organised, you look the part and you've bags of energy. I can't think of anyone better suited.'

Deep below the layers of apathy, the old Jill began to stir. A local councillor. Her father had not become one till he was twice her age. Her parents would be impressed with that. But still the thought of dragging herself out of the swamp was beyond her. She cast about for excuses, not realising that even doing that was beginning to exercise her brain a little.

'What about Robin? I can't go out on the knocker with him.' Already her voice had lifted just slightly above the flat monotone of a few minutes ago.

'Why not? There's nothing like a baby for grabbing people's sympathy, and they'll know that you have real understanding of their problems.' Mark was not going to let that stand in her way. He demolished the next argument before she had a chance to bring it up.

'And if you do need to leave him, my mother would be only too delighted to look after him. She's dying for the chance to show him off to all her friends.'

'Oh, I don't know— ' Jill said.

But the seed had been planted. Mark was wise enough to let it rest there that night. He waited for her to bring the subject up again, which she did a couple of days later. By the end of the week, she had agreed.

It took a great deal of courage for Jill to present herself before the selection committee. It was only the thought of letting Mark down that carried her through. Once accepted, she then had the whole of the local party expecting her to do her bit, which goaded her into further action. But once she started campaigning, the ashes of her fighting spirit rekindled. She had found her place in life.

Jill loved it all, the public meetings, the doorstep canvassing, the planning late into the night. It was a close-run contest, against a well-established

Labour candidate who had served the area efficiently for several years, and the outcome was uncertain right up to the count.

The atmosphere was tense as the last papers were added up. Jill held tight onto Mark's hand. Their faithful supporters, decked out in blue ribbons and buoyed up with excitement, waited with them. There was a silence as breaths were held. The result was announced. Mrs Jill Lovesey was returned as councillor for Milldown ward.

In an eruption of cheers, Jill flung her arms round Mark.

'We've done it! We've done it!'

Mark hugged her back.

'You've done it, darling. Congratulations.'

The full meaning of the triumph gradually came home to her. She had done something her parents would understand and be proud of.

'I can't wait to tell Mummy and Daddy.'

She phoned them from the Conservative Club. Her mother answered.

'Oh, hello Jilly dear. How are you?'

'Couldn't be better, Mummy. I've just won the election! I'm now the official representative of Milldown Ward.'

'That's nice, dear. Well done.'

Her mother might have been commenting on a messy painting brought home from infants' school. Jill felt as if she had been kicked in the stomach.

'Is Daddy there?' she asked faintly.

'No, he's still at the Club. They're still chewing over the results. I've only just got in myself.'

All the sour resentment of her childhood gathered in Jill's heart.

'Hasn't it gone too well in Brackstead, then?' she asked.

Was it possible that her father had lost his safe position? She craved to hear that he had.

'Not the best of results,' her mother admitted.

'Your father's all right, of course, but three of the marginals have gone.'

'Milldown was Labour last time, but I won it,' Jill persisted, trying to press her point home.

'Really?' Something of her ache for recognition at last transmitted itself to her mother. A spark of real interest coloured her voice. 'Your father will be glad to hear that. I'll tell him when he gets in.'

That was as much as Jill managed to extract.

It was the same all along. Whatever her triumphs, personal or political, always the same faintly patronising approval. Though they never actually said it, she always heard the qualifying words to each stilted message of congratulations. '. . . Quite good, for you, but Jennifer would have done better.'

So Jill spent her time juggling the needs of her family with an ever-growing ambition. It was soon recognised that she was destined to go further than the local council. Mark was quite happy for a nanny to be employed once Emily appeared on the scene. Jill was not cut out to stay at home looking after babies. He much preferred the battling, enthusiastic Jill to the downtrodden mother. But he did miss her company. Jill rearranged appointments and sometimes even turned down opportunities she would have liked to have taken up, so that she could spend more time with him. For even Jennifer could not have found a better partner. More important, maybe, but for once Jill was wise enough to know that this did not matter. Where Mark was concerned, her parents could think what they liked. She was happy with him.

It was this problem of dividing herself that caused her much heartsearching over whether she should try to get into national politics. She knew that this was what she wanted to do. Local government had given her a taste of what it was like, but she did not want to stand still. There were new mountains to conquer. Besides, though she did not quite admit it in so many words, to go for a seat in Parliament was to go beyond what her father had achieved. Her parents must sit up and take notice then. But how would Mark feel? If she did get in, it would mean spending days at a time in London.

'If that's what you want to do, then do it,' he advised. 'You won't be happy if you don't, now that you've started the idea.'

He was still dazzled by her at times. On the platform she was magnificent, carrying all before her. He was immensely proud of her, while knowing all the time how vulnerable she was underneath. If she failed to take up this challenge, he knew she would regret it.

It took rather more discussion than that, but in the end Jill was convinced. She served her apprenticeship fighting and losing in a depressed industrial constituency, then got her chance of a marginal, and won.

'It's a great day for the Party, Jilly,' her father boomed down the telephone line when she told him the news. 'We've got the pinkos on the run. They won't be able to do a thing now. What's that you say? You've got in? Well, there you are, heads are rolling all over the country. Lucky for you you were in on this.'

Of course, Jennifer would have been given her minister's portfolio by now. A backbencher was small beer. Jill swallowed her disappointment with difficulty and set her eyes on the next goal. She would do it yet.

CHAPTER TWELVE

The decorating project was going better than Carol had ever hoped. She had taken Sid into her confidence, and since he needed work, he was willing to go along with her fiction inasmuch as he did not contradict anything she said about the work they were supposed to have done in the past. As he was not the world's most talkative man at the best of times, Carol was fairly sure he would not drop her in it. The daft Kevin had been given his marching orders, much to her relief. She certainly could not have trusted him to keep his mouth shut. Carol flitted in and out of Andrea's house with her drawings and paint charts and fabric swatches, pretending to be working on other projects when she was at Mrs Cleve's, and thoroughly enjoying herself. It was a long time since she had flung herself into a situation like this, and she had almost forgotten what fun it was. Not quite as good as having an affair, but something of the same excitement.

Andrea was unstinting in her praise.

'You are clever,' she enthused, as the paper began to go up. 'I would never have thought of chocolate and cream for a bedroom, but it looks really stylish.'

'Dark colours are very restful, and sophisticated. It's all too easy to fall into the pretty-pretty trap with bedrooms and end up with one that just looks like everyone else's,' Carol said, quoting loosely from one of Mrs Cleve's glossy magazines.

Andrea gravely agreed.

'I would probably have gone for flowers and pastels, and it wouldn't have looked anything like as terrific as this. It's no wonder you're making a success of your business.'

Sid, halfway through pasting the next sheet, coughed and stopped to roll another cigarette. Andrea offered to make some more tea.

'Have you time to stop for a cup?' she asked Carol.

With only a week of washing and the unmade beds waiting for her at home, Carol said she might be able to spare ten minutes or so.

'I've shown the room to several of my friends,' Andrea said, as they sat looking over a garden bright with spring flowers. 'I hope you don't mind. They were all very impressed. I think you might be getting a few more commissions.'

'Oh great,' Carol said, trying to work out whether this was good or bad. Could she keep it up? Why not? And it was all money. It had to be better than slaving for that cow Cleve. 'I can always do with more work,' she went on, then suddenly remembered that she had tried to get out of doing Andrea's room by saying that she had too much on. That was the trouble with lying, you had to remember what you had said. Quickly, she fabricated, 'I thought I had quite a lot lined up, but some of them have fallen through. You know how it is – win a few, lose a few.'

'Yes—' Andrea looked thoughtful. She drew breath as if to speak, changed her mind and took a sip of tea, started again. 'I was wondering – well, it was just an idea, I don't know what you'll think but – you see, I've got some time on my hands now and I'm going to have more as the children get older, but I haven't any particular talent like you. I've been a secretary, and a mother, and that's just about it. But I was a good secretary, I was efficient and organised and I didn't flap under pressure, and I thought, perhaps you might like some help with the office side of your business. I could do all the paperwork and the books and dealing with the phone calls and correspondence and that would leave you free to do the creative side—' she trailed off, her face anxious. 'I don't know what you think, though.'

Carol was trying to think very fast. How was she going to get out of this one? Why had she ever got into it? Why didn't she just keep her big mouth shut?

'It's a terrific idea, Andy, but I don't think there's enough for you to do, really. I mean, there's only me, and Sid of course, and I just sort of muddle through with the paperwork. It wouldn't be worth your while, it's not like I'm a big company or anything. But thanks all the same. If ever I get to be really successful, you're the first person I'll ask to join me.'

'I don't mind it's not being a big company,' Andrea said. 'To be honest, I don't want to go back to that sort of set-up. That was the attraction of your business. I'd really be part of it, but I'd still have time to look after the house and family properly. It seemed the ideal solution.'

The wistful expression died and was replaced by one of determined confidence. She gave Carol a level look. 'And as I said, I could be a very useful partner. I am in a position to put quite a lot of work your way. Most of our friends are quite comfortably off, and they know other people who are similarly placed, and it could build into a very nice new source of commissions for you.'

'Well – I – er – I'm quite sure you're right, Andy. Look, give me a bit of time to think it over, eh? Must rush now. Look at the time! I'll come back and make sure Sid's OK tomorrow, then we'll start on the blinds. Should really start coming together then.'

She made her escape.

All through the rest of the afternoon and into the evening, the problem niggled at her. She could just keep putting Andrea off, of course, but the prospect of really going into this interior design lark tempted her. Was Andrea obliquely threatening her with her rich friends? Count me in or I'll not pass your name on? No, Andy wouldn't threaten a two-year-old. She wasn't the type. But it would be nice to do this sort of thing all the time. Swan around making drawings and buying expensive stuff all with other people's money. She might even give up working for that old cow. While the boys came and went and were finally nagged into going to bed, and Samantha moaned about some teacher she didn't get on with and then went out to see a friend, and the dirty dishes piled up on the draining board, Carol dithered. At last, when the house was quiet, she picked up the phone and dialled Penny's number. Penny had got her into this, she could think of what to do next.

'Hello?' Penny's voice was crackling with so much nervous tension the handset practically sparked. 'Oh – Carol – I wasn't expecting – what is it?'

Not the most encouraging of greetings. Carol nearly made an excuse and rang off. Instead she waffled on with the usual enquiries.

'Oh fine, fine. Look, did you want something, Carol?'

Carol explained, in rambling detail.

'Well do it, then,' Penny told her shortly. 'What's the sweat? Go ahead with it.'

'But Andrea— '

'Count her in as well, if it makes her happy.'

'But I'd have to tell her— '

'Tell her then. Sod it, Carol, I can't make all your decisions for you.'

'No, I know, but— '

'Look, I've got to go. Do you mind? I'm sorry. Best of luck and all that. 'Bye— '

' 'Bye.'

Feeling rejected, Carol replaced the buzzing

receiver. So much for friends. You ask for advice and get your head bitten off. She wandered into the kitchen, looked at the mess and decided she could not face it, ambled into the lounge and pressed the channel buttons on the television. Nothing very interesting. For want of anything better to do, she watched a repeat of the serial episode she had seen on Sunday. What was she going to do about Andrea, and this decorating business? She just couldn't make her mind up. Samantha came back in, banged around and disappeared into her bedroom. It was no good discussing it with her. The phone rang.

'Carol?' It hardly sounded like the same Penny. Her voice rippled with happiness. 'Oh Carol, I'm so sorry I snapped at you earlier. I was waiting for a call and I thought you were it – him. I was just so strung up. I am sorry, darling.'

'That's OK.' Carol could guess the rest of the story, it was obvious in her breathless joy. 'He did ring, then, after me?'

'Oh yes. Oh Carol, it's so wonderful, I can't tell you. I'm so grateful to you I could kiss you. Hug yourself for me, will you? Remember that evening we went out? I would never have gone there then if it weren't for you and then I would never have met him, or not so soon anyway. Perhaps we would have done sometime, yes, I think so, I know it really, it was meant to be, this one – am I making sense? I don't know what I'm saying. I feel as if I've drunk a bottle of champagne— '

Carol felt a pang of jealousy as she listened. It had been so long since she last experienced those giddy, delirious first stages of love. By contrast, her emotional life seemed flatter and duller than ever. When did she last want to dance in the street?

'It's that guy you were talking to at your table, is it?' she asked.

'Yes, Duncan. Duncan Randall.' There was a world of tenderness in the way she spoke his name. 'We started off all wrong, and then Justin nearly wrecked it, and then this week he's been in New York and I could hardly bear it, Carol, he was so far away and all those beautiful competitive American women around him with their perfect teeth. I kept thinking, supposing he doesn't come back? Supposing he's offered a job over there? That's why I was so short with you, darling, he was flying back today and I was desperate to hear from him. And then he called me from the airport. Oh, I could turn cartwheels! This is the best thing that's happened to me in years. He's free, Carol, actually free. Not even an ex-wife! I got so sick of all those married men. I couldn't face it, not after the last one, Gerry, that really screwed me up. I said, never again, no more affairs, no more "my wife doesn't understand me", not even if it means there's never anybody in my life again. And then this. I still can't believe it.'

Funny, Carol thought, listening to the catalogue of Duncan's virtues, how people don't change. Penny always fell heavily, completely and generally disastrously in love. There had to be something wrong with this one. No man was that perfect. Why hadn't he married? In Carol's experience, any guy who got to be fortyish and not married had to be AC/DC.

'What grade does he get?' she asked, reverting to their teenage method of rating boyfriends.

'A+,' Penny claimed.

'Pen, nobody gets A+.'

'Duncan does. And I know a great deal more about it than when I was seventeen, believe me. When I say A+, I mean A+ in everything.'

'Christ,' said Carol. So much for AC/DC. 'How come nobody's got their hooks into him before now? Has he been in a monastery or something?'

'He's just not committed himself. He's lived with one or two people, of course. And he is a bit younger than me.'

'Ah.' So that was it. 'How old is he, then?'

A slight hesitation on the end of the line, then, 'Twenty-nine.'

'You cradle-snatcher, Pen!'

'I really don't see that it matters. Age is only relative, isn't it?' She sounded so cold that Carol had to agree.

'Oh yes, right. I was only joking. He looked gorgeous to me, from what I saw of him.'

Reassured, Penny said, 'I've been rabiting on, you must forgive me. Carol darling, I really phoned about you and Andrea and this decorating thing. Look, why don't you go into it? You've got the talent. And it would be a very good idea to have Andy along, she'd keep you organised, you'd make an excellent partnership. And I could probably put some business your way, when I hear of friends who are in the money and thinking of having alterations done. Why don't you? You've nothing to lose.'

'Yes— '

They chewed it over for a while longer, until Carol was convinced. Yes, she would do it.

'Tell you what,' Penny suggested. 'Get some cards printed and send one to Jill. MPs might moan about their pay but they're not short of a penny or two. She could be a very good contact. And think how pleased she'd be to hear how you're using your gifts. You might not have made the Slade, but it is something artistic.'

Chuckling at the memory of Jill's efforts to direct their lives, Carol agreed. She would do it. She would talk to Andrea about it tomorrow.

When it came to the point, though, she was more than a little nervous. What was Andy going to say when she found out the business was all a pack of lies? She almost backed down, but Andrea pinned her down till she had to answer.

'What about my idea of coming in with you, Carol? Have you thought about it? What do you feel? It is a good suggestion, isn't it?'

'Well, er, I was going to talk to you about that,' Carol said. 'You see, er, it's not quite what I said. I mean, the business isn't quite as big – in fact there isn't one.' She stared over Andrea's head, not daring to look at her.

'*What*?' Andrea was flabbergasted. 'What do you mean? I don't understand.'

'I made it up,' Carol confessed. 'Well, you were so successful, you and Penny. What with her sitting there in that fantastic outfit looking like a million dollars and going on about television series and locations and what-not, and you with this lovely big place and all, and then Jill getting to be an MP and having that great posh house and the horses and everything, I felt a right prat. I hadn't done anything, so when you asked me I just – made it up.'

She waited for the righteous indignation.

'Oh.' Andrea still sounded puzzled. 'But our guest room – you did that, all the plans and everything, and Sid coming to do the work – how did you— ?'

'Sid was working for the woman I clean for,' Carol confessed. 'I got him to keep quiet. He needed the job.'

'Oh,' Andrea said again, frowning. There was a dreadful silence while she considered the matter. Carol was just about to jump in with more justifications when Andrea delivered her verdict. 'I do know how you felt. I sat there thinking I'd done nothing with my life as well.'

'You?' Carol said, amazed. 'But you've got all

this.' She waved a cigarette at the house around her.

'It's all Robert's,' Andrea pointed out. 'Don't get me wrong, I love it. I love my family, but – well, it would be nice to have something of my own. And yours of course. You know, I'm rather glad you made it all up. That means we could build it together, I could be in at the beginning. We are going to do it, aren't we? I really think we could make a go of it.'

'I guess so,' Carol agreed. After all, with Andrea to do the boring bits, and Sid to do the actual work, it would be a real doddle. 'Right,' she said. 'We'll do it. What does your Robert think of it?'

'He's treating it as a joke. He thinks I'm only doing it because my friend Camilla keeps nagging me to get out of the house. Camilla's a bit like Jill, always trying to organise me. Robert's probably hoping it will just be a flash in the pan. But it won't be, will it? We'll make a success of it. I've lots of ideas. I think we should have a launch party, and invite everyone who might be a potential client.'

For the whole of the afternoon, they moulded the project into something they could both be happy with. Andrea had all the practical side covered, premises, letterheads, expenses. Carol began to feel her brain cells stir. Long ago, when she was part of the Swinging London of the Sixties, she had worked for a while in a small promotion agency. She added her own flamboyant suggestions to Andrea's sensible ones, and gradually something that had been a defiant lie took shape as a real entity. When she finally left to collect Carly from school, she felt a new woman. This past year she had almost lost faith in her conviction that something always turned up. Her luck with money had always been very patchy, but never had she been without a man for so long. Well, now the money side was picking up again, and who knew what opportunities might happen along in the talent field from the decorating business? She remembered Penny's happy voice from yesterday evening. That was what she wanted. The new job was OK, and it certainly beat cleaning for a living, but she needed someone to love her.

The next day, Saturday, brought a phone call from Andrea. Would she mind coming over and talking to Robert? She could bring the children and they could play with Andrea's three. Carol's boys both had something far better to do than go out with their mother, but Carly was glad to come, and went off happily with Andrea's Sally to her room.

The moment Carol met Robert, she was glad she had put on the new shirt and skirt Penny bought her, and bothered to take time over her hair and make-up. He was rather tasty. She liked older men when they were business types, and had firm handshakes and authoritative voices, as Robert did. She gave him her most winning smile, and was sure she saw an answering gleam of speculation in his grey eyes. This could be interesting.

They all talked in a civilised fashion about the proposed partnership. Robert was obviously worried that Andrea would be taking too much on, committing too much time and money to something that might well be a flop. Carol had to work hard to convince him that it was a viable project, especially as she had gone into it so haphazardly herself. For almost the first time in her life she was being made to think about the future, plan it carefully. It was not the way she usually went about things.

All the while, she was aware of another level of communication, of being assessed not as Andrea's partner, but as a woman. The prickles of excitement brought a new glow to her skin, a shine to her eyes. Instead of slumping back or perching nervously on the edge of her chair, she sat with her ample figure gracefully arranged, her legs crossed at the knee to show a fetching expanse of calf. Thank God her legs were still good. The outfit disguised some of her worst faults and the buttons left casually open on the shirt revealed just enough of her bust to look inviting. With a shiver of pleasure, she noticed that Robert couldn't keep his eyes from straying there. Perhaps he was a boobs man. If so, her luck was in. And then Andrea suggested another coffee and she pulled herself up. It was her friend's husband she was thinking of, she must stop it. Regretfully, she turned her attention to Andrea, asking about her children, talking about her own, reducing herself to boring middle-aged mum again. All the fun went out of the morning.

'You've had quite an interesting life, from what I hear,' Robert remarked, when Andrea disappeared into the kitchen.

'I've been about a bit,' Carol admitted.

He leaned forward a little, edged along the sofa to be nearer her chair.

'But you're on your own at the moment?'

Christ, Carol thought, he wasn't what you might call subtle. But he was rather nice. She wavered, tempted, exhilarated by the knowledge that the next move was hers. She had not played this game for ages, it was great to know that she still could, that someone still fancied her. She had been beginning to wonder whether she had lost it. She held his gaze, teasing.

Down the stairs came the thud of feet. Giggling, Carly and Sally burst into the room, full of some game they were making up. Abruptly, Carol switched the invitation off.

'I'm not married to anyone at the moment, no,' she said, and then put him off finally, 'but that's not to say I'm on my own.'

He was saved from having to cover his disappointment by Andrea's coming in with the tray.

'I am glad you two are getting on together,' she said, putting it down on the coffee table. 'After all, we're going to be seeing a lot of each other in the future.'

Carol certainly saw a great deal of Andrea during the next three weeks. They planned the launch party for Designs Unlimited, as they had decided to call themselves, down to the last detail. Replies to the invitations started to roll in. Most of the guests were Andrea's friends. To keep her end up, Carol had asked a few people but had no hope of them turning into customers. As a defiant gesture, she gave a card to the Cleves, but they already had something on that day. Penny was coming, and had given them quite a long list of names to invite, of whom some had accepted. Andrea and Carol were both hoping she would bring Duncan along so they could find out what she saw in him. And, as Penny had suggested, they sent an invitation to Jill.

'I wonder if she'll come?' Carol mused.

'She must be very busy,' Andrea pointed out. 'But it would be marvellous if she did.'

'Bet you she doesn't. She's avoiding us.'

In the event, Carol was right. A short note of empty regret was all they received.

'Told you,' Carol said.

'Oh well, there's plenty of others, after all.' Andrea looked at the long list of guests with its ticks, crosses and question marks. 'Do you think it will be a success?'

Carol thought of the food already prepared and stacked in the freezer, the cases of wine out in the garage. With plenty of food and booze, what could go wrong?

'Yeah, sure,' she said. 'They'll all have a wow of a time.'

CHAPTER THIRTEEN

When Duncan and Penny arrived at the party, it was just beginning to warm up. The first stiff groups had begun to mix a little and the occasional burst of laughter could be heard. Penny was in the mood to enjoy herself. Just to have Duncan so readily agree to come was enough to make her day. Accustomed, from painful experience, not to make demands on a man's time, she still could not get used to the fact that there was no wife to take first claim, no sensitive teenagers who must not suspect, no friends who might see them and report back home.

'I doubt if there will be anybody you might find useful here,' she warned as they walked up the driveway.

'Stop digging at me, Penny-lope,' Duncan said, mock-aggressive. 'I'm not on duty the entire time, you know. Sometimes I do things for sheer pleasure.'

They held hands, fingers laced, as Penny rang the bell.

Andrea took their coats and Robert, looking slightly amused by the whole affair, gave them drinks. Carol came to greet them, her abundant figure packed into a Dallas-style suit of pale grey silky stuff with one silver revers. She looked quite stunning, the Carol Penny used to know, but more so. All the old confidence was back.

'Penny! And this must be Duncan – nice to meet you. Penny, you're a real friend. All these people you talked into coming! Andy's mates have got their eyes out on stalks.'

Penny smiled, happy for her.

'You're glad you took the plunge now?'

'You bet!' Carol turned her seductive eyes on Duncan. 'Do circulate and impress people, won't you? They'll all think it's so exciting, meeting a real reporter from a daily paper.'

Duncan assured her that he would, but to Penny's relief seemed unmoved by Carol's opulent style.

'We seem to have been given the role of Rentaglitz,' he remarked. 'Do you think you can take it on?'

'For Carol and Andy, yes,' Penny told him. 'Besides I feel partially responsible for this, so I must do my bit towards making it a success.'

As well as the revamped bedroom, there were 'before and after' displays to look at. Somebody – Carol, Penny supposed – had taken pictures of various grotty rooms and had them blown up to poster size, then alongside each one was a drawing of how it would look after the Designs Unlimited treatment. Penny was impressed. It all looked most professional. Nobody else at the party would have guessed they were the work of a woman who had not put pencil to paper for years. Jill was right, she admitted. They did have talent, all four of them. It just needed bringing out. And it had been Jill who had been the cause of this renewed blossoming, however remotely. Her eyes sought Duncan, charming a group of Andrea's friends on the other side of the room, and her heart convulsed with brittle happiness. If it had not been for Carol's wanting an evening out . . . she followed the chain of cause and effect backwards, Carol lying at the party, Andrea getting them together again, Jill having an article written about her. It all came back to Jill again. For a brief moment, she felt that life was not just a random mess, but that it had a pattern and an order to it, if you could stand far back enough to see it. Maybe there was a reason for it after all.

'Penny, darling!' It was one of her old boyfriends, the only one she had ever managed to stay on civilised terms with. She switched on her party face.

'Roy! Sweetie, how nice of you to come along. Lovely to see you again. I didn't know whether you were busy at the moment, but I thought you might like an invitation.'

He sidestepped the chance to tell her what he was doing, thus giving away the fact that he was resting.

'You know me, darling, biggest liger in the business, though it isn't exactly Grosvenor House, is it? Who are all these people, for God's sake?'

There were plenty more like him there, Penny knew, just along for the free food and booze. Roy would lend his face and his air of success to the occasion, get smashed out of his mind and go home and forget the whole thing. Did Carol and Andy realise this, she wondered, innocents that they were? She hoped they were not expecting orders from even half the people here. If they got just one definite they would be lucky. Promotions like this only sowed the seeds. She steered Roy over to a couple who were looking lost and got them talking. Roy could be relied upon to entertain them with anecdotes about himself. He knew his obligation as a freeloader, and would throw off some tale about how wonderful Designs Unlimited was even if he couldn't remember exactly who his hostesses were.

Carol was on a glorious high. She had suffered a dreadful crisis of confidence for the last twenty-four hours, but with a couple of gins and the arrival of the guests, she bounced back with her full share of heedless optimism. It was all going wonderfully, she knew she looked great and people sounded very impressed with her displays. She replenished drinks and answered questions about the new company and lied shamelessly about her previous experience. What did it matter? She knew now that she could deliver the goods.

At the bar she ran into Robert, also doing his good host bit.

'Did I tell you how particularly gorgeous you're

looking today?' he asked, opening a fresh bottle of whisky.

Carol just could not resist it.

'No, but you can say it again if you like,' she invited. After all, it was a party, wasn't it? Everyone tried it at parties.

He ran a hand over the slippery surface of her suit, lingering on her bottom. 'Very nice,' he commented. 'Looks good on you. I like a woman to look like a woman.'

Carol leaned towards him till they were almost touching.

'I like a man who feels like a man,' she purred, then picked up the tray of glasses she had refilled and threw him a parting smile. 'See you, tiger.'

She bubbled with suppressed laughter as she handed round the drinks. She had not lost her touch. She could see it in the eyes of the husbands of Andrea's well-groomed but sexless friends. They stopped what they were saying to give her that swift appreciative look. Starved of attention as she had been this last year or more, she opened out and gave back for all she was worth.

Andrea saw only that her new partner was mixing well, getting round to all the guests. She seemed to be talking and laughing a lot, perhaps she was persuading them to give Designs Unlimited a go. She ran an experienced eye over the number of heads, and decided that all that were going to come had arrived by now. She began uncovering the mouthwatering array of food, then noticed a woman standing alone looking out of the window and went over to draw her into the crowd.

'Hello, Julie, I haven't seen you for ages. How's the family?'

'Oh – Andrea. Fine, thanks. We're moving, you know.'

Andrea scented business.

'Really? Where to? Nice place?'

'Oh lovely, just what we've been looking for, four bedrooms, and a double garage and you should see the kitchen! It's got everything. The only trouble is the garden. The previous owners did absolutely nothing to it except mow the lawn. I was just looking at yours, it always looks so beautiful. I really don't know where to start with ours, and John's no help, he's never at home, and when he is he's certainly not gardening.' She made a wry face and turned away from the window. 'You're blossoming out, aren't you? How are you going to find time to run a business and a home? I say – I've just had a thought! I suppose your Designs Unlimited doesn't do gardens, does it? Or are you just concentrating on interiors?'

For a moment Andrea's mind went blank. There had been so much to think about these last few days that the new idea took a while to root. Then she pulled herself together and tried to look intelligent.

'Well – yes,' she heard herself saying. 'We – er – we're not pushing the landscaping side today because we want to get the interiors off the ground, but we are offering a complete design service, inside and out.' She was amazed at how the words came out. She sounded so confident she almost believed herself. She picked up one of the pads of headed paper that had been left lying conveniently about. 'If you're really interested, I can come along and see the garden and discuss what sort of general ideas you have in mind – you know, easy maintenance, children's area, outdoor entertaining and so on – and then I draw up three alternative plans for you. You choose which you like best, then we put it into action for you.'

She looked at Julie, pen poised hopefully over the pad. Julie seemed impressed.

'That sounds very fair. It would certainly solve

the problem. I'd have to ask John, though.'

Spotting the classic get-out line, Andrea found a tenacity she did not know she possessed.

'Bring him over and see what he thinks. He is here today, isn't he?'

While Julie went to find her husband, Andrea signalled frantically at Carol, who strolled over.

'Carol! I think I may be making a sale. For a garden design! We never thought about gardens, did we?'

Carol stared at her.

'I don't know a bloody thing about gardens.'

'But I do. We can't let this one slip. Look, can you get this food uncovered while I follow it up? I've got Julie interested, but I'll have to persuade her husband. Have you got anything definite yet?'

Carol had to admit that she hadn't.

'Plenty of them are interested, but none of them actually asked me to go round and have a look.'

'There you are then, we must get this garden one.'

Ten minutes later, she was back at Carol's side again.

'I think I've done it! They've booked me to go round in a fortnight's time, after they've moved in, and discuss what needs to be done. Isn't it marvellous?'

'Wonderful!' Carol threw an arm round her shoulders and gave her a kiss. 'Clever old Andy Pandy. We're on our way!'

Andrea was still tingling with the excitement of success when Camilla Hastings approached her plate and glass balanced expertly in one hand, as overbearing as ever. Andrea greeted her with a confident smile. No more nagging from Camilla now. She was a businesswoman in her own right.

'Andrea!' Camilla took her arm and led her to a fairly quiet corner. She lowered her voice dramatically. 'Andrea dear, you're not really going into partnership with that woman, are you?'

Astonished, Andrea gaped at her.

'Well – I – yes, of course. That's what this is all about. I'm getting out of the house, Camilla, doing something worthwhile, using my talents.'

Her friend sighed, the woman of the world talking to the young innocent.

'My dear, she eats men! She had a go at Martin, but of course he didn't rise to it, he doesn't go for the overblown type. She's been all over old Jimmy Dobson and he lapped it up until Sheila came and dragged him away, and now she's trying it with Dave Ripley. But it's not them I'm worried about, it's your Robert.'

'Robert?' Andrea looked wildly about the room. 'Why?'

'My dear, you must have noticed. He's been drooling over her all afternoon. He can't keep his eyes off her. You really are asking for trouble, you know.'

Andrea spotted Robert on the other side of the room. A wine bottle in each hand, he was chatting to a small mixed group of their friends and refilling their glasses. Nothing out of the ordinary there, just Robert being the good host that he was, quietly seeing that everyone had all they wanted. She searched out Carol, and found her offering a plate of canapes to three women from the Flower Club. She could see them all nodding and smiling, obviously agreeing about something. Another woman joined the group, and was drawn into the conversation. Nothing could have been less threatening. She turned back to Camilla.

'I think you've been reading too much Jackie Collins. Carol's one of my oldest friends, we went to school together. And she's a very gifted artist. Designs Unlimited is going places, you'll see!'

Camilla gave her a sad look.

'I do so hope you're right. I'd hate to see anything happen to you and Robert. You're such a sweet couple.'

'Thank you, Camilla, but there really isn't anything to worry about.'

She excused herself and walked away, all the pleasure gone out of the party for her despite the fact that she did not believe a word Camilla said. She was just causing trouble, of course, like she tried to once before, suggesting that Robert was having an affair. Perhaps she and Martin were going through one of their bad patches again. Perhaps Martin was even having an affair. But not Robert, and certainly not with Carol. The idea!

As if called by her thoughts, Carol appeared.

'It's all going very well, isn't it? You're famous for your food, did you know that? Your Flower Club ladies have all been saying what a good cook you are. Have you seen Penny? Doesn't she look terrific? Being in love suits her.'

'Yes,' Andrea agreed. 'Yes, it does.'

They both looked at Penny, shining as she chatted to some people by the window. Carol and Robert? It was just Camilla's nasty mind. She hadn't enough to occupy her, for all her part-time work. Carol and Penny and Andrea were friends to the death, hadn't they vowed it on the banks of the reservoir?

'Mind you, you can see why,' Carol was saying. 'That Duncan's rather lovely, isn't he? I didn't realise he was so young, I only saw him in the half-light before, but then I was tied up with someone else.'

'Yes,' Andrea said again. She considered Duncan as he walked across the room and slung an arm round Penny's shoulders. 'But it doesn't matter, does it? Lots of women go out with younger men these days. As long as Penny's happy, and she is, you can see that.'

The two of them smiled indulgently, glad for their friend.

'Funny how things work out, isn't it?' Carol said, the nearest she ever got to philosophising about life.

Penny said much the same thing later on, when she and Andrea paused for a moment.

'Isn't it strange how our lives have all taken a turn for the better since we met up again? It must be meant. We all need each other, there's something that has to be worked out between us.'

'But what about Jill?' Andrea asked.

'I don't know,' Penny admitted. 'She must come into it somewhere. She's still influencing us even in her absence. But I suppose she doesn't need us. We were only ever foils for her, after all.'

She could not have been more wrong.

Jill was fighting against the almost irresistible force that pulled her towards the others that day. Circumstances seemed to be conspiring. Her mother had gently twisted her arm until she had to go and see her father again, home from hospital now with a nearly clean bill of health but creating a dreadful fuss over the healthy diet he was supposed to be following. Jill tried to convince him that fresh fruit and fibre did not have to be boring, but her mind was hardly with him. Behind his head the many faces of Jennifer smiled at her. The invitation she had received beckoned. Andrea and Carol – Designs Unlimited – twelve noon onwards – and it was only twenty minutes away, at Woodlands Park. When she escaped from her parents, the car seemed almost to drive itself, nosing round the manicured gardens of substantial new houses dressed to look old in leaded light windows and solid oak doors. She did not know this area, it had only been built in the last five years. She would just drive through she told herself, then get home. Mark and the children were waiting for her. There was a constituency bunfight this evening.

The street name jumped out at her, then she saw the cars parked thickly on both sides of the narrow road. She pulled up at the corner, shaking. People were still arriving. A couple with a child in tow rang at the door even as Jill watched, and a woman answered it. Andrea, unmistakably. Jill was sweating with what she vaguely recognised to be fear. There was the past, the thing that she wanted to face but was afraid to, terrified of what she might find. Andrea smiled, welcomed her guest in, an Andrea strangely untouched by the passing years, more poised maybe, but looking almost exactly the same. Jill sat holding onto the steering wheel as if to a lifebelt, wanting and not wanting to get out, to knock at that door, to be taken back into that close, exclusive little circle that had once been her shell. The door was closing as Andrea looked out again, along the road, straight at Jill. She snapped into action, switching on the ignition, shooting away before she realised that Andrea was gazing not at her, but at the next group of guests just turning into the street. But it was enough, the spell was broken. Mrs Jill Lovesey MP was on her way back home, back to the sanity of her own safe family.

CHAPTER FOURTEEN

Just as Penny had feared, the location filming of *Traitors* was even worse than the studio work. Living in each other's pockets night as well as day, the team had time and opportunity to intensify the dislikes and rivalries that had been apparent from the start. The director was at his wits' end and even the unit manager, a calm northerner who never had been known to flap in his life, was finding it difficult to cope.

'Look, sweetie,' he growled at the leading actor, 'I find the locations, that's what I'm paid to do. If you think you can do better then come and take over my job, and I'll do yours.'

He stomped off, clipboard in hand, to consult with the lighting director, leaving the leading man under the dripping pine trees with Penny.

'Why do they always have communist countries covered with sodding forests, and why do we always come to sodding Wales to film them?' he demanded, hunching his shoulders against the cold.

'Could be worse. Could've really gone to East Germany,' Penny pointed out.

'Nothing could be worse than this godforsaken place.'

Penny mumbled in agreement. She did not want to be drawn into another argument, she had to think herself into the part. This was her big scene, when her duplicity was finally discovered. She had to get the emotion right. Stamping her feet against the creeping chill, she burrowed into her character's head, taking on her fears, her obsessions, her hang-ups. The woman started to drape round her like a cloak, until Penny was standing differently, breathing more shortly, casting the muscles of her face into a new mould. The lights came on, the stage manager fussed over a detail to do with the props, the unit manager's radio crackled with impatient orders from the director. The last-minute changes were sorted out. Penny glared resentfully at the leading man, who was still grumbling on. He did not need the same time to step into his part, he just switched it on like a light.

'OK, let's go— '

Penny got into position, glad that the action was starting. It was all right while she was working, she could blank out everything else and become her character. She pressed herself against a tree, listening, waiting for the car that was to come along the forest track towards her. The first take of the day began.

By the evening, she was drained. As usual on location she had eaten too much, driven by the cold of the Welsh mountainside to take the comfort of the endless offerings of hot food. She was not happy about her performance. She had not done all that she had wanted to with it, it had not come out quite as she had envisaged. On the coach back to the hotel she sat wrapped in her own problems, ignoring the bickering going on around her. At least they did not try to draw her in so often now. She had gained a reputation for being stand-offish, but she did not care. She did not want to be part of it. She looked forward to a long hot bath and a quiet evening. No phone call tonight, though. It was the phone calls that kept her going, buoyed her up so that she felt detached from the rest of the team, walking in a little world of her own. But this evening Duncan was covering a first night and would not be in till the early hours. There would be no loving voice in her ear, reassuring her that she was not forgotten, listening to the latest tale of trouble amongst the team. Instead, she told herself, she would stay in her room with a book, and refuse to get in with the crowd at the bar. She would rest. God knew, she needed it. Her legs were beginning to buckle at the knees. She took out a hand mirror and scanned her face. She looked positively haggard.

A bath, a meal and a face mask later, Penny lay on the bed in her hotel room, failing to read the book she had promised herself. However hard she tried to concentrate, the image of Duncan in his velvet jacket and bow tie haunted her. There had been huge publicity for this new musical. Everyone who counted would be there for the opening, and everyone who wanted to be noticed by everyone who counted, including beautiful young girls who would do anything for a mention in the papers. She could not shake off the mental picture of a lithe eighteen-year-old with a Page Three figure hanging on Duncan's arm and gazing at him with eyes full of promise.

Her hand reached out for the phone. She had to talk to someone. Andrea? She would hardly understand, cosily married as she was. Carol? Carol knew how it felt, she had been through it enough times herself. She got an outside line and dialled.

'Pen! Lovely to hear from you. How are you?' Carol's voice rang cheerfully down the line, as clear as if she had been in the next room.

'Oh fine— ' Penny said automatically, then warmed by the prospect of a sympathetic ear, 'well, a bit fraught, really, cooped up with all these bloody people.'

'I wouldn't mind being paid to stay in a luxury hotel and do what I enjoy doing all day long,' Carol said.

'Darling, you've no idea—' Penny went over the squabbles on set, her worries about Justin, now staying with Mike and Wendy for the duration of the filming, and finally came round to Duncan.

'I mean, I know I don't own him. Far from it. But

God, I do miss him, Carol, and this evening there he is in the middle of some of the most beautiful women in London. It has to be a temptation.'

'They're all bastards underneath,' Carol agreed.

Penny hardly found this comforting.

'Not all of them,' she said loyally, though she knew Carol was right.

'Poor old Pen. This is the one, is it?'

'Yes,' Penny admitted. 'I've thought so in the past and I've been wrong, but this time – yes, I really think he is. Oh Carol, what am I going to do?'

A chuckle rolled down the line.

'You know bloody well. Hold on to him, you lucky cow. He's not married, is he?'

'No, no he's not.'

'Well, there you are then. And he loves you?'

'Yes, I think so. But not – not as much as I love him.'

'Do they ever? What are you worried about, Pen? You've got it all going for you. I could do with your problems.'

What was she worried about? Penny wondered. Just everything, that was all.

'You're right,' she said. And realising that she was being selfish, asked after Carol's affairs. How was Designs Unlimited going?

'Not bad,' Carol told her. 'Andy's doing a garden, and now there's a hall and stairs turned up, so we've got enough to keep us going.'

'That's great. And you're getting on all right still? You must see almost as much of Andy as we used to in the old days.'

'Yeah— ' Carol's voice became full of meaning. 'See a fair bit of her Robert, too.'

'*Carol!*' Penny was jolted out of her own pit of anxiety. 'You're *not!*'

'Well – let's say he'd like me to. He's quite tasty, is Robert, in a conventional sort of way.'

'For God's sake, Carol, don't be such an idiot!'

'Well really, Pen, I don't know what you're getting so steamed up about. You've put it about a bit yourself, haven't you?' Carol sounded put out.

'Sure, but not with friends' husbands. Not even to get on in this shitty business. It just isn't on, Carol.'

Huffier than ever, Carol tried to justify herself.

'I don't see the harm in it. I tell you, if it wasn't me, it'd be someone else. I don't think Andy Pandy gives him his oats. Not the way he likes it, anyway.'

'Let it be someone else, then.' Penny was genuinely worried for her friends. Andy would never get over it if she found out, and Carol needed Andy far more than she needed her husband. Or he her, for that matter. 'Look, Carol, don't get me wrong. Play six in a bed if you like, that's fine with me, but don't mess up this friendship just when we've all got it together again. You'll ruin Designs, too, if you're not careful, and that would be a pity.'

'Oh rubbish. You're a real old worryguts, Pen. It's only a bit of fun, I'm not going to run off with him. It'll put new life into their marriage, you'll see. I've seen it all happen before. Nothing like a bit on the side to make a man turn to the hearts-and-flowers bit. Andy'll be grateful to me.'

'I doubt it,' Penny said. But nothing she could say could move Carol. They finally rang off on a note of discord.

The call had a useful effect, in a way, at least it turned Penny's thoughts to other people's problems. She had not realised just how totally thoughtless Carol still was. It had not seemed to matter so much when they were young. Carol had been quite happy to drift through life snatching enjoyment where she could until Jill decided to organise her. Then she had managed to sabotage all the plans by getting pregnant. Even her abandoning of the baby

Samantha and her marriage was forgivable in a way, she had after all been only eighteen at the time and did not mean to do it. But to drift into an affair with a friend's husband just because he happened to be there? Penny could not condone that, for all her own varied past. Wendy had once been a friend of hers.

It had all gone so well at first. Penny, tired of the constant moving about after jobs, the killing rests when nothing was offered, saw security in Mike. She was disappointed in the progress of her career. It had not taken off as she had hoped in those heady days after leaving drama school. She was still chasing tiny supporting roles in provincial theatres and odd spots in adverts while some of her contemporaries were beginning to get leads. Then, when she was at a particularly low point, she met Mike at a party.

'An actress?' he said, on asking the usual questions about her. He was clearly impressed. 'What are you playing at the moment?'

Penny was doing precisely nothing, but did not admit to it. Instead she told him all about the roles she had done in the past. Mike listened with solemn wonder. They drank, and danced, and talked some more. The evening was over before Penny realised she did not know a thing about him. She had spent the entire time basking in his admiration, and it had been very good for her battered ego. When they next met, she asked what he did.

'I'm a social worker,' he told her. 'I'm concerned with old people's welfare.'

'Oh really? Is it interesting?' Penny disliked old people. They made her uneasy. She did not listen very closely to Mike's halting description of his work.

'But that's enough about me,' he said, with a self-effacing gesture that she was to come to know very well. 'You're much more fascinating. Tell me about that play you did in Liverpool.'

And she did. He was a good listener. It was his one big talent. They were married within three months, and a month later Penny found she was pregnant. They were both delighted. Of course, Penny thought, she could not look for work now, not with a baby on the way. Her agent told her she was mad to give up now, just when she might be on the verge of making a breakthrough. Penny told him she had heard it all before, and spent her afternoons browsing round Mothercare.

'We'll have a big family,' Mike enthused. 'At least four, boys and girls. They'll be so proud of their beautiful mother.'

They bought a flat on the ground floor of an Edwardian house in Lewisham and furnished it with a mixture of Habitat and renovated junk shop bargains. Justin was born and started their big family. Penny enjoyed wheeling him round the shops for a while, but by the time he was six months and no longer keeping her awake at night she began to get restless. She ordered *The Stage* from the newsagents and began memorising parts, just to keep her hand in. Mike could not understand it.

'I just don't see why you spend all this time learning words you'll never speak,' he said. 'If you want something to do, why don't you start a mother and toddler group? There's a great need for one round here, you know. Mothers tend to become isolated.'

'Don't tell me that, buster, I know already.'

She felt isolated from her own world. It had been such a relief at first to get away from the competition, the bitchiness, the recurrent poverty, but now she missed the excitement of it all, the nerves and the exhilaration and most of all the close camaraderie of a good production. She devoured the news and the gossip in *The Stage*, and scanned the adverts, tempted. Just a two-week run in a provincial theatre, just a bit-part in a television series.

Mike could cope by himself for that amount of time. But Justin – she would look at the baby, sitting up now amongst his bright plastic toys, and he would wave his arms at her and laugh. How could she bear to leave him? It was slowly borne upon her that she was no longer one person, but two, that any decision she took on her own life affected Justin as well, and that his needs had to come first because he depended upon her, and she loved him. She scooped him into her arms and felt the softness of his wispy hair and warm hard head against her cheek.

'Don't worry, Jussikins,' she told him. 'I'm not really going to leave you, not ever.'

But she could not help watching the television of an evening with an eye to parts she could have done, and done better.

Then her agent phoned. Was she still availabe for work, or should he take her off his books? She could not sever the connection altogether.

'Yes, I'm still available,' she told him.

And as luck would have it, just when she stopped chasing parts, they began to materialise. Mike gave in to her coaxing and agreed to take a day off while she went up to Television Centre to audition for one of them. Within a week, she had been given the job. Just one episode of a costume drama, but it was a start. Mike took a week off work this time to look after Justin while Penny went to rehearsals and recordings. It was a happy, close-knit company, the big-name stars mucking in with the supports. Penny was hooked. From then on she took whatever was offered, worrying all the time she was away whether Justin was all right, whether he was missing her, worse still whether he was not missing her. The girl in the flat above theirs was always willing to mind him. She was on her own with a toddler to bring up and needed the money, and Justin seemed happy enough with her. Only Mike made any complaints.

'You'll have to give it up once we have another baby.'

'I don't want another one,' Penny told him. 'I'm happy with Justin, he's all I want.'

It escalated into a full-scale row. The next evening, Penny found that her contraceptive pills had been thrown away. She went out and got some more, keeping them hidden. Nothing was said between them, but she knew that Mike was disappointed every time she started a period. He retaliated by getting a job in Hammersmith and suggesting that they bought a house now that he was earning more. No doubt he hoped a larger home and the lack of a convenient babyminder would keep Penny in, but he was out of luck. Their new neighbours were a couple called Wendy and Jim. Wendy had just miscarried and was feeling very low. She and Penny spent long hours drinking coffee and talking. Wendy, a maternal soul, drooled over Justin, who took to her immediately. She was more than willing to look after him when the chance of a lead in Manchester came up. Mike found himself out-manoeuvred.

It set the pattern for the next three years.

'You know what,' Penny remarked one day as she and Wendy sat in the garden idly watching the children grubbing in the earth. Wendy had produced two little girls in quick succession after the first tragedy, 'all you and I have to do to solve our respective problems is to change husbands.'

Wendy gaped at her, startled.

'What?'

'It's true. Just think – Jim thinks these are more than enough— ' she nodded at Wendy's daughters – 'wheareas Mike would like half a dozen. And the question of working, too. Jim would like nothing better than to see you out there earning enough to buy him a new car every year, and Mike wants a nice home-bird ready with his pipe and slippers every evening. He was enchanted with the idea of marrying an actress once upon a time, but he doesn't actually like living with one. He'd much rather have someone who bakes bread and has babies.'

Wendy looked apologetic. She had left some bread rising in her kitchen.

'I suppose so. It wouldn't work, though.'

'Idiot!' A sense of humour was not one of Wendy's strong points. 'I was only joking.'

Inside, the phone rang. It was her agent.

'Penny, darling girl, this is it, this is the big one.'

The thing she liked about Lewie was his boundless optimism.

'Oh yeah? Got Hollywood on the line, have you?'

'Better than that, darling. West End. It's a corker, Penny, you've got to do it. You are doing it. Audition one o'clock Tuesday, I've said you'll be there.'

Penny could hardly breathe. The West End!

'Did they ask for me?' she squeaked.

'They asked for you. So you are going.'

'Lewie darling, just try stopping me. Tell me more. What sort of production is it? Who's in it, any big names? What sort of part am I going for?'

By the time Lewie had finished explaining, Penny felt as if her head was about to burst open with the excitement. It was a political play, the sort that was described in the press as 'significant', with eight players, the leads being taken by two well-known TV and stage actors who were sure to draw the crowds. Penny was to audition for the younger female part, the girlfriend of the minister who was at the centre of the story.

When Mike heard about it, he tried to put his foot down.

'It could go on for months,' he objected.

'Yes, I hope so,' Penny said.

'But what about Justin? What about me? Don't you think of us at all?'

'Mike darling, don't you see? Once the rehearsals and the provincial try-out are over, I'll only be working in the evenings. I'll have all day to be with Juss. It's just perfect. I'll be able to be a mother and an actress.'

She out-argued him of course, she always could. Mike had to resort to sulking and the occasional tantrum. Penny tried hard to ignore him. Indeed, once the play got to Shaftesbury Avenue that was quite easy to do, for she was home when he was at work, and working when he was at home. When she got in some time after midnight Mike was usually asleep. It was only at the weekends that they saw anything of each other. Penny found that that suited her very well. She could stand Mike in small doses, in fact it was quite restful to talk to someone who did not think the world had ended when the play got a bad notice, who thought there were more important things in life than being upstaged or finding that the box office returns were falling. She did not notice that when he was not irritable he was silent. She was wrapped up in her own world. The play and Justin were enough.

Then one night when her taxi drew up even later than usual, she noticed that the lights were still on next door. She had hardly reached the front gate when Wendy came rushing out in a state of hysteria.

'Oh Penny, Penny, I'm so glad you're back. Can you come in? Please. I know it's late, but— '

Penny spent the next two hours listening, sympathising, soothing. Jim had left. He had gone to live, predictably, with his secretary who was everything that Wendy was not, cool, sophisticated, immaculately groomed and childless. Wendy was devastated. Penny hit on the one thing that she knew would be any comfort.

'You've still got the girls,' she pointed out. 'They're the ones that really matter. You've got them and you've still got your home. Jim will have to pay maintenance. I'll get you round to a really good solicitor first thing in the morning.'

'I don't want that,' Wendy wailed. 'Not that. Not dragging it all through the courts.'

'You'll have to, for the girls' sake,' Penny told her. 'Think of them. You have to think calmly and logically about this to keep their home together.'

She finally crawled into bed at gone three in the morning, exhausted.

It seemed that Penny's and Wendy's fortunes were at a joint low ebb. The week after Jim left, the theatre management announced that they were taking the play off. It was no longer breaking even, let alone making a profit. The cups of coffee were changed for bottles of wine. They got mildly drunk over the kitchen table and tried to sort each other out. Wendy was short of money and a man, Penny was soon to be out of work. Then came the offer of a short tour of the West Country.

'There we are!' Penny exclaimed in triumph. 'Two out of three accounted for. I'll go on tour and you must accept proper market rates for looking after Juss. Can't fix your love life for you, but I'll work on it.'

'I don't want anyone else,' Wendy sighed.

Penny actually believed her. Maybe it was the truth when she said it. But by the time she came back from a sun-soaked jaunt round all the main towns and seaside resorts of Devon and Cornwall, Mike and Wendy had discovered that what they both needed most in life was each other. Penny was nothing but an obstacle in their path.

The shock was total. She could not see that it was the most natural thing in the world. Mike and Wendy were ideally suited. She only remembered all those hours she had spent putting Wendy back together again after Jim's departure. Mike's having a girlfriend she could accept, but not that that girlfriend should be Wendy. Feeling utterly betrayed, she took Justin and left, dossing down in friends' flats till she found a place of her own. Anywhere, just so long as it was away from those two.

Then the battle over Justin started, first between their respective solicitors, then in court. Penny won, but she had never felt secure.

No, she thought, lying gazing at the ceiling of the hotel bedroom, she must not let Andy and Carol be drawn into that scene. Even if it did not get that far, and she rather thought that Carol might be right, and that it was just a brief fling, Andy must certainly never know. It was no good just telling Carol not to play with fire. She had already tried that, with total lack of success. Perhaps she could lure Carol away with the prospect of more glamorous men, of the world of fast living and gossip columns. Who did she know who might be used? Somebody must owe her a favour somewhere. She was so busy racking her brains for an answer to the problem that she almost forgot to miss Duncan's call.

Two more days of this dump, she told herself as she got ready for bed, and then home, to London, to Duncan.

CHAPTER FIFTEEN

In the corner of the dining-room that she had turned into an office, Andrea sat looking at the paperwork for Designs Unlimited. There was not much to look at. The In and Out trays were both empty, the correspondence file was painfully thin, the accounts were simple in the extreme. Andrea dealt with everything immediately it arrived, in the efficient manner that had first brought her to Robert's notice when she worked at his office. She sat with her elbows on the desktop, fingers laced, and considered what they had done so far. The hall and stairs that had been commissioned around Easter was now finished, and dear Camilla and Martin had come up trumps. They wanted their dining-room done Art Deco. Carol was at the library now, finding books.

'What's Art Deco, for Gawd's sake?' she asked, when Andrea first told her.

'Oh come on, Carol, even I know that. It's Thirties stuff, black dancing ladies holding white lamps, that sort of thing.'

'Sounds foul,'Carol said, but trotted off to find out about it quite amiably. One thing about Carol, she was quite easy to direct, if you went about it the right way. The trouble was, she got bored very easily. Andrea almost hoped they would never get a whole house to do. Carol would never stay the course.

She did not worry about the lack of orders, like Andrea did.

'Something will turn up,' she said, when Andrea tried to point out how uncertain everything was.

So far, something had turned up by the time each job was finished, but then they had only been at it a very short while. Andrea, the lover of security, wanted to see everything laid out in front of her. Carol did not look further than the next week.

Andrea sighed, and took down one of her gardening books. The gardening side, surprisingly, was doing just as well as the decorating. Even people who prided themselves on their artistic ability inside the home did not think further than a lawn and border when it came to the outside. Andrea's plan for Julie's garden had been much admired. They had been helped by a feature in the local paper on property. It had said that after fitted kitchens and bathrooms, what helped sell a house was a landscaped garden. Andrea was currently working on two. One just wanted the plan drawn up, the other wanted the work done as well. Andrea already had the sub-contractors lined up.

She worked happily at the more complicated one all afternoon, consulting plant guides, arranging trees, estimating costs. By the time she stopped to go and collect the children from their various schools, she was pleased with what she had achieved. She tried to tell Robert about it when he came in.

'. . . And then there will be naturalised bulbs under the fruit trees, crocuses and daffodils and narcissi,' she explained, 'and the beds in the centre will be used for bedding plants, to give bright colour in the summer.'

Robert nodded absently and patted her on the shoulder.

'Sounds very nice, dear.'

Andra felt a spurt of irritation. He sounded so patronising.

'You don't take Designs seriously, do you?' she asked.

He looked at her in surprise.

'Of course I do, dear. You're doing very well. I'm

very glad you've found something that interests you.'

Andrea supposed that it did all seem rather petty beside the decisions he had to take and the enormous responsibilities he had at work. In comparison, Designs was just what he took it to be – a harmless hobby to keep her occupied during the day. She served up the beef in beer, confident of his praise. Robert liked meaty dishes with plenty of flavour. She had been very careful not to let the standard of her cooking and housekeeping slip because of Designs.

He ate a few mouthfuls, then laid down his knife and fork.

'I'm sorry, darling, it's very nice, but I really can't manage it. I should have phoned to tell you – I had a heavy lunch today.'

'Oh.' Andrea felt rejected. 'I made it especially. I thought you liked it.'

'I do normally, dear. You know that.'

'Oh well— ' Andrea gathered herself together. 'Not to worry. Was it an important lunch? Did it go well?'

'Yes, I think so. You know how these things are.' He gave her a brief resumé of the discussion, which Andrea did not really follow. She was wondering whether some ground-cover was going to be needed on the dry spot on the south facing side of her garden plan. She came to find Robert looking at his watch.

'Look – ah – darling, I've got to go out. Do you mind? Chap I see on the train, Bill Chambers, you've heard me mention him, asked me out for a drink.'

Andrea stared at him. Robert never went out in the evenings. He was always too tired after his day's work. He was certainly not one for going out to the pub for a drink. They had plenty here.

'Oh,' she said. She could think of nothing else to say.

Robert looked vaguely uncomfortable.

'Bit of a sad case. Trouble at home and all that. Think he gets lonely.'

Andrea was touched by this unexpected piece of consideration for others. She kissed his cheek.

'I think that's very sweet of you, darling. You go off and keep him company.'

As she cleared the plates away, she could hear the shower running upstairs. Robert looked into the kitchen as he was leaving. He had combed his hair – what was left of it – differently, and he smelt of aftershave. Then she noticed his trousers.

'They're nice,' she said. 'I haven't seen them before. When did you buy them?'

'Oh – the other day. You said it was about time I got something new. Don't you remember? You said— ' he sounded almost defensive.

'Yes, yes, I did. They're nice.' Andrea laughed. 'You look quite trendy.'

Robert gave an odd smile.

'Yes, well – 'bye, dear.'

It was only afterwards that it struck her that he had gone to a great deal of trouble just for a drink with a friend. She was in bed by the time he got in. It was well past closing time, and Andrea was getting worried. Supposing he had been stopped by the police? Supposing— ?

'Sorry I'm late, darling.'

He kissed her forehead. His breath was heavy with whisky.

'I wondered where you'd got to,' she said.

'Went on to some club he knows afterwards,' Robert explained. 'God, I'm shattered.'

He got into bed and lay back with a great sigh that sounded more like vast contentment than exhaustion. He was asleep within minutes. Unaccountably disturbed, Andrea lay awake listening to his breathing.

Carol arrived late the next morning. Andrea,

already irritable, pointed out that they were supposed to be at the Hastings' in less than ten minutes.

'All right, all right,' Carol snapped back. 'It doesn't take that long to drive round there, does it?'

'We ought to get everything straight first, so we know what we're talking about when we arrive,' Andrea told her.

Carol shrugged, a gesture that Andrea was finding more and more annoying.

'So what's to talk about? It's no different from the other jobs, is it?'

Andrea changed tack. 'You do know what Art Deco is now, I hope?'

'Sure, sure, I've got the general idea. I still think it stinks, but if that's the way they want it, the customer is always right and all that.' She rubbed a hand over her face. 'You haven't got an aspirin or something, have you? I've got the mother and father of a headache.'

Andrea looked at her more closely. Under the make-up, she did look rather jaded.

'PMT?' she asked, instantly sympathetic.

'Er – yes,' Carol lied, not wanting to admit to a hangover. 'Gets you sometimes, doesn't it?'

'Oh, I know. I used to suffer terribly from water retention, until my doctor gave me these marvellous tablets. You ought to ask yours. Have you got the sort of doctor who listens to you?'

'Yeah well,' Carol played along with it. 'I'll do that.'

They arrived at the Hastings' with a unified front.

Andrea was hard-put to keep Carol's nose to the grindstone during the next week. The new project bored her, and producing three different designs in the same style was purgatory.

'Why can't they have something modern?' she asked. 'It's a terrific room, all that space, all those windows. I could do something really eye-catching, instead of this old-fashioned rubbish.'

'At least they are employing us, or will do if they like the drawings,' Andrea pointed out. 'There's nothing else on the interiors front at all. I think we ought to advertise. All those people we invited to the party, and all the food and drink we poured inside them, but not much came out of it. We'll have to put a regular ad in the local paper.'

'Get Pen to chase up some of those rich friends of hers,' Carol suggested. 'I bet they wouldn't want this Deco stuff.'

'We've already asked Penny to do so much. She was really marvellous at the party.'

'Yeah, but like you said, none of the people she brought along have put any work our way, have they?'

'I know, but all the same— ' Andrea stood gazing out of the window, tapping her teeth with a biro. There was a limit to what you could ask a friend to do. Her real friends had rallied round. First Penny, now Camilla – 'Jill!' she exclaimed.

'What?'

'Jill. We'll chase her up. I'll do it now.'

She got through to Jill's secretary. No, Mrs Lovesey was not in the House today, she was engaged in constituency work. Could a message be forwarded?

'If you would.' Andrea gave her name and Carol's, and that of Designs Unlimited. 'Will you tell Mrs Lovesey that we were very sorry she could not attend the launch party, but as we are sure she'll be interested in the company, we are forwarding one of our brochures to her.'

The secretary was politely non-committal. Andrea thanked her.

'Well, that didn't get us very far,' Andrea commented. 'Funny how none of us actually gets to talk to her. Anyway, I'll send off some of the things we produced for the party, with a personal letter. That might get some reaction from her. Then I'll see what the rates are for an ad in the paper. You'll have to help me with the layout of that.'

'What? Oh – right.' Carol was staring blankly at the wall in front of her, a dreamy smile on her face.

Andrea came over to see how far she had got.

'Oh Carol, you've not done anything! We promised the drawings within ten days.'

'Keep your hair on, for Chrissakes! I've only just started. Give me time to think.'

'Sorry.' Andrea went off to make some coffee. She sometimes thought that it might be better if Carol did her side of the work at her own house.

She said as much to Robert over dinner that night.

'Be a pity if you fell out,' he said. 'But if this is all getting too much for you— '

'It's not getting too much for me, it's just that I find Carol a bit frustrating at times.'

'Well of course I don't really know her, but perhaps it might be better if you saw a little less of each other,' Robert suggested.

'I think you might be right,' she agreed. 'Darling Robert. You always know how I feel, don't you?'

He looked almost embarrassed.

'Mm, yes,' he muttered, and changed the subject.

It was later, when she looked in the cloakroom to check that the boys' wellingtons were properly marked, that she noticed the new sports bag on the floor.

'That's funny,' she said, showing it to Robert. 'I wonder where this came from?'

'Oh – er – it's mine,' Robert admitted.

'Yours? But you don't play any sports.'

'That's no reason why I shouldn't start, is it? You know what Camilla says about keeping fit.'

There was a defensive note in his voice. 'Thought I'd take up squash. Might join the leisure centre.'

'Squash? But that's an awfully energetic game, isn't it? You want to be careful not to overdo it at first, darling. After all, you're— ' she stopped herself just before reminding him that he was over fifty now.

'I'm not drawing my pension yet,' Robert snapped, and went to pour himself a whisky.

He went to bed early that night, and was asleep before Andrea was out of the bathroom. Andrea looked at his face, slack against the navy flowered pillowcase. The poor darling had been overdoing it, she decided. But she had the distinct feeling that her life was getting a little ragged about the edges.

The reply from Jill arrived within the week, and was disappointing. Rather formally, she wished them well in their enterprise. There was no mention of even attempting to put any work their way. Andrea found it strangely disturbing. The old Jill would have jumped in with both feet, applauding the idea, adding several of her own, goading them into bigger and better schemes. Maybe she just had too much else to concern herself with. There was, after all, both her demanding job and her family. Why should she be bothered with a potty little business like Designs Unlimited? That was it, Andrea told hereself. She simply had more important things on her plate than this. But then, in the sixth form, Andrea had thought the clever and original Jill Somers had more important people to take up, and yet she had gone out of her way to make a friend of her. It had been one of the great surprises of Andrea's life.

Jill opened a new world for Andrea. She had long been vaguely discontented, suspecting, as all teenagers do, that there were better things out there if only she could get hold of them. But it was not until Jill drew her into her inner circle that Andrea realised what a small, restricted life she had been leading. Instead of the old round of chapel, Sunday school, youth club, homework, there was a huge range of exciting new possibilites. Now that they were in the sixth form, they were allowed joint club meetings with the boys' school next door. So there was the Debating Society, the International Society, the Film Club and the Literary Society to go to. Jill soon had a say in all of them, particularly the Debating Society. She was hauled up before the headmistress, along with her fellow conspirators, for arranging such subjects as 'This House believes that marriage is a restriction on a free society' and 'Religion is the only opiate that should not be allowed to the people.' The administrations of both schools had not yet come into the Sixties. Jill was especially contemptuous of her headmistress.

'What she thinks she's running is a Seminary for the Education of the Daughters of Gentlefolk,' she declared. 'It's about time she woke up and realised that we're not in the Edwardian era any more.'

To Andrea's horror, Jill suggested that the next debate should be 'This House believes that contraception should be freely available to all over the age of twelve.'

'Jill!' Andrea squeaked. 'You'll be expelled!'

'Good,' Jill said. 'Can't you see the headlines in the local paper? "Councillor's Daughter Expelled over Pill Row". Fabulous!'

For Jill's warfare with her parents was total. Any weapon was admissible. Andrea watched, appalled. The lengths Jill would go to to score a point made her own small battles seem quite harmless by comparison. And battles there were. Jill saw to that. First it was minor things like bedtimes.

'Andy, *nobody* goes to bed at half-past ten on a Saturday night,' she insisted.

'My parents do. That's why they like me to be in before then.'

'Well for God's sake, you've got a key, haven't you? This is a party, not a kiddies' tea. It won't get going properly till ten.'

'But I don't know these people. I haven't been invited.'

'Of course you haven't. Neither have I. We're gatecrashing.'

Andrea quailed inside. It was all too much to take in at once. What on earth was she going to say to Mummy?

'Where have you told your parents you're going, then?' she asked.

Jill gave a wolfish grin.

'Romano's.'

Andrea gasped. Romano's was a cellar coffee bar with a wicked reputation. Rumour had it that drugs were to be had there, and it was regularly raided by the police. Nothing had ever actually been found, but the unsavoury stories made it very popular. Jill would not have dreamed of going there really, since it was patronised by the plebs from the Technical College, but it was very handy for worrying her parents.

'Look, if you really need evidence, I'll give you some,' she offered, ever inventive in the cause of rebellion. 'I'll write you an invitaion.'

Which she did, and in the end Andrea showed it to her mother, since not to go would have brought the full force of Jill's disfavour down upon her head. She promised to be in by eleven, knowing that she would not, and finally arrived home at one. Her father had phoned the police by then. When she got to school on Monday, she found Jill exulting in the latest set-to with her own parents.

'Dad heard from some police crony that there

was going to be a raid on Romano's, so he went down there to get me out! Imagine! My dad down that dive. I nearly died laughing. And when I wasn't there, they thought I'd been spirited off by white-slave traders or something, because someone saw somebody that looked like me go off with these Arabs from the language school. They were having forty fits. It was fabulous.'

The episode had given Jill the full attention of both parents for nearly all of Sunday. She was high on it for days.

Sex was another device Jill used. Although far too insecure and frightened of the consequences to take the plunge, Jill persuaded a girl whose father was a doctor to get some leaflets on contraceptive methods for her, and left them in her room, just hidden enough to be found. That caused another huge row. Had they not been fearful of becoming gossiped about, Jill's parents might have consulted the Child Guidance people. As it was, mindful of maintaining their position, they tried to handle it themselves.

Andrea never quite got over being shocked at Jill's behaviour towards her parents. An only child herself, she had often wished for a sister, and could not understand Jill's consuming jealousy of Jennifer. She would have been proud of a big sister so beautiful and clever. She would have been someone to admire. But then Andrea was not Jill, she was content to sit in others' shadows. That was why Jill liked her.

Now, after ten years of watching her own boys compete for attention within the family, Andrea could understand it better. What if she and Robert had always given all their love and praise to Anthony, the elder and brighter of the pair? Matthew already had a chip on his shoulder about Anthony being clever, despite the fact that he had always been encouraged to develop his own interests and had constantly been assured of their appreciating his worth. If they had treated the boys as the Somers treated Jennifer and Jill, maybe Matthew would have been driven into rebellion by now.

She sat and pondered the problem one evening when Robert had gone out to keep the unfortunate Bill Chambers company. Carol's accusation once more came to mind, that Jill had not tried to rescue Jennifer at all, but rather had held her under. No, she could not believe that that was true. And yet – that would be a very strong reason for not having anything to do with the rest of the gang now.

CHAPTER SIXTEEN

It was not often that Jill watched the television, and then only the current affairs programmes. Now, after a gruelling day, she sat back to see what Newsnight had made of the events of the last twenty-four hours. She was a few minutes early in switching on, and a trailer for a new drama series was running, a spy story, as far as she could see. She watched it without interest, too concerned with her own inner turmoil to care much about the figures on the screen. Then as if summoned up out of her own consciousness, there was Penny, furtive, suspicious, searching through a microfiche, listening to the two main characters talking. To Jill, she seemed to be spying on her, creeping into her flat, poking at the hidden corners of her mind, asking, asking. She punched the off-button and the image died, but the hunted feeling stayed with her.

They would not leave her alone, Penny, Carol and Andrea. Ever since January, when that article in the magazine came out, they had been pursuing her, working on the almost unbearable burden of guilt that she carried. She thought she had learnt to cope with it, even in part to accept it. The continual feverish work pushed it into the background, Mark's love and his belief in her took the weight from her soul. She thought she was strong now, that she had conquered it, until they came back, ghosts out of the past, to haunt her.

First there was the invitation to the reunion lunch, that had been bad enough. Then Penny's voice, mercifully on the answering machine, but unnerving all the same. After that it was this decorating business, more invitations, phone calls, brochures. Now Penny was getting into her very home, her fastness. Jill had begun to develop a nervous habit of glancing behind her, afraid that one of them might be there. She ought, she knew, to go and consult a doctor about it before she started seeing them everywhere, before she became too scared to open doors, thinking that one of them was standing on the other side waiting for her with accusation in her eyes.

No, all she needed really was Mark's reassurance. She had been away from home far too much, the strain was beginning to tell. She would not let these fantasies get a hold on her. She was not paranoid, she was a normal, well-balanced woman. It was just a manifestation of stress. She must take more time out to relax. Perhaps she should take up some sport, or exercise. Jogging, aerobics. She led a very unhealthy life, rushing about, staying up late, trying to be in two places at once. She must take control of herself. She pushed the on-button, and watched Newsnight with all her considerable powers of concentration.

But sleep eluded her that night. The past stalked all around her in the dark and the present questioned her in bright, friendly voices. How was she doing? Would she like to come to a party? A lunch? Perhaps she would like to look at these brochures? Have a room redecorated? Meet up again? Let us back into your life? Questions, questions. False, insincere. She knew what they really wanted to know. What did you do to Jennifer? What happened? What happened?

'No!' She sat up in bed, shouted defiance at them. 'Go away!'

She went into the bathroom, swallowed two sleeping pills, read in bed until she began to feel them take effect. Only when her eyes would hardly stay open did she switch off the light.

She woke feeling heavy and oppressed. Something had to be done about this, she decided, as she stood under the shower trying to wash the bonds away. She had to face it, since running away was not working. She must look it in the eyes and fight it. Meet the others again, Penny, Carol and Andrea. Then they would go away and leave her in peace. As she dried and dressed, and ate her breakfast, the idea seemed feasible. Difficult, but feasible. But when it came to picking up the phone and making the first step, she found that she just could not. Try as she might to lecture herself into it, her hand would not pick up the receiver. There had to be some other way.

'The reservoir,' she said out loud.

That was it. She would go back. Not just drive past it, as she did that time on the way back from seeing her parents, but stop and stand by the shore, and lay the ghosts. That was the answer.

This resolution she was able to stick to. The next Saturday morning saw her there.

A new generation of young people came to the water now. Unlike Jill's contemporaries, they did not see an exciting world ahead just waiting for them to come along and take what they liked from it, but a hostile place from which a living had to be wrested. Even here in the prosperous outer suburbs jobs were not there for the asking, as once they had been. And yet, looking at them, they seemed to be enjoying themselves. Jill was glad, with the part of her that was not absorbed in her own problems. They were still larking about on the grassy banks, groups of pretty girls in shiny swimsuits, boys showing off, music blaring. Ghetto-blasters now, not the weak trannies that used to annoy the staider members of the public so effectively.

Jill looked out across the water, glittering in the summer sunshine, inviting, innocent-seeming. The Mirror dinghies were still there, but they were outnumbered by the sailboards that skimmed across the dancing waves at breathtaking speed, their helmsmen spreadeagled, braced against the pull of the wind. Jill's heart stopped each time one collapsed, flopping into the waves, but always they climbed back, dragged up the jointed mast, raced off again. A safety launch puttered about, but had no rescue work to do, no limp figure to haul desperately from the water. Her mind veered away, refusing still to recall. When she finally returned to the car to drive home, she had still got no further than setting out across the reservoir with Jennifer by her side and the threatening dark clouds above. Beyond that was a gate through which her memory would not go.

Penny also had a problem with the past, the very recent past in the form of her performance in *Traitors*. Due to rescheduling, the first episode was to go out much sooner than had been planned, and the publicity machine, such as it was at the BBC, had rolled into action. She saw herself briefly on the trailers and hated it. Duncan, who had seen the previews, told her she had nothing to worry about.

'You're terrific, Pen, really terrific. The whole thing's good, it grips the viewer from the start. The bad working atmosphere might even have been a help, because the creeping suspicion comes over. You doubt the most innocent-seeming people even by the end of the first episode. I think you may well find you've got a hit on your hands there. Just you watch the ratings and see if I'm right.'

'Mm,' Penny said doubtfully. 'I sure hope so.' What she really wanted to know was how she had done.

Duncan understood all about the performer's voracious ego. He put his arms round her.

'And you, darling, you are great. Even though you don't have a lot to do in that first episode, you really come over. You're a simmering presence. Just wait till a couple have gone out, then I'm sure I can get a piece in about you. It's going to do you a lot of good, is *Traitors*, it could be the start of a real upswing in your career. Believe me.'

She wanted to.

'I've thought that so often before, and it's never really happened,' she said.

'It will this time. Think positive, love. You will succeed, you have a vast talent.'

His tremendous confidence was a continual tonic to her. He believed absolutely in himself and his own abilities, and the belief flowed out into her life. When she was with him, she felt she could do anything, solve any problem, sweep obstacles aside. Nothing presented any lasting difficulty, for together they were irresistible. It was only when they were apart that she doubted, wondered how long this could last, trembled to imagine how empty her life would be now without him. No amount of success in her career could ever compensate for that.

'Come round and watch the programme with me, and hold my hand, and then I know it will be all right,' she asked him.

'I was hoping you'd come and see it at my place. I wanted to celebrate a star performance.'

Sadly she shook her head. She knew that if Duncan had planned to mark the occasion, then it would be something to remember always. But there was one huge obstacle, that she did not even want to remove.

'I always watch with Justin.' she explained. 'It's a sort of ritual, staying up to see Mum on the telly. I've done it ever since he was about two, as long as the piece was at all suitable. I don't want to stop it now, especially not now, when he's being so difficult. You do understand, don't you?'

'Oh sure, sure— '

But she could see the line of impatience tightening round his mouth. Unlike some of her boyfriends in the past, Duncan made no attempt to win Justin over. He accepted him as an integral part of her life, chatted on the odd occasion when Justin was in one of his communicative moods, and even on one isolated evening helped him with some homework, but he certainly did not turn up with expensive bribes or ask Justin what he would like to do at the weekends.

Penny felt the terrible fear of losing him clutch at her heart again. There were so many other women out there, without truculent teenagers ever present to spoil an intimate evening.

'I can send him off to bed directly it's finished,' she said, 'he won't be in the way for long, it's not on late— '

'All right, Pen, it's OK. It's a movable feast, I'll just bring along some Coke for Justin as well.' He kissed her creased forehead. 'Don't look so worried, love. You worry too much. You'll worry yourself into a nervous breakdown one of these days. Relax, loosen up.'

She smiled into his eyes.

'I'll try.'

'That's better. Nothing's insoluble, you know.'

'I know.'

'Just leave it to me.'

'I will.'

To him, nothing *was* insoluble. That was what worried her. If the time ever arrived when he came to see her as a problem, he would simply step round her. There was a hard edge to him that she admired, but was afraid of.

She was twitching with nerves by the time the evening came round. She never liked watching her own performances, always vowed she would never do so again, but when it came to the point she had to. She could not pretend that something that had dominated her life for weeks just did not exist. Duncan arrived with a large box of food, which he insisted that Penny should not look at, two bottles of champagne and a six-pack of Coke.

'Something for everyone,' he said. 'How's the star? Got first-night nerves?'

'It wouldn't be so bad if it was on stage,' Penny said. 'You can improve a live performance if it isn't quite right at first. But there's nothing I can do about *Traitors*, it's all in the can. If it's dreadful, all I can do is emigrate.'

'You'll have to go to the Gobi Desert, then. They're planning to sell this one all over.'

Penny groaned. Millions of strangers, all round the world, watching her make a cock-up of a perfectly good part.

'Des said he was going to watch it,' Justin put in.

'Oh great.' Penny said. That was all she wanted, the ghastly Des grinning at her and making comments next time he turned up.

They sat waiting for it to begin, looking like a perfect family group, Justin sprawled over an armchair, Penny and Duncan sitting on the sofa with fingers linked. Penny made a sudden hopeless wish that it could always be like this, the three of them on amicable terms, living a normal life like normal people. But she knew it was just an illusion. Her life did not work out like that. Duncan squeezed her hand and she smiled at him. Live for the moment. She had him here now. Just enjoy it.

Duncan was right in his analysis. It was good. Penny sat squirming with embarrassment at all the things she felt were wrong with her performance, but still it came over very strongly.

'Oh God,' she groaned at one point, 'look at Graham, isn't he a ham?'

Justin shushed her.

'I can't hear, Mum, when you're going on.'

She knew then that it was going to be all right. Justin was an excellent barometer. If he was hooked, the rest of the viewing public might well be. She relaxed, leaning back against Duncan, letting him put an arm round her shoulders. The story unfolded. Even knowing the plot backwards as she did, it was still gripping. And everyone had given of their best, despite the circumstances.

'I think you're right, you know,' she said to Duncan. 'The bad atmosphere must have helped, it has put an edge on everyone's performance. Look at Geoff, he's really pulled it off, and Peter's put flesh on some pretty sparse lines. It's so involved, though. Do you think people will be able to follow it?'

'Don't underestimate their intelligence. They've cut their teeth on John le Carré, remember.'

The closing credits rolled. Duncan fetched the champagne out of the fridge.

'Put that disgusting muck down and have a proper drink,' he told Justin. 'Your mother's very talented lady. I think the phone's going to be ringing with quite a few offers that can't be refused these next few weeks.'

He poured three sparkling glasses.

'To the star,' he said. 'Long may she shine.'

'Cheers, Mum,' Justin responded, and his face lit with one of his rare smiles.

They drank, laughing, the three of them united by their pleasure in Penny's success. It was one of those perfect moments that should be frozen in a crystal bubble and kept for all time.

'Food,' said Duncan, and unpacked the contents of his cardboard box. Smoked salmon, French cheeses, exotic salads, patés were heaped on the dining table. 'You won't get Red Cross parcels like this in the Gulags,' he told Penny. 'You'd better watch that Anderson character, I think he's working for the KGB.'

'There's far more to it than that,' Penny laughed. 'Just you wait. Deals and double-deals till you don't know which way anyone's facing.'

Justin picked up a little pyramid of Valancay, his lip curled in disgust.

'What's this?'

'Goat's cheese. Put it down.'

'Yuk. Smells foul. It's all dirty.'

'Justin!'

'No-one asked you to eat it, sunshine,' Duncan told him. 'If you don't like what the management provides, you can always go down the chippy.'

'Thanks, I will,' Justin said.

'Oh Juss— ' Penny could see the perfect evening slipping away before her eyes. 'There must be something here that you like.'

Justin finally sorted out a plateful and went to eat it on the sofa with a computer magazine spread out before him. Duncan ignored him. Penny drank two more glasses of champagne but instead of getting light and giggly could feel a maudlin hopelessness welling up. The prospect of success meant little when her life was such a mess. She ought to be used to it by now. Give with one hand, take away with the other. Yet she still went on expecting that one day it would all come together.

She realised that Duncan was talking about his job, and focused her attention. She must not let herself slip into self-pity.

'. . . like working with a piledriver. I've met some self-made thrusters in my time but this one beats them all.'

'I thought you thrived on challenge,' Penny said.

'So long as it doesn't come up and hit me on the head.'

They talked for a while about alternative openings. Duncan mentioned getting back into television again, he had access to the grapevine and there were rumours of interesting projects starting up. But Penny was sure he was holding something back. She sent Justin off to bed.

Duncan held out a hand to her, drew her into his arms.

'Darling, darling, you're so tense. You let that boy wind you up like piano wire. You'll snap one day if you let him get to you. Relax, let go a little.' He ran his hands over her back, soothing the crackling nerves.

'You don't understand,' she told him. 'You can't, you haven't children of your own. I know he seems like a sulky little horror to you, but he's my son and I love him. I love him so much it hurts.'

'Yes, I know that.'

She felt a small sigh escape his chest and looked up at him. For once the careless confidence was missing from his face.

'Hey— ' he smiled, 'this is supposed to be a celebration, remember? Come and sit down.'

Penny removed the remains of Justin's meal from the sofa and they curled up together.

'It's going to be all right, you know,' Duncan assured her, in between kisses.

'What is?' Penny asked. She still had half an ear alert for noises from Justin's room. She did not like making love when he was in the flat.

'Everything.'

He reached for the remote control set and turned on the television, adjusting the sound level to blot out any noise they might make.

'There,' he said, 'Safe. Now forget it all. Forget everything except you and me. Stop thinking.'

She did not believe it would be possible, but it was. First the outside world disappeared, and then her internal worries dissolved, until there remained only the two of them, and the pleasure they gave and took, and made for each other.

Penny lay drifting at last on a dark sea, happy in every cell of her body. The reality beyond herself and Duncan came trickling slowly back, but it no longer mattered. Just as long as he was here, the rest of the world could go hang.

'Best ever, ever, ever,' she murmured, tracing the lines of his body dreamily with her fingers.

He caught her hand and studied it. It looked oddly dressed, with rings and nail varnish, compared with the nakedness of the rest of her.

'So far,' he said. 'The best so far. There's no limit to you and me.'

'Yes. I feel that as well.' She gazed at him, drinking in again the features she carried constantly with her. 'I love you.'

'I love you.'

She knew it was the truth. He was not one to pretend out of a sense of payment for what had gone before. He was deeply honest with his emotions, sometimes painfully so. The possessive female in her wanted him to go on, to speak of the future, to commit himself, but she managed to curb it. He would tell her when he was ready, he was not one to be pushed.

'Darling?'

She caught her breath, the slight hesitation in his voice making her heart turn over.

'Mm?'

'I'm going over to the States again.'

'Oh.' She was filled with a terrible fear. 'When?'

'The day after tomorrow. I only knew this afternoon.'

So that was what he had been holding back earlier, when they had been talking of jobs.

'How long for?' She was surprised to hear herself speaking so calmly.

'About a week. I've got to do some interviews.'

'I shall miss you.'

Such a vast understatement. A whole week of empty days stretched out before her, with a great question mark at the end.

'I shall miss you, my darling. It's a big lonely place. So I wondered – could you come too? You could leave a number with your agent. And I wouldn't be working all the time. We could do the town, see what's happening on Broadway. You could go shopping on Fifth Avenue.'

It was a prospect of such dizzying pleasure that she could hardly contain it. A whole week together, and in New York! She could not speak.

'You've never been there, have you?'

'No,' she managed to whisper.

'You'd love it. There's so much I want to show you – places, people. I can't describe the atmosphere. You have to be there to feel it.'

She listened, spellbound, as he rolled out New York in front of her feet, inviting her to step right along. For a short, delirious time she walked with him, believing in the dream.

'So you'll come? You've got a passport? I can hurry a visa for you.'

'Oh darling, I'd love to, you know that. There's nothing I want more. It would be wonderful— '

'But?' he supplied, a dangerous note in his voice.

She shivered, unable to meet his eyes.

'You won't leave Justin?'

She shook her head.

'Good God, Penny, it's only a week, he's not a baby. You left him to do that location work.'

'I know, that's just it, don't you see? I've already left him only a few weeks ago, and there were all those days when I was recording in Birmingham. If I go again, he'll be with Mike and Wendy practically more than he's with me.'

Duncan said nothing, but his face was tight with anger.

'And it's his exams coming up. He needs some support then, he's not academically inclined. I can't just abandon him with that in front of him.'

'You wouldn't be abandoning him. It's only a week, and he'd be with his father.'

'But that's just it.'

There was a long crackling silence.

'OK, if that's the way you want it.'

Duncan picked his shirt off the floor, began to dress.

'Oh darling, please— ' Penny reached out to touch him. 'Please don't take it like that. Try to understand. I'm so afraid of losing him.'

In silence, Duncan zipped up his trousers, then turned to look at her.

'You'll lose him one day. He'll grow up, and leave home. And then what will you do? You'll have spent all this time giving up everything else in your life for him, and he won't thank you for it. If there's one thing calculated to turn a child against you it's telling him you've sacrificed everything for him. It's an emotional burden, and one that most teenagers find far too much to carry.'

Penny bit her lip, refusing to recognise the truth, but knowing that he spoke from experience. He might not be a parent, but he had been an only son with an adoring mother.

'You get on all right with your mother now,' she pointed out gruffly.

'Now, yes. But not when I was growing up, having that held over my head the entire time. What's my mother got to look back on now? Nothing but a cuttings file. I don't live near her, I don't visit her that often, I certainly haven't given her any grandchildren, and she's very little else in her life. It makes me feel guilty, but it still doesn't make me go back any more frequently. I've got my own life to live. Do you want Justin feeling guilty about you, thinking that he ought to find time to go back and see the old girl?'

Her eyes filled at the cruelty of it.

'No,' she said, blindly searching for her dress. She felt unprotected, arguing like this with nothing on. How could this happen? How could two people who had been as near to being one as you can get on this earth spring so far apart so suddenly? 'I do have a life of my own,' she pointed out, trying to defend herself.

'A career, yes. But is that enough?'

She felt transparent. He could see through all her pretences, strip off her self delusions. Of course it was not enough.

'No,' she admitted.

'Well, think about it.' He retrieved his jacket, and not waiting to find whether he had won or not, made for the door. 'I'll call you when I get back.'

Penny was too crushed even to try to stop him.

All through the next day, she dithered about the flat unable to do anything. Every time the phone rang she jumped out of her skin and rushed to pick it up, her hands trembling. But always it was just another well-wisher, saying how much they had enjoyed *Traitors*, and what a brilliant job she had done with the part. Penny thanked them all mechanically, and put off all offers of celebratory drinks, meals or parties. A dozen times or more she nearly rang the paper. Twice she actually dialled, only to slam the receiver down again. What could she say? Not that she was going to go with him, and that was the only thing he wanted to hear. By the evening, she became desperate, and rang his flat. No reply. She was left wondering where he was. She told herself that she ought to go out, that hanging round waiting for the phone to ring was the ultimate mug's game, but still she stayed, even though she knew the call would not come. He knew her too well. He was letting her regret it.

'That creep Randall coming round again?' Justin enquired, as she prowled restlessly from room to room.

'No. And don't call him that.'

'He's a right poseur. All that foreign food. Yuk.'

Penny felt close to screaming.

'Well you won't be forced to eat any for a while, he's going to the States tomorrow,' she said, her voice tight.

'Good.'

Justin tucked into the Cornish pasty and chips she put before him, pausing only to shake on another dollop of tomato ketchup.

'Mum, can Des come round?'

'Yes, yes— ' Penny was not in a state to refuse anything.

'Good, only I've got this new computer game I want to show him.'

She managed to focus her interest on this. She

knew Justin had no money left, he had spent his last penny at the weekend.

'How did you get that?'

'Dad gave it to me.'

He wolfed down the Angel Delight and disappeared into his bedroom.

The next day, after the plane had taken off and there was nothing more to hope for, Penny went out and spent a lot of money on new clothes, but even that failed to have its usual therapeutic effect. What was the use of new clothes if Duncan was not here to take them off her?

Justin failed to come home after school. He rang from Mike and Wendy's.

'Mum? I thought I'd stay over here for the weekend.'

'Oh Juss— !' She couldn't keep the wail out of her voice. She took a shuddering breath and tried to sound reasonable. 'Darling, we were going to go out. remember? I thought you might like to go to Thorpe Park. You enjoyed that last time. All those rides— ' She knew she was resorting to bargaining with him, but could not help it.

'Thanks, Mum.' Justin sounded gruff. Penny remembered Duncan's words. She was putting an emotional burden on his shoulders. 'Another time, eh? I mean, I'd like that, but— '

'All right, darling.' She smiled at her reflection in the mirror, projecting happy unconcern. Her face felt stiff. 'Another time, perhaps. Do you need any clothes? You didn't take anything with you, did you?'

'It's OK, I've got enough here.' He was relieved now, let off the hook. 'See you Monday, Mum.'

It was the fact of his having sufficient clothes for a weekend already at his father's that hurt most of all. He hardly needed to move in, he was halfway there already. Penny slid slowly down the wall and sat on the floor. The flat was silent and empty, as empty as her life now that both Justin and Duncan had gone out of it. She crouched unmoving for a long, long time, staring into the abyss. There was nothing to get up for.

CHAPTER SEVENTEEN

That same Friday afternoon, Carol was also wandering about the house in an aimless fashion, though she was pretty sure the call she was waiting for would come through in the end. First Carly, then the boys, then Samantha came in from school, and the house filled up with noise. More boys arrived, friends of Rory's, and the cheap stereo crackled into life. The sound of Meatloaf pounded through the thin walls. Carly burst into tears and threw herself at Carol, complaining that she couldn't hear her television programme, and then Samantha stormed downstairs, yelling at all of them.

'For Chrissakes, I can't hear myself *think*! I've got exams coming up, I've got to work. I can't concentrate with all this row going on. Mum, can't you do anything about them?'

Carol looked through the open door of the lounge at the group of boys. They grinned back at her in defiance.

'Can't you turn it down?' she suggested.

They pretended not to hear.

'Right!' Samantha strode across the room and pulled out the plug, to a chorus of protest. 'Stuff it,' she told them. 'If you want to play your moronic music, take it somewhere else.' She glared at one of the visitors. 'Go to *your* house.'

'Can't,' he told her. 'Me mum's not home and I'm not allowed in till she gets back.'

'You tell your mum that we're not a bloody childminding service,' Samantha said. 'Now bugger off, the lot of you.'

They argued further, to save face, but in the end they went, grumbling.

Samantha turned down the volume on the television, which sounded loud in the sudden silence, and spoke to Carly.

'You shut up snivelling and watch your programme,' she told her, not too unkindly since she was another female. Carly obeyed.

Finally, Samantha looked at Carol.

'There. That's the way to deal with them,' she declared, and went back upstairs. Two minutes later, the sound of Bonnie Tyler belting it out with full power vibrated down from her room.

Carol sighed. There was no doubt that Sam got what she wanted, but did she have to be so aggressive? If that was being a feminist, she could keep it. She cut herself a slice of Swiss roll and leaned against the sink, thinking of the evening ahead. Would he be able to get away?

The phone rang.

'Hallo?'

The sweet thrill of excitement at the sound of Robert's voice.

'Is that my favourite little artist lady?'

'That's me, baby.'

Samantha appeared at the top of the stairs.

'Is it for me?'

Carol covered the mouthpiece.

'No, it is *not*! Shove off!'

She waited for the bang of Sam's bedroom door before speaking again.

'Sorry, darling. Just my nosy daughter. Where are you? At work?'

'Of course. I've given my secretary a whole heap of last-minute jobs and told her I'm not to be disturbed, and now I'm sitting here getting all excited just thinking of you.'

Carol gave her most seductive chuckle.

'No good just thinking about it, darling. Shall I smuggle myself in, then we can see what we can do under the desk?'

Robert made a noise of agreement, and they spent several minutes playing with the idea.

'Now see what you've done to me,' Robert complained at last, mock serious!

'I can't see, but I can imagine,'

'Wicked! Just wait till I get my hands on you.'

'Can't wait, darling. That's the problem.'

'Just keep yourself under control till this evening.'

Carol shivered with delight. He was going to make it.

'This evening?' she asked, all innocence. 'What's so special about then?'

'This evening, my gorgeous, it is going to be just you and me. No interruptions.'

Despite all her coaxing, he would tell her no more, but she could hazard an intelligent guess. He had fixed up a room. Either a hotel, which she was not keen on, or a friend's place, which was fine so long as she did not know the friend. It was amazing how they always managed it, after a few frustrating sessions in the backs of cars. Then she smiled to herself. Next, it would be the weekend away. She always enjoyed that. She hadn't had a weekend with a lover for – how long? Since before Carly was born.

'Sounds delicious, whatever it is,' she breathed. 'Till then, Tiger.'

Humming to herself, she went to tackle Samantha. Nothing was to stand in the way of this one. If need be, she would pay her to babysit. If she was studying as she said she was, she would be in anyway. After a brief round of bargaining, which Sam won, Carol was able to devote herself to deciding what she was going to wear. She drifted happily round the kitchen, pricking sausages and opening cans of beans, and thinking of the evening ahead. Now she would really see what Robert was made of.

The phone rang again.

'Carol?'

It was Andrea. Carol's stomach churned with fear and guilt.

'Oh – hello, Andy,' she managed to say. What the hell did she want? 'What's the matter? I thought we got everything sorted out this morning.'

'Yes, we did, I just wondered whether there was anything we missed.' Andrea sounded vague and distracted, not her usual businesslike self.

'I can't think of anything. We went all through the checklist, didn't we?'

'Yes— ' Andrea hesitated. 'I – er – I wondered if you'd like to come round again. Have a drink and supper. We could have a girls' chat. All we ever seem to talk about now is Designs.'

Carol swallowed. Andy suspected something! She was checking up.

'It's a great idea.' she said, trying desperately to think of a good excuse. The brassy blare of Sam's tape throbbed through the ceiling. The kids. Of course. Andrea would readily accept that they came first. 'Only I've got this meeting up at the school I've got to go to.' she said. It rolled glibly off her tongue. 'You know what these things are like. Go on for hours and they never tell you anything, but you got to go, haven't you, or they think you're not interested.'

'Oh – yes – of course,' Andrea agreed. 'You can't miss that. Another day, perhaps.'

'That'd be nice,' Carol agreed. Elated by the easy

success, she asked, 'Isn't Robert home this evening, then?'

'No.' It was impossible to make out what she felt from her voice. 'He's working late. They've got a big deal coming up, apparently.'

'Oh, I see. No wonder he thinks Designs is just a game we're fiddling around with.'

Carol could get no more clues out of her. She certainly did not sound suspicious. But you never knew with Andrea. She seemed so quiet and butter-wouldn't-melt, but often there was a lot going on underneath. Pondering, she went back into the kitchen, just in time to rescue the sausages from burning.

'Bugger it,' she said, looking at the burst skins. 'Well, they'll just have to lump it. There's nothing else.'

She pushed Andrea to the back of her mind and shoved some slices of bread under the grill.

Two hours later, the children fed and squabbling over which programme to watch and the plates dumped in the sink, Carol emerged from her bedroom a different woman. After careful consideration, she had decided not to wear something that could be easily slipped out of, but quite the opposite. Various layers of clothing and underclothing would keep Robert in a state of anticipation. There was nothing like it. Carol was bursting with confidence. Somebody wanted her. And now that she had her hair done and her make-up on and had overhauled her wardrobe, she knew she could beat any woman in sight. She kissed Carly, told the boys to behave themselves and thanked Samantha. Only Carly took any notice of her, but she was not bothered. Kids you were stuck with, men were worth playing for. The sight of the telephone in the hall caused a slight misgiving as she thought of Andrea's call, but she stamped on it firmly. Andrea had money, Andrea had that big posh house, Andrea had a husband to keep her. She could let Carol have a little bit and not miss it at all. The taxi that Robert had ordered tooted outside in the street. Closing the front door on her responsibilities, Carol set out for an evening of pleasure.

That flat to which she was driven became the focal point of her life for the next month or more. Situated further up the railway line than Brackstead in a gentrifying area of town, it was ideally placed for their meetings. It belonged to a colleague of Robert's who was off on a factfinding trip. The only other person with a key was the cleaning lady who came in each day and cleared up the evidence of their occupation. It could not have been a better arrangement. Carol was unstinting in her admiration.

'You're so clever, darling, finding this,' she purred, revelling in the comfort and the privacy. 'It's just perfect. Only you could have fixed somewhere as lovely.'

Robert glowed in the warmth of her praise. He never failed to respond to a boost to his ego.

'Only the best for my beautiful tigress.'

It was a strangely anonymous place, part of a converted Victorian house with large rooms and high ceilings, immaculately done out in dark masculine colours. It was like one of Carol's designs when just completed, without any of the personal clutter of everyday life. Even the pictures on the walls looked as if they had been placed there to harmonise with the stage set, rather than collected for their own merits. Carol, peering curiously into one of the wardrobes one evening, found the very clothes hanging stiff and new like merchandise in a shop. There was nothing old and worn, nothing to show the personality of the absent owner.

'He's divorced,' Robert told her, when she pressed for details. 'This is just a place to lay his head. I don't think he spends much time here.'

Carol looked at it all with envy. Men always got the best deal. Divorced women ended up in crummy council houses with a horde of kids.

But she had to admit that she had very little to complain about at the moment. She had sussed out Robert and had him on a string. Though he was gentleman enough not to admit it in so many words, it was evident that Andrea permitted no more than the missionary position twice a week. Carol, with a taste for the exotic and a variety of experience to draw on, could do a whole lot better than that. She held out the prospect of new and exciting adventures the next time, and the next—The only problem was Robert's staying power. Unused to such abundance, he rarely lasted the course. But Carol was adept at letting a man think he was the best ever. With everything to gain, she made sure he left her arms for the pale delights of home considering himself the greatest since Casanova.

He was more than generous in his tokens of love and gratitude. First the conventional gifts of flowers and silk underwear, then, at Carol's cleverly dropped hints, more practical items. A new washing machine was delivered to her door within days of her old one being pronounced beyond repair. She had no doubt that if she could keep it up a few weeks longer, she could even swing a fur coat. She had not had a fur since she sold her treasured fox jacket to pay half a year's gas and electricity bills at the end of a disastrous winter seven years ago. Life was going fine for Carol, and she intended hanging on to the luck while it lasted. You never knew, maybe this time it was here to stay. Stranger things had been known to happen. Half a lifetime of being let down by men had not killed her dream of finally finding someone who would stick by her. Not marry her, she had had that scene. She could do without the smelly socks and the early-morning rows and the complaints about the cooking. No, what Carol wanted was for an affair to go on for ever, with the candlelit meals, the presents, the anticipation.

'A kept woman,' she said out loud, with a happy sigh. That would be the life.

Robert ran a hand over her as she lay on the bed.

'Satisfied, Tigress?'

She gave a throaty purr.

'You bet – till the next time.'

Maybe next time she would get him to hold on long enough for that to be the truth.

Andrea put the phone down and prowled restlessly round the big house. Working late again! That was the third time this week. Worry gnawed at her. Robert was doing too much, it must be a strain on him. He was over fifty, at least a stone overweight and very rarely took any real exercise. Add stress to that and it put him in the danger zone. In her overwrought imagination, she could hear the phone ring again, the cool hospital voice on the other end, the news that Robert was in intensive care. She pulled herself up short. She must not think like this. He did not look like a man under stress. In fact, he was particularly sprightly at the moment. She had remarked on it only the other day.

'Nothing like a challenge to bring out the best in you,' Robert had told her.

'It's not another redundancy scare, is it?' she asked, remembering the last time he had repeatedly worked all hours.

'No, no,' he assured her. 'It's all going fine. That's the cause of all this. There's so much happening I just have to devote extra time to sorting it out.'

But all the same, she could not help wondering just what it was doing to his constitution. There were worrying symptoms. He was not at all interested in sex, falling into an exhausted sleep every night, often before Andrea had even got into bed.

There was a scrunch of wheels on the gravel driveway, and Andrea's heart sank. She knew without looking who it was. Camilla had her own distinctive way of pulling up, two inches from the bay tree outside the front door. She considered for a moment not answering the ring at the bell, but remembered that she was standing in the middle of the through lounge. She could be clearly seen by anyone coming in. Reluctantly, she went to open the door.

'Andrea, dear! Are you busy? I don't seem to have seen anything of you for ages.' Camilla, tanned from a twice-weekly sunbed, looked amazing in a white t-shirt dress with Yes! printed in large letters across the bust.

'Camilla, what a nice surprise, do come in.' Anyone less thick-skinned would have been put off by the lack of enthusiasm in her voice, but not Camilla. She bounced into the hall and made her way out through the kitchen.

'Let's sit outside, shall we? Enjoy the sun while it's here. I do love your garden, you'll have to come and do something with ours.'

She stretched out on the padded lounger and accepted the drink that Andrea offered.

'Just Perrier with a slice of lemon and some ice for me, darling. Must think of the figure.'

Andrea found herself actively disliking Camilla. She had for a long time, she realised, handing the tall glass to the recumbent woman. It was just that she had never admitted it to herself until now. She sat on the edge of the second lounger and sipped her orange squash, making no attempt at conversation. No doubt Camilla had plenty to say.

She did, but in a roundabout way.

'How's the business going, then? Not out working today?'

'We're a bit quiet at the moment,' Andrea admitted. 'All the interior work is finished for now, but I'm busy with the drawing stages of a garden.'

She expected Camilla to leave the subject, having made a token gesture in that direction, and launch out on some tale of her own, but she did not. She asked about the current plan in detail, then about what Andrea was considering for the future.

'Sounds to me as if it's the garden side of it that's going to be successful, rather that the interiors,' she said.

'It comes and goes,' Andrea told her. But it was true. There was at least one more client almost certain to give them a garden to do, and they had a contract to maintain one of those that had just been completed. Not a vast amount of work, but a lot more than seemed to be materialising for the decorating.

'Really, you could do without that Carol,' Camilla said.

Andrea tried to convince her otherwise, but Camilla was not to be moved.

'You just don't like her,' Andrea accused.

'With reason, honey. She's dangerous.' Camilla dropped Carol as suddenly as she had picked her up. 'What does Robert think of the business now?'

'Oh, he's very interested,' Andrea said. Robert did always ask after her day, but absently, as a matter of habit. He took no more notice than in the days when she had nothing more riveting to report than a trip to the shops. Without meaning to, the thought uppermost in her mind spilled out. 'I'm a bit anxious about him, actually. He's got so much on at the moment, I'm afraid he's overdoing it.'

There was a small, perceptible silence.

'Overdoing what, precisely?'

'Why, work, of course. Three times this week he's had to stay late. It can't be good for him.'

Camilla's long red fingernails chinked against the side of the glass.

'Andrea dear, don't hate me for this, but I think there's something you ought to know— ' she hesitated, avoiding Andrea's eyes.

Andrea felt a chill starting in the pit of her stomach, but simultaneously a guard went up, resisting belief in whatever was about to follow.

'Oh yes?' she managed to say.

'Yes— ' Camilla scanned the bright summer garden, uneasy even behind her large sunglasses. 'You know Martin's been doing a job up in town these last couple of weeks? Well, he quite often gets the same train back as Robert. The five forty-two. Not always the same carriage, of course. But one day they did travel down together, and when they got to Minster, Robert suddenly said he'd forgotten to make a phone call and bolted out.' She paused and looked at Andrea.

'So?' Andrea's face set in mutinous lines. She did not want to hear any more, but knew that nothing she could do would prevent Camilla from spilling it all now that she had started.

'So, there's nothing very important in that, I know, but – what days was Robert working late last week?'

'Tuesday, Thursday and Friday,' Andrea admitted.

'Yes, well, that was Thursday. On Friday, Martin just got in the last carriage as the train was pulling out, and when it reached Minster, he saw Robert heading for the exit as he went past. And again this Wednesday.'

Wednesday. The day before yesterday, when Robert had not got in till gone eleven. Andrea fought against the rising tide of evidence.

'Perhaps they've opened a branch there,' she suggested.

'Oh come on, Andrea! Men in Robert's position don't go making personal visits to branch offices.' Camilla dropped her usual hectoring tone and became almost gentle. She leaned across the space between them and placed a hand over Andrea's tightly clasped ones. 'Face it, darling, he's meeting someone. He must be. It's all so obvious, so corny. Men always follow the conventional pattern. Has he smartened himself up lately, taken a new interest in his appearance?'

Andrea nodded.

'And taken to bringing you presents?'

There had been flowers on Wednesday.

'That was to apologise for all the late evenings.'

'I'll say it was. Evenings spent where, I wonder?'

Andrea choked back burning tears of anger.

'It's not true! I don't believe a word of it. There's sure to be a simple explanation.'

Camilla shrugged and sighed.

'If that's the way you want it, OK. But you'd do far better to face up to it and fight back.'

'There's nothing to fight! Robert would never cheat on me, I know it. I'm as sure of him as I am that I'm sitting here. Robert loves me.'

'I expect he does, Andrea, but— '

'Stop saying these things! I won't listen to any more! It's horrible.' Andrea curled up, putting her hands over her ears. 'Go away!'

She felt Camilla's hand squeeze her shoulder, sensed rather than saw her walk off round the side of the house. Only when the car engine started did she let the tears go. But still she refused to believe it. Camilla was a trouble maker. She liked stirring things up.

By the time she had to go and pick Sally up, she was outwardly calm. She went through the usual teatime routine, and saw that Anthony was ready for Scouts on time, ironing his scarf and checking that he had cleaned his shoes. But all the time Camilla's words were chasing round her head. However often she told herself that she did not believe a bit of it, she could not stop repeating the accusations over and over again. The hour came and went when Robert would have come home. She sent Sally to bed and left Matthew watching the television while she cleared up the kitchen. Then the answer came to her, so obvious that the relief made her weak inside. Phone. She did not even have to speak to Robert, since she certainly did not want him to think she was checking up on him. She could put the phone down once she had got through.

With new decision in her movements, she dialled. Only when she was halfway through the number did she remember that the switchboard might not be operating at this hour of the evening, but by then it was too late. She had to go through with it. The ringing tone went on and on. Then a click.

' 'Allo?'

'Oh – er – hello,' Andrea was disconcerted. 'Is that Western Consolidated?'

'That's right, dear.'

'Oh – can you put me through to extension 207, please?'

'He ain't there, dear. I just been cleaning that floor, and they've all gone.'

'Ah.' But he might not be in his own office. They

might be having a meeting somewhere else in the building. 'Are any of the staff still working?'

'Don't think so, love. Last lot left about ten minutes ago.'

That was it. It had not taken as long as Robert had thought. He was on his way home now.

'Thank you,' she said, 'thank you very much.'

She glanced at the clock. *Ten to eight.* Even allowing for the trains being less frequent at this time of the evening, he would be back in under an hour. Practically skipping with delight, she went to search the freezer for something really delicious. The poor darling would be starving.

Nine o'clock rolled round, then ten, but no Robert appeared, weary from his long day. They had gone out for a meal together, Andrea told herself, converting the worry into anger. They had finished the day's workload and gone to relax. He might have told her! Here she was, thinking he was overdoing things when all the time he was sitting in some expensive restaurant somewhere in town. How inconsiderate!

It was nearly eleven before the car could be heard going into the garage. Andrea sat very still, taking deep breaths. She would not make a scene. If she kept calm, he would explain and apologise. She must pretend that she thought he had been working all this time, for she must not let him think that she had been spying on him. That would ruin the trust between them. So she got up and went to him, as she always did, holding her face up for the ritual kiss.

Robert briefly brushed her lips with his. There was a whiff of wine on his breath.

'Hello, darling. You must be exhausted,' Andrea said. 'Come and sit down. Would you like anything to eat?'

The trout armandine she had prepared earlier

was ruined. She had timed it for a quarter to nine.

'No thanks, just a cup of tea. We sent out for a meal.'

Robert switched on the television, dropped onto the sofa, closed his eyes. Andrea stood in the lounge doorway, unable to think clearly. At last she asked, 'Did you say "sent" or "went"?'

Robert looked at her for a moment as if he wondered who she was.

'What? Oh – sent – you know, they deliver the stuff.'

'Wine as well?'

His look was guarded now.

'Wine as well,' he agreed. 'Got to keep our strength up, you know.'

'Yes, of course,' Andrea replied automatically. 'I'll make you some tea.'

It had only been one of the cleaners she had spoken to, she reasoned, as she filled the kettle. They did not know what was going on. They could not be expected to. If she had managed to get on to the right extension, she would have found Robert's little group. Everything was perfectly all right. It was just a bit of a misunderstanding, that was all. Nothing to start worrying Robert about, he had quite enough on his mind.

When she carried the tray into the lounge, he was already dozing off, a smile on his lips. He jerked awake as she set the cup beside him.

'Successful session, was it?' she asked. 'You look pleased with yourself.'

'Very,' he told her. 'Well worth the effort. Going to take a while longer yet though.' He sipped the tea. 'Lovely. Just how I like it.'

Andrea asked a few general questions about who was in on the project, but only received the vaguest of answers.

'Look, darling,' Robert said at last. 'I really can't tell you much at this stage. You do understand, don't you?'

Andrea did not. He always shared at least some part of his work with her. But she nodded, all the same.

'There's my girl. Now, if you don't mind I think I'll turn in. I'm whacked.'

By the time Andrea came out of the shower, he was already asleep. She lay beside him awake into the small hours, the events of the day keeping her brain running in overdrive. It all seemed to be explained, she knew there was nothing to worry about – and yet . . . The niggling ends of sentences wore at her mind. Better to face it and fight it. There was nothing to fight. Just accusations. Shadows. But the shadows were very real at three in the morning. Minster station. All gone home. She finally dropped into an uneasy, dream-filled sleep, and awoke in the morning feeling unrefreshed. She could not live with this doubt, but neither could she face Robert with it. She would have to find some way of laying the fear once and for all.

CHAPTER EIGHTEEN

What she needed to do, Andrea realised, was to talk it over with a friend. Certainly not Camilla, but someone who knew both Robert and herself and could give a sensible opinion. Carol was the most convenient candidate, but Andrea did wonder a little at the value of her judgement. Her attitude to men and marriage was so totally different from Andrea's that she might not fully understand how Andrea felt. But as the weekend progressed and the questions she wanted to ask Robert but could not grew more pressing, she found herself longing for Monday morning and Carol's arrival.

Carol breezed in late, as usual, and flopped down on a chair in the dining-room.

'Gawd, those kids drive me crazy. Rory's been bunking off, so now I got to see he gets to school. I don't know what I'm going to do with them. They're a right pain, those boys, just like their father.'

'Who was their father, Carol? You never have said much about him.'

Carol got out a cigarette, lit it and drew a deep breath.

'That's better. Keith, well, there's not a lot to say about him really.'

Andrea recalled that Carol had given the impression at the lunch that her second husband had been a good provider, though dull. But then Carol had said a good deal at the lunch that subsequently turned out not to be true.

'Where did you meet him?' she asked. Carol's irregular life fascinated her, and right at the moment she felt that Carol's view of men might help her focus more clearly on her own vague apprehension.

'At a party. It was when I was living in London. Can't even remember whose house it was now. You got a coffee on the go, Andy? I'm gasping.'

Coffee mug in hand – with sweeteners now, not sugar, Andrea noticed – and cigarette half-smoked, Carol was ready to start.

'I was going with this really boring guy at the time. Like really boring. But rich. All he could ever talk about was his business, which was importing some rubbish from Hong Kong. He went on and on, you've no idea. I only stuck with him as long as I did because he took me to all the places I always wanted to go to, but by the time we went to this party, I was getting right fed up. Anyway, there was Keith, and he was quite good-looking, and he fancied me, and he had a good line of chat. He was a salesman, you see, a rep, so he was good at talking. So I ditched this other guy and went home with him.'

It all sounded so easy, the way Carol put it. Off with the old, on with the new.

'And you ended up marrying him?' she said.

'Yes, I did, to cut a long story short. Didn't happen as quickly as that. He was off round the country selling washing machines during the week, so I only saw him weekends. I didn't have time to get fed up with him that way, in fact I really missed him. And I was missing Sam as well, of course, so when he asked me to marry him and said he didn't mind us having Sam with us, I jumped at it. I really did love him then. I mean, it's not every man who'll take on a child like that, is it? They do now more, because everyone's splitting up all over the place, but it was different then. I was over the moon. Nice little house on a new estate with all new carpets and furniture. I was fed up with living in grotty flats with a load of other girls. It was heaven, having a place of my own.'

Carol sighed, stubbed out her cigarette, ground the butt into the ashtray.

'What went wrong?' Andrea asked.

Carol shrugged.

'I'm a lousy housewife, that's what. The boys are only eighteen months apart and I let things go. When he came home at weekends, the place was always a mess and I'd spend my time nagging at him. In the end he cleared out. Found himself someone else up Birmingham way.'

'Just like that?'

'Yeah, just like that. So I gave up on marriage after that. Not my scene.'

'But Carly?' Andrea could not help asking. 'Where did she come from?'

Carol laughed.

'You don't need a wedding ring, mate. Even you must know that. Carly was a mistake, like Sam. I'm glad I've got her, though. She's a pet.'

'But her father? I mean— '

'Why didn't he Do the Right Thing? He was married already, that's why. The whole bit – nice house, three kids, dull wife. Didn't even say she didn't understand him, just that she was boring. But you could see he wasn't going to leave all that nice comfortable security for my rabble. He was quite nice about it. Gave me some money. But you could see he was scared stiff I'd turn up one day and tell his wife.'

A nice house, Andrea thought, three kids, dull wife. Was she dull? Was that why Robert was stopping off at Minster on the way home, if he was?

'And did you?' she asked.

'Give me a break, Andy! I may be pretty stupid, but I'm not a stirrer. What's the point? Let her keep her old man. I'd've got fed up with him inside of a year if he'd stayed, and he'd've hated the nappies and broken nights bit all over again. I mean, he wanted me to get rid of it.'

'But you didn't want to?'

'No – well – I was horrified at first, when I discovered I was pregnant. Thought I'd done that one, along with marriage. But then I nearly miscarried her, and I found I really wanted her. Got really broody over Carly, I did. Loved every moment of that pregnancy.' Carol paused, lit another cigarette, looked back into the past. When she spoke again, her voice was thick with tears. 'It's fantastic, isn't it? I mean, really – wonderful, that moment when they first put the baby into your arms and it looks at you. I don't care what they say, I'm sure babies can see you. They stare at you. Carly did. That was the first time I really loved one from the start. I just loved her from the moment I first saw her.'

Andrea nodded in silent agreement, her view of Carol adjusting. She was not as shallow as she liked to have everyone believe, it was all a defence. She cared, cared very deeply.

'Oh well— ' Carol put down her empty coffee mug, drew a deep breath. 'Can't go on having them, can you? Four's enough. Eat you out of house and home. Have we got anything to do? Any new work in?'

Andrea had to admit that they had not.

'I've got the garden job to finish off, but there's nothing else, I'm afraid. We'll have to step up the advertising.' She did not want to start talking about work. There was still the problem of Robert on her mind, and Carol seemed to be in a particularly receptive mood. 'But do stay,' she urged. 'Have another coffee, I'll put some on.'

But Carol was standing up, dropping her lighter into her handbag.

'Sorry, Andy. It's a nice idea, but I didn't think

we had anything on, so I booked a legwax.' She grinned, savouring a coming victory. 'That old cow Cleve'll be in at the salon today. Can't wait to see her face when I come in. The times she left me slaving at her place while she went swanning off to have something done to her. I think I might have a facial next week. Got to keep the old body in running order, haven't we?'

Have we? Andrea wondered, looking at herself in the hall mirror after Carol had gone. Her unmade-up face looked back at her, clean, not too lined – dull? She stepped back and inspected her figure. Not much to be seen, for she was wearing a shapeless old pair of jeans and faded shirt, ready for the gardening job. At least she was not fat. In fact she was nice and slim, it was just that the slim models in magazine photographs managed still to have curves in the right place, which Andrea had not. She looked critically at the place under the shirt where her bust ought to be. She had always been rather small-breasted, and now after three children they had shrunk to almost nothing. Did it matter? Robert never mentioned it. She ran a hand over her hair. Neatly cut, it fell back into place. Neat, yes, but alluring? She had not really thought about it before. Robert always commented with approval when she was dressed up ready for a dinner or an evening out. He liked the way she looked. So why was she worried?

Robert was home at the usual time that evening, but appeared abstracted. Several times Andrea made a remark which he simply did not seem to hear.

'Is everything all right at work?' she asked him at last.

Silence, then, 'Mm? What?'

'Work. Is everything all right?' Andrea repeated. 'You seem worried.'

'No, no, it's fine. Just got a lot on my mind, that's all.'

'I wish you'd share it with me, darling. I know I don't know all the ins and outs of it, but I do understand something about the company.'

Robert patted her hand.

'Very sweet of you, dear, but I can't at the moment. Look— er— ' he made a visible effort to focus his attention on her. 'Tell me about what's-it's-name, Designs Unlimited. How are things going there, eh? Still enjoying being a businesswoman?'

Andrea went through what there was to tell, but knew she was being put off. He was hiding something from her, and she did not like it. The secure ground under the feet felt horribly shaky.

The next day, it happened again. Another late meeting.

'Don't cook anything for me, darling. We'll be taking these American chaps out to dinner.'

'Oh,' Andrea said. 'Well, thank you for letting me know.'

'You don't mind, do you? You know how it is, have to keep the wheels oiled.'

Andrea suddenly saw the chance to get a piece of the action, and grabbed at it.

'Why don't you bring them back here? I can fix you up something by this evening. How many of them are there?'

'That's very sweet of you, but it really isn't necessary. I've got a table booked now.'

Andrea held on. Normally, she would have been pleased not to have to produce a cordon bleu meal in one afternoon. Now she wanted desperately to do it. She had to see these Americans for herself. If she could get them to her house, eating her food, she would be certain of their existence.

'You could always cancel it. I expect they'd love the prospect of a meal in a real home instead of all the hotel and restaurant food they've been eating. I could do them something traditionally English, Americans always like that, and we could have the patio doors open, so that the smell of the roses drifts in. The garden's looking lovely now, they'd go wild about it. Do bring them, Robert.'

'Well now— ' there was an edge of unease to Robert's reassuring voice. 'I can't put you to all that trouble, not at such short notice— '

'It's no trouble, and I've done it at shorter notice before now. Remember those Germans? And that nice Swedish man? You swore I swung the deal for you with the meal I cooked for him.'

'I know, dear, you were wonderful. But the circumstances are rather different this time. Ronnie's coming along, and you know how he doesn't like having plans changed at the last minute. Not where his food's concerned.'

Andrea was finally foxed. Ronnie was the managing director, and an exacting and very knowledgeable gourmet. She had fed him once in the past, but had taken a week to prepare the feast.

'Oh well— ' she said, defeated. 'If that's the case. I'll expect you when I see you, then.'

It was only after she put the phone down that she wondered why he had not told her about Ronnie at first, instead of bringing him in as an afterthought. It sounded almost like an excuse.

She wandered aimlessly round the house, straightening a cushion here, blowing at a speck of dust there, turning it all over in her mind. Something was wrong. Robert was not behaving normally. She stepped out into the fragrant warmth of the garden, but even that failed to soothe. There was nothing to distract her thoughts. Designs seemed to have ground to a halt, she had even rung Carol earlier to tell her not to bother to come in. She knew she ought to be out there hustling up some new business. At the very least she should place some more ads in the paper. But the question mark above Robert drained all her sense of purpose. The success or otherwise of the business meant nothing if her marriage was threatened. She must do something.

The phone in the hall attracted her. She stood looking at it, racked with indecision. Ring Robert back on some pretext? Speak to his secretary, sympathise with all the late nights she had been working and see what her reaction was? Ring Carol? This seemed far less threatening, so she tried it, but nobody answered. Andrea replaced the receiver and stood chewing the dry skin at the side of her fingernail while a far more radical plan formed in her head. The dead piece peeled back to the living flesh and a drop of blood started up. Andrea picked up the phone again and dialled Camilla's number. First she must confirm what Camilla had said the other day. She must be sure. Again nothing but the endless unanswered trill. Desperate now to talk to someone, she tried Penny, and jumped when she got through after only two rings.

'Hello?' There was a trembling eagerness in Penny's voice. 'Oh – Andrea. What can I do for you?'

'Oh — er — ' She hardly knew where to begin. She could not just launch into it all. 'Just calling to see how you are. I'm loving *Traitors.* I watch it every week. It's very involved, isn't it?'

There was a polite exchange over the series, neither of them really listening to what the other was saying.

'Have you got anything else lined up?' Andrea asked.

'No – well, there's been plenty of interest. I went to an audition for a West End production. Just what

I want, really. I thought you might be my agent, or even the producer. But it's difficult to think about work when everything else is in such a mess.'

'I know,' said Andrea. 'I feel just the same.'

'You?' Penny was shrill with disbelief. 'Good God, whatever's wrong? You can't mean Robert, surely? I'd put you two down as the original well-matched pair. Whenever I feel cynical about marriage, I think of you and Robert and tell myself that it can work for some people.'

'It can, truly,' Andrea told her. 'It's just that – oh, I'm sure it's all a silly misunderstanding on my part. We've just got our wires crossed somewhere, that's all— '

A wave of sympathy came over, lapping Andrea in its warmth. She knew she had been right in phoning Penny. There was nothing like engaging a friend's help.

'Come on, Andy, out with it. What's worrying you? Tell me.'

So she did, from her first suspicions to the latest phone call.

'Mm,' she could almost feel Penny picking her words carefully. 'It doesn't look too bright, does it?'

That was not what she was hoping Penny would say. She wanted to be told that she was making a fuss about nothing.

'No,' she agreed, aware of a sick feeling in the pit of her stomach.

'Look, Andy, it probably is just as he says, you know. Has he worked late like this before?'

'Sometimes, yes, but never so consistently. There was one other time, a while ago, but afterwards he said they had been threatening to cut down on management and he had been in danger of being made redundant and didn't want to worry me about it.'

'Ah – yes – very considerate of him.' Again the slight hesitation, then Penny said, 'Andy, I really don't think you've got too much to worry about. I was right in what I said just now, you two are very well suited. You've got a very good relationship, something you've built over the years. Even if there is something going on, it won't last. He'll come back, believe me. They always do. They might promise the earth, but they always stay with the wife and family in the end. You've got everything on your side.'

Somehow, Andrea did not find this particularly reassuring.

'I suppose so,' she said. 'But it's this terrible suspicion. I can't bear it, not knowing. I did think of ringing his secretary, but he might have her primed, she's very loyal.'

'Quite probably,' Penny agreed.

'And then I thought, perhaps I could drive down to Minster station and meet his train— '

'Oh Andy, do you think that's wise?'

'No. Oh, I don't know. But anything's better than living with this suspicion.'

'But what would you do if he saw you there, checking up on him? If there's nothing going on, he'll be terribly hurt. You'll destroy the trust between you.'

'It is destroyed,' Andrea said, facing it for the first time. She had tried to set her mind against it, but still it had eaten away at her. She did not believe every word that Robert said to her any more. She weighed up his statements and found them wanting.

'Oh Andy. Oh, this is dreadful . . . You seemed so happy, you two.'

'We were,' Andrea said. 'We still could be. It's probably all my fault and I shall be ashamed of it. But I'd rather hate myself for suspecting him than keep wondering what he's up to all the time like this.'

When she finally rang off, she found she had sorted it out. She had not needed Penny's advice, just a sounding board against which she could bounce her thoughts. Her mind was now made up. She must find out, one way or another. She picked up the phone and began to make arrangements for the children to go to friends after school. Then with everything taken care of, she drove up to Minster station, still not quite believing that it was she who was doing this.

The place lay sullen in the gritty heat. It smelt of dirt and Jeyes fluid and dead cigarettes. The glare of the evening sun glanced off the rails and hurt her eyes. She put on the dark glasses she used for driving and felt a fool. What was she doing here? It was ridiculous. Supposing she met someone she knew, what on earth would she say to explain her presence?

She bought an evening paper and sat down on a grimy bench, intending to hide behind it, and felt even more of a fool. People did not act like this in real life, it was like a cheap American movie. She would go home. But she did not. The element of resolve in her that had held out for Robert in the first place against parental opposition came into play. She would prove it one way or the other. Jill would approve of such decisive action. She sat on her uncomfortable bench and waited.

The rails hummed and twittered with life, jangling the nerves on her spine. The loudspeaker crackled and spat some garbled information over the platform. The platform vibrated and Andrea's stomach churned in awful anticipation. Then with an agonising squeal of brakes the train pulled in and the idling engine throbbed as people got down and doors slammed.

Andrea scanned the tired faces with desperate anxiety. He mustn't be here, he mustn't, he mustn't – so many middle-aged men, wilted in their dark suits and crumpled shirts, walking heavily as they made for the exit, wanting only to get home and relax. But none of them had that familiar step, that particular set to the body. The last passengers plodded through the gate. Andrea sagged limp in her seat. It was all right, he was not there. Tears of relief started in her eyes.

A fast train thundered through, sending the litter gusting into the stale air. Andrea breathed deeply, her unread paper slipping from her hands, and stared blindly at the crenellated edge of the platform roof. She felt drained by the tension of the last few days, empty of everything but a vast sense of release. The ground was still steady under her feet after all. Her security was not threatened. All was well. She smiled weakly, savouring the moments of quiet, not even wanting to get up and leave. Everything was all right. The minutes slipped by unheeded.

She hardly noticed the next train pulling in. Gaggles of brightly-dressed typists, pale clerks, the occasional shopper trooped past her. A youth tripped over her outstretched foot.

'Sorry,' he muttered, marching on, hands in pockets.

Andrea jerked into awareness. The youth had already disappeared through the exit, followed by a couple of businessmen, followed by—

'Robert!'

She jumped to her feet, started after him. There was a hold-up at the gate while a man argued over an excess fare. Disgruntled passengers pushed their way past. Heart thudding wildly, Andrea shoved through the knot of people and out into the booking hall. Robert had gone. She ran to the entrance, looked desperately up and down the street. There were queues for buses, taxis leaving, a line of cars waiting to pick up tired commuters, people going in all directions. Then she saw him, on the other side of the street, walking briskly, a spring in his step, an air of purpose in his stride. In a daze, she followed.

Another shock. He went into a shop, into several. Little specialist places, of different ethnic groups, open all hours. Robert, shopping! She stumbled after him as he swung along, laden now with carrier bag in one hand and briefcase in the other. He was quite oblivious of her presence. At one point he stopped suddenly to look at something in a window, and she nearly ran into him. Her heart stood still as she caught the sound of his voice. He was singing, singing to himself as he looked at the shop. A cry rose in Andrea's throat, but died before it reached her lips. Robert never sang.

He dived down a side road of terraced Victorian houses with a clutter of old cars parked along the pavement, then into another of rather larger properties, still old, mostly divided into flats. Plane trees lined the street and music drifted out of open windows. A group of children sat on a wall like so many pigeons, watching two of their number stunting on shiny BMXs. Robert hurried past, turned into the front path of a smartly converted place, its pale brick cleaned, its paintwork renewed, its small garden tastefully planted with a selection of shrubs surrounded by cobbles. Just in time, Andrea stepped back behind the privet hedge of the place next door. He did not stop to ring. The part of her brain that was still able to function deduced that he had a key. She heard the gentle thud of the door closing.

She sank onto the low stone-topped wall beneath the hedge, heedless of the twigs sticking into her back. She was too shocked to cry. She certainly could not think. There was just a numbness, a blank misery that swallowed her up. She sat, a still, cold island in the sticky heat of the summer evening, aware only of the crumbling of her life's foundations. There was no past or future, just the dull thump and click as the door of the flat shut behind Robert, leaving her on the outside.

She did not see the woman approaching from the direction of the station, tripping along confidently in her high-heeled sandals, swinging her bag, did not notice her stop suddenly in shock, stare, hesistate, start forward then turn and hurry back along the street. The tap-tap of her hurrying feet hung on the heavy air, but Andrea did not hear her. She was unaware that she had just missed knowing the one thing that would have made the betrayal even worse to bear.

CHAPTER NINETEEN

There was still a notice nailed to the fence of the dinghy park. 'Property of the Brackstead Sailing Club'. Jill looked at it, wondering if it was the same one that she scrawled on, all those years ago. Her fingers itched. The rebellious girl in her was so near the surface now that she could hardly be controlled. She opened her bag, found the red marker pen, held it, chunky and satisfying, in her hand. The notice was clean and white, so inviting. A bubble of glorious excitement rose within her. She stepped forward, reached out. 'Property is Theft', she wrote.

'There,' she said out loud, and laughed. That would show them.

Behind her on the grass verge was her new car, symbol of the fact that she was one of Them, the capitalists, the supporters of law and order, the pillars of the system. She was everything her parents represented, and more. Mark's firm was bigger and more successful than her father's little business, she had gone on to become an MP while her father had stayed at council level, they lived in a larger, more opulent house than her parents and sent their children to private schools. She had done what all ambitious parents hope their children will do, had taken several steps up the ladder. She had done what they hoped Jennifer would do. But still she was not Jennifer.

She sat on the bank and watched the water, her eyes dazzled by the glare of the sun on the waves. It was quiet today, the last week of the school term. Her own children, breaking up earlier than those at state schools, were already at home, but the need to return to the past was so strong that she had left them in the care of the latest au pair and driven down to Brackstead as soon as Mark was out of the house. Mark knew there was something wrong, but for the first time in her life, she could not tell him. He thought he had laid the ghosts for her long ago. He would be so hurt if she told him that they had never gone away. They just lurked beneath the surface, waiting. And now they were reaching out their hands, dragging her under, pulling her down, just as Jennifer had sunk below the white-topped waves, her long hair floating like seaweed.

A solitary dinghy bobbed across the water, a Mirror, just like the one she and Jennifer had owned, red-sailed as most of them were, a figure in a bright orange lifejacket sitting at the helm. It was even painted blue, as theirs was.

'*Allegro*,' Jill whispered.

Jennifer, the musical one, had chosen the name.

'Pretentious,' Jill had declared. 'It sounds more like an ocean racer than a dinghy.'

'What does it mean, Jenny?' their mother asked.

'Swift and lively.'

Both parents looked impressed. They knew nothing of music, their taste ran to the Black and White Minstrel Show. They were slightly in awe of their daughter's familiarity with musical theory and classical composers.

'Swift and lively,' their mother repeated.

'Just right for a boat,' their father decided.

Jill muttered 'Pretentious,' again, but nobody listened. When the dinghy was launched, with a bottle of Babycham, she was named *Allegro*.

But she was always more Jill's than Jennifer's. That was what drew her to the reservoir, every weekend and all through the holidays. It was the one thing she was better at than Jennifer. Out on the water, contending with the vagaries of wind and waves, there was no room for brooding on the injustices of her life. In precarious harmony with the elements, she found escape.

What had happened to *Allegro*, she wondered. She had not returned to the reservoir after that day, had not been able to face the water, let alone sail the boat again. She supposed it must have been sold, or given away. She had never asked. Perhaps she was out there somewhere, in the black depths of the water, along with the other ghosts. The reservoir had drowned a village. In the drought summer, skeletal walls of the outlying houses had appeared. Jennifer was there too, waiting. They had dragged her body back, but that was just a limp, empty thing. The real Jennifer was there still, beautiful, brilliant, playing a sparkling prelude, writing an erudite essay, hitting a winning ball. If Jill went to find her, if she brought her back, maybe then at last she could have some peace. She had tried so hard to replace her. She had been trying for eighteen years, for half her life, to fill the yawning gap, to be the daughter her parents had lost. She had done everything they had wanted for Jennifer, and more, but she had failed. She was not her sister. She never would be. She was just Jill, the other one.

She stood up, and walked down the steep slope to the water's edge. She took a step, and the ripples lapped over her sandalled feet. If she could find her, out there, if she could bring her back, she could undo the terrible thing she had done. Out in the middle of the lake, Jennifer danced in the glancing sunlight, laughing. Jill took another step, and the water came to her knees.

'Wait!' she called. 'Wait for me!'

Andrea did not know why she was driving out to the reservoir. The car just seemed to go that way. She needed to get out of the house, that much she did know. She tried to work, knowing that this was supposed to be a great comfort in times of trial, but it did nothing for her. She could not concentrate. Even filing the minimal post in the In tray was too difficult to achieve. She merely opened the two letters and left them on the kitchen worktop. One appeared to be an enquiry about a design job, but her mind would not take it in. She wandered about the garden, twitching at the odd weed, deadheading the occasional rose, but could settle to nothing. The terrible revelations of the evening before possessed her.

Robert had arrived home just after eight.

'Hallo, darling.'

He hovered in the kitchen doorway as she fiddled around with saucepans.

'Hello.'

She banged open cupboards, took dishes out and put them in again. She did not dare turn to look at him.

'You're not as late as you thought, then,' she managed at last, her voice high-pitched and raw.

'No – ah – got away earlier.'

The boys were still up, and would be for another hour. If she said anything now, Andrea knew she would end up in tears, or worse. She was not going to hurt and bewilder them yet. That much she had determined on. Robert was not to be allowed to cause them pain. She produced a scratch meal, laid a place for one, spoke only when spoken to and that in monosyllables.

At nine-fifteen they finally faced each other.

'How long has it been going on?' she asked.

He avoided her accusing gaze.

'Only a few weeks,' he muttered.

'So you don't deny it, then?'

He shook his head.

'How did you find out?'

'Martin Hastings saw you, getting off at Minster.'

'Martin Hastings! God, that's rich. He's been— '

Andrea saw she was about to be sidetracked, and the anger that had been growing slowly below the surface suddenly boiled up.

'Never mind him! It's you we're talking about. Oh Robert, how could you? How could you do such a thing? I thought we were so happy!'

'We are – I am – it just, just happened— '

Andrea glared at him, standing a yard away from her in the middle of the lounge, refusing to react to her, giving away nothing. Her hands closed into fists.

'You can't just happen to have an affair that goes on for weeks. You planned it all out. All those lies, all those late nights. They didn't just happen!'

'No,' he admitted.

'Who is it? Somebody at work?'

'Yes. Yes, somebody at work.'

She knew he was lying.

'It's someone I know.'

'No. Really. You don't know her.'

'What's she like? Young? Pretty?'

'No, no younger than you.'

Scalding tears gathered from sheer frustration. How could he stand there so rocklike, so unemotional? Didn't he know what he was doing to her?

'Then why? Why did you do it? What's she got that I haven't? Where have I failed you? I've tried to be a good wife, I've done everything I could for you, I've backed you up in every way— ' The words flooded out, chased round and round, came back always to the first question: why? She was fighting wildly against an unknown enemy, and he would not tell her where she had gone wrong.

'Andrea, please— '

He held her shoulders, trying to calm her. Andrea twisted away.

'Darling, listen. I'm sorry, truly I am. I didn't want to hurt you, that's the last thing I ever wanted to do. If it hadn't been for Martin Hastings, you would never have found out. But it's over now, I promise you, and it won't ever happen again. I do love you, you know that.'

Andrea stared at him, half of her wanting to believe him, the other half astounded that he could imagine that it could all be wiped out with one apology. Anyone would think that it wasn't important, that he had merely run over one of her rosebushes, not shaken the foundations of their marriage.

'And that's all you've got to say, is it?' she asked, her voice wavering dangerously beyond her control.

Robert did not answer. She could tell he was holding something back.

'Is it? You still haven't told me why. There must be a reason. Why wasn't I good enough for you?'

Robert went over to the drinks cabinet, poured

two large brandies, pressed one into Andrea's hand.

'Look, sit down, darling, and drink that up.'

Andrea resisted for a long moment, then dropped into an armchair. Robert squatted before her on the footstool, took her free hand in his.

'Listen, you're a wonderful wife, the best in the world. I was an idiot. But it's all over now, finished, I promise you. It was just a passing madness.'

She knew she should accept that, take the chance to steer out of dangerous waters, probe no deeper. But she had to know. There must be some way in which she fell short of his expectations, or it would never have happened. She kept on, asking, guessing, trying to make him tell her.

'Darling, please. Just leave it, will you? I don't want to discuss it any further. It's over, it's in the past.'

There was an edge of desperation in his voice now, and she knew she was getting through. At last, after suggesting every possibility she could think of, she hit upon the obvious one.

'Was she better than me in bed, was that it?'

'Andrea, please. Don't go on.'

But she did go on, persisting with a masochistic pleasure, knowing that she was not going to like what she heard. And at last she forced him into admitting it.

'In what way was she better? What did she do that I don't?'

'All *right*. If you *must* know— '

Robert got up and paced over to the window, looking out into the summer night. With his back to her, he began to detail everything he and Carol had tried in the last few weeks. Once he had started, he could not stop. It all came out.

Andrea could not take it. She fled upstairs, locked herself in the newly decorated spare bedroom, spent the night haunted by images of Robert doing all those – things – with some other woman. There was only one thing of which she was certain, and that was no comfort. Nothing would ever be the same again between her and Robert.

They parted with stiff formality the next morning, he setting off for work as always, she unloading the dishwasher. Outwardly, the day followed its usual pattern. The children got ready for school, so excited by its being the last day of term that they did not notice the strained atmosphere. Andrea dropped off first the boys, then Sally, drove home, left the car on the driveway. Now that they were all out of the house and there was no need to keep up a mask of normality, she was lost. It was then that she knew she had to get out.

She drove aimlessly at first, through the new estate of which their part was the most exclusive, out onto the dual carriageway that would take her away from the suburbs. Then she saw the notice – 'Brackstead Reservoir' – and the newer one under it – 'Sailing Centre' – and turned into the side road without taking a conscious decision. Back into the past, before Robert, before the responsibilities and problems of adulthood. She parked at the dam end in a picnic area and walked across the worn grass to the water's edge. Part of her vaguely apprehended that it was a beautiful summer's morning, that the place was empty and quiet, the lake spread out before her glittering in dancing ripples. But that was only the background to her thoughts. She searched inwards and backwards, running away from the situation she did not want to face.

It was not always sunshine and laughter then, she realised, picturing four girls lounging on the grassy bank with a transistor radio jangling beside them. They were always nagging her about her shortcomings then. Don't wear that awful mumsy dress, stop worrying about what your parents will say, loosen up, don't be so inhibited . . . She had been inhibited then. In spite of two years of Jill's admonitions, ably assisted by Penny and Carol, she still felt ill at ease at times, that last summer. She could not quite behave as the others did, could not fling herself into each new project with never a thought for anything but the excitement of the moment. Always the constraints were there, holding her back.

Was that the problem now? she wondered. Was she still holding back? She began to walk along the lakeside towards the sailing club, hardly seeing where she was going. But if that was the reason, why hadn't Robert said anything? Had he been dissatisfied all these years and done nothing, said nothing? If only he had told her, she would have tried. Unwanted, his words of the evening before returned. She tried to imagine herself doing some of the things he described, and baulked at it. Horrible! She was not entirely naive, she had heard of such practices, knew that some people enjoyed them, but not Robert, not herself—

It was not until she was only fifty yards or so away from the dinghy park that she noticed the woman sitting there looking out across the water. She stopped, not wanting any contact with another, unable to cope with even the briefest exchange of glances. She nearly went back, was in the act of turning away, when a certain familiarity in the figure tugged at her mind. She looked again, stared, afraid that she was in the grip of a hallucination, conjuring up spirits from the past.

'Jill?' she whispered, unbelieving.

It was not Jill of the long mane and the frayed jeans, but the successful MP in a stylish flower-splashed dress. Andrea hesitated, caught between two opposing forces. She wanted to run away, to be by herself, and yet she could not resist Jill's magnetic pull. So she stood, and stared, unable to move.

Jill seemed to be wrapped in her own thoughts as well, gazing so fixedly at the middle of the reservoir. Then as Andrea watched her, she stood up and walked to the edge, until her feet were actually in the water. Her voice floated back on the warm air. 'Wait! Wait for me!'

Like a blow to the senses, Andrea realised that something was wrong. She started to run, stumbling on the tussocky grass.

'Jill!' she cried, then screaming, '*Jill*! Come back!'

She was running in a nightmare, her feet leaden, the goal too far away. The woman wading ever deeper into the lake was oblivious of her, seeing only some distant beckoning phantom. Andrea turned her ankle, yelped and ran on, plunged into the water and caught Jill by the arm, tugging her back.

'Jill, stop, please! You must stop.'

Like a sleepwalker she looked at her, face blank. Then recognition dawned slowly in her eyes.

'Andy?'

'Yes, it's me, Andrea. Come back, Jill. Come and sit down.'

Incredulous, Jill gazed at her, then at the hand gripping her. For a long moment they stood, the water lapping their legs.

'It is me, Jill.' If Andrea had been shocked to see her there, how much more so was Jill, finding a ghost appear suddenly at her side. Andrea pulled gently at her, speaking firmly as she might to one of her children. 'Come on, it's all right now. Come and sit on the bank.'

But the faraway expression returned. Resisting, Jill made to break away.

'Jennifer, I have to find Jennifer.'

Andrea was paralysed. Oh God, she prayed, 'what do I do? What do I say?'

'She's not there, Jill. She's not in the water. Jennifer's not there. You must come back, you must.'

'Not there?' She sounded puzzled.

'No. Please Jill, come away.' Then, in a flash of inspiration, 'Jill, I need to talk to you. I want your advice.'

If there was one thing Jill always enjoyed above everything else, Andrea remembered, it was giving advice. If she did not have the appropriate experience or information, she was quite willing to forward you on to someone else, but she did like to be regarded as the one to whom you came first. Slowly, she returned from the distant time she travelled to, breaking out of the fog of unreality. Andrea could see the words dropping into her consciousness, taking effect. Clarity tightened the lines of her face, she gave that quick decisive nod that Andrea remembered so well.

'Right,' she said. And as if it was the most natural thing in the world, waded back to the bank and sat down on the coarse grass.

Andrea flopped down beside her, limp with relief. Now how to carry on? Let her talk about it, or strike out on something quite different?

'That's a very pretty dress,' she commented.

Jill glanced down at it, unmoved.

'Yes,' she agreed.

She never did care for clothes, Andrea recalled. They were badges, symbols. Once she dressed to look like a rebel, now she evidently wished to appear prosperous and efficient, but the garments themselves were merely a means to that end. The passion that Carol and Penny expended on fashion, Jill put into ideas.

Trying another tack, Andrea asked about Jill's children. She answered at some length, but Andrea could tell she was not thinking about what she was saying. She finally stopped and regarded Andrea properly for the first time.

'You're still the same old Andy, aren't you?' she said.

That faintly patronising tone was still there, stinging Andrea. Yes, still the same old dull boring Andy Pandy. Inhibited Andrea, who could never let go and really enjoy herself, who had never learnt the art of abandonment and because of that had lost her husband's interest.

'That's right,' she agreed. 'You'd have thought we'd have changed after all this time, wouldn't you, but we haven't, any of us. Half a lifetime gone by, and all we've done is get worse. Penny's still so tied up in her career that she can't handle relationships properly, Carol just lives for the moment, I'm so uninteresting that nobody notices I'm there, and you— ' she tried to stop herself, but having started on a course of brutal honesty the words came out of their own accord '– you're still trying to outshine Jennifer. The only difference is that now you're trying to beat her by playing her own game, instead of setting up in opposition.'

She took a deep breath, surprised by the sense of liberation. It was amazingly invigorating, speaking the truth instead of cloaking it in kindness and tact. Jill was staring at her, white-faced, but she did not let it stop her. She felt her way forward, letting out all the half-formed thoughts that had lurked at the back of her mind since that first reunion meeting.

'There's something wrong with all of us,' she said, 'We're all locked in the past, we're not developing properly. It's as if we all need to hold each other's hands still.' Then it came to her. She gripped

Jill's arm in excitement of discovery. 'That's it! We must all get together again for one last time, and you have to be there. You're the key, you and Jennifer. It didn't work with just the other three of us. You've got to come, and we have to talk about it, about that day Jennifer died.'

'No.' Jill edged away from her, fear in her eyes. 'No, I can't.'

'But you must, Jill. Don't you see ? If you don't, you'll never be free, you'll always be in Jennifer's shadow, and we'll always be in yours. You must do it, we all must.' With a decision worthy of Jill at her most thrustful, she pulled her friend up and propelled her back along the lakeside towards her car. 'Come back with me now. We've got all day. I'll phone the others and make them join us. Carol's got nothing on that I know of, and Penny's not started on another job yet so they've no excuse. They'll have to drop whatever else they're doing. It's just a question of convincing them that it's vitally important. I think it would be better if you called them. Yes, that's it, of course it is. They'll listen to you, they always did. If you tell them, they'll come.'

CHAPTER TWENTY

Penny was throwing her energy into an orgy of cleaning. Already that morning she had scoured the kitchen and the bathroom, now she was washing down all the paintwork. The flat had not had its hidden corners so thoroughly investigated for months. She had Radio One on loud, and sang along with the endless banal lyrics, trying to make the noise and the physical effort take over and switch off her head. But still she could not stop listening for the phone. Somewhere out there, in a pub, in a producer's office, in a plush lounge, a decision was being made that would affect the next few months of her life.

She had arrived at the audition on top form. Duncan drove her to the stage door of the theatre, kissed her long and lovingly before letting her out.

'Go for it, darling. Give it all you've got.'

She smiled back at him, charging up on his belief in her.

'I'll do that.'

He gave her a last squeeze, leaned over and opened the car door.

'Break a leg!' he called, as she walked across the pavement.

Penny laughed and waved. She was not superstitious by nature, but before an audition it was best to propitiate all the gods of the theatre.

'I will!'

She ran up the steps to the stage door brimming with enthusiasm and confidence. She knew she could do it.

The part was a gift, the break she had been waiting for, the female lead in a clever comedy set on a health farm. The author was known for his memorable characters and witty lines, the director a past master at getting the best out of both play and players. It was a West End production, and likely to run. Penny went out onto the stage and projected every last ounce of ability. It was the best audition piece she had ever done. The competition was stiff, two talented actresses with more stage experience than she, but Penny knew she was in with a very good chance.

She rubbed at the skirting boards in the hallway, removing every last trace of dirt. If she could just get that part, then something in her life would be settled. Everything was in such a state of flux. There was nothing she could rest her mind on with confidence. Justin was bouncing back and forth between her and Mike like a tennis ball, spending all of every weekend there now, and sometimes staying over till Monday night. Mike was beginning to point out that the school near to him was much better than the one Justin was attending now. Penny suspected Wendy of pushing this angle, since she knew it was her weakest point. If it was to Justin's advantage that he changed schools, Penny had to consider it. She considered it for the length of time it took to clean the hall, but still came to no firm conclusion.

And then there was Duncan.

No phone call from the airport this time when he arrived home from New York. He was home for twenty-four hours before Penny heard from him. She knew he was back, because she rang up the paper and found out. For all of that evening, she hesitated on the point of contacting him, but did not quite dare to. Then at last, the next morning, he rang her.

'How was the Big Apple?' she asked, trying to sound bright and friendly.

'Amazing,' he told her, and proceeded to terrify her with tales of his wild week. He did not actually say that his nights had been as fully occupied as his days, but the implication was there. Then he suggested that they should meet that evening.

It was an invitation that stopped Penny from quite hitting the bottom. She had not completely blown the whole thing.

Later, as they lay on his bed with the warm night air drifting in through the open windows, he admitted that he had been desperately lonely.

'You know I wanted to come,' Penny told him.

'Oh sure,' Duncan said.

He turned his head to look out at the lights across the river.

'Darling, I did, really. I hated it being here while you were away. You couldn't have been more lonely than I was.'

She leaned over to look at him more closely, but his face was unreadable in the half-light.

'You had Justin.'

It caught her like a kick in the stomach. He was young and free, he had talent and drive, he was not going to wait around for ever. He had his eyes on the next step up the ladder. A woman tied by a teenage son would only be a drag on him. She wound herself round him, took his head between her hands and kissed him until she felt him respond.

'I need you, Duncan. I love you.'

'And I love you. You're one on your own, I've never met a woman like you before.' He ran a hand over the smooth lines of her body, and she could sense him choosing his words. 'I think we could have something real, but – you're as elusive as water. You've got to get your head together, Pen. You can't run in all directions at once.'

Beyond that he would not elaborate.

Penny was torn between joy at knowing that he did see a future that included both of them, and fear at what he was asking. For he wanted her to choose, and she could not do it.

'Why can't I have both?' she asked now, kneeling

on the hall floor with a damp J-cloth in her hand.

Why not Duncan and Justin, and a career as well? Other people managed it. For the last three weeks she had avoided the issue, but she knew it was coming to a head. Neither of them mentioned it. Instead, Duncan disappeared up north for a couple of days, for an interview, he said. Whether he was asking the questions or being asked, he did not say. Penny did not dare to find out, in case it was a job he was going after. In the meantime, her agent told her of the part going in the play, and Duncan was most enthusiastic, encouraging her to go for it. Now it occurred to her to wonder why. Was he making sure she had a life raft in the event of his leaving her?

Beside her ear the phone rang, making her jump. Heart thudding, she picked up the receiver.

'Penny? Andrea.'

'Oh – Andy. Hello.' It took her a moment to adjust. Then she remembered yesterday's call and the anxiety about her friend surfaced. 'Is everything OK?' she asked, fearing the worst. She had tried several times to ring Carol and find out if she knew anything about Robert's erratic behaviour, but had only reached Samantha.

'Well, no, but that's not what I'm ringing about. Listen, can you come here right away? It's very important.'

There were a thousand reasons why she could not just drop everything. Two, anyway. She might hear from Duncan, she would almost certainly find out today whether or not she had got the part.

'What's it all about, Andy?'

'I can't tell you now, it's too involved. But Jill's here, and it's essential that we meet, all four of us.'

'*Jill?*' Penny repeated. 'Where on earth has she sprung from?'

'You'll find out later. Just come, Penny. Please.'

'Is Carol— ?'

'I'm just about to ask her. You will come, won't you?'

Penny could not refuse. Going into the bathroom, she tried to make sense of it. Jill! And what had happened yesterday? Was the wonderful Robert up to anything? One thing was certain, if Carol was involved Penny would never forgive her. If only she had been able to get through to her yesterday. She stripped and stepped under the shower. Even in an emergency such as this seemed to be, she was not appearing in public looking less than perfect.

Carol felt like a wreck. She peered at her face in the lounge mirror and groaned. She looked like a wreck. She had spent a sleepless night, racked with fear and guilt. She would never forget the shock she had had yesterday evening, seeing Andrea like that waiting outside the flat. After the first disbelieving stare, she had turned and run, not knowing what to do apart from get away. Back at the station again, she had collapsed on a bench and tried to think. What to do? She was almost certain that Andrea had not seen her, but did Robert know she was there? Had Robert told her, and was she now waiting for Carol to arrive? It then occurred to her that she must phone him and find out.

His surprise at hearing her voice was enough to let her know he suspected nothing.

'Listen,' she told him. 'Just go and look out of the front window, will you? See if anyone's sitting on next door's wall, under the hedge.'

'What?' He laughed, thinking she was joking. 'You're not serious.'

'I'm dead serious. Honest.'

'Very well.'

She heard the receiver being set down, then clearly across the room came Robert's horrified cry.

'Christ! Andrea!'

Hurried footsteps back to the phone.

'Carol, it's Andrea. She's sitting outside.'

Carol explained what she had done and where she was.

'Well don't come back here. Oh God, what am I going to do? How did she find out? I can't go down there. I can't face her. Oh God, what am I going to say to her?'

His panic was even greater than her own.

'I don't know,' she snapped. 'I suppose she can't sit there for ever.'

'What if she knocks at the door? What shall I say to her?'

'I don't know,' Carol repeated. 'Just don't tell her it was me, that's all. Do you hear me? Don't tell her it was me.'

'No, no, I won't— ' he was hardly listening.

The pips went.

'Look, I'm off home,' Carol said. 'I'll see you.'

'But Carol— '

The line went dead.

When she got home, Samantha was bawling the boys out. When she noticed that her mother was back, she actually stopped and made a cup of tea.

'You look terrible, Mum. Is there anything wrong? You're back ever so early.'

Carol mumbled some garbled tale about having a row with the person for whom she was supposed to be working.

'Tell him to stuff his job,' Samantha advised. 'Oh, I forgot to tell you. Someone called Penny rang earlier. She said to call her back.'

Carol groaned. The last person she wanted to speak to was Penny. She had made it clear ages ago that she disapproved of affairs with friends' husbands. If only she had listened to her. She drank the tea, then went on to gin and lime, but it did nothing to deaden the worry. What if Andrea found out?

The same thought was still on her mind the next morning as she wandered about the place in her housecoat. She could not summon up the strength to get dressed, but she knew she would have to make the effort. She only had one cigarette left and she couldn't last out until the boys came home to get some more for her. She picked up the empty gin bottle and made a face at it. She could have done with another drop of that, too.

'God,' she said, 'bloody men.' Why were they so stupid? Why did he let Andrea find out? Everything had been going so nicely, she had an interesting job that was paying quite well in fits and starts, and she had a rich lover. Now what was going to happen? Even Carol could not believe that it would all go on as before, though she did hold on to the hope that Designs might not fold up. She really enjoyed that, despite Andrea's nagging, and if Andrea did not know that it was she whom Robert had been seeing, perhaps she would get away with it.

She lit the last cigarette and looked at the state of the kitchen. Samantha had yelled at the boys until they cleared away and washed up last night, but the breakfast things were still lying about. All the same, it looked better than it usually did. Sam might be a pain, but you had to admit that she did get things done. She would never get herself into a mess like her mother. Carol leaned against a work-stop and looked out into the unkempt garden. God, what was she going to say when she next saw Andy? Perhaps she could manage to keep away for a week or two until the worst of it had died down. Perhaps it would be better to fade out of her life altogether.

The phone rang. Carol stiffened with foreboding. Now what? She let it ring, but in the end the noise got on her nerves so much that she had to go and answer it.

'Carol? Andrea.'

Carol nearly dropped the receiver.

'Oh,' she croaked.

'Are you all right, Carol? You sound a bit odd.'

'I— er— ' Carol tried to think. If Andy was asking after her she must still consider her a friend. But Carol still did not want to see her for a while. 'I'm feeling a bit rough,' she said. It was true, after all.

'Oh, I'm sorry. But listen, Carol, can you possibly get over here? It's very important.'

'No!' Carol squeaked, before she could stop herself. 'I mean, I really don't think so, Andy. I was just going back to bed.'

'Are you really that bad? Carol, can't you take some aspirins or something? It won't be for long, I promise, but it is essential that you come. Jill's here.'

'Bloody hell.' Had she dragged Jill into it now? Oh God. 'Sorry, Andy, but I can't.'

'But you must! Listen, Penny's already on her way, but it will take her at least half an hour, probably more. Obviously you won't feel like walking if you're not well, but I'll send a taxi for you. OK?'

'No, it isn't OK. I feel like death.'

'Carol I am sorry, but you just must come. The cab will be there to pick you up in twenty minutes. 'Bye.'

Carol was about to start on another line of defence, perhaps involving one or other of the children, but the line went dead.

'Send as many bloody taxis as you like, mate, but I won't be in them,' she muttered. Andrea,

Penny *and* Jill! No thanks. It sounded as if they were setting up some sort of a court. She wasn't having them standing in judgement on her actions. Maybe they had had a hold over her when they were all eighteen, but not now. Her stomach quaked with fear at the thought of the three of them staring at her with accusation in their faces. It was all right for them, they did not know what it was like to be on your own. At least, Penny did, but Penny had told her to lay off Robert, so it was no good looking for understanding from her. Carol fled upstairs and shut herself in her bedroom.

Then it occurred to her that she would be trapped. If she did not turn up, Andrea would be sure to ring again. She might even come round. They might all come round. It was easy enough when you had a car of your own. She imagined them walking up her front path, sneering at the weedy lawn and the peeling paint on the door. No, she could not face them here.

'Oh God,' she wailed, 'what am I going to be?'

She looked wildly about the room, and once more caught sight of herself in the mirror, hair all over the place, face pale and unmade-up, saggy mauve housecoat gaping where the buttons were missing.

'Get dressed,' she told herself. 'Get dressed first.'

She rushed round frantically, splashing water over her face, dragging on clothes, slapping on foundation. A comb through her hair, lipstick round her mouth, sandals on her feet. She still looked like nothing on earth, but at least she felt a bit better. Just doing something had made an improvement. Now what? She ran downstairs and retrieved her handbag. She must go out. Yes, that was it, she would get away from them. She hesitated in the hall, biting her lip as she looked at the phone, half afraid it was going to ring again. She could almost hear Andrea's voice, or perhaps even Jill's, telling her that she must come.

'Oh no,' she said. 'Oh no, I'm not going, and that's flat.'

But she knew that she would. Running away was just a pretence. Sooner or later they would catch up with her. They were all so much stronger than she was, she could not stand up against them. She had to go.

Outside, a car drew up and hooted. Hands shaking, Carol opened the front door and stepped out.

CHAPTER TWENTY-ONE

Jill was sitting in a blue dralon-covered armchair in an unfamiliar room. She could not remember how she got there, but she was not afraid. There was something reassuring about the place. Photographs of children were grouped on the oyster-coloured wall opposite her, standard school shots with blue backgrounds and gold-rimmed mounts. There was something she recognised about the younger boy, but she could not place it. At the end of the room, patio doors opened onto a sunlit garden which sloped down to fields and woodland. She could walk out if she wanted to, but she knew she must not, for there was something she had to do. She was waiting to meet—to meet—

A door opened behind her and someone walked in.

'Here we are.'

A woman placed a tea tray on the tiled coffee table. Jill stared at her.

'Andrea!'

Andrea smiled at her. She poured out the tea.

'Sugar?'

Jill shook her head.

'No thank you.'

Of course, it was beginning to come back to her. She was at Andrea's house. Andrea lived here. She looked about with more interest. It was a nice place. Fancy old Andy doing so well. But she still could not remember how she had got here. She kept quiet. She had the feeling there was something lurking at the threshold of her consciousness, something she did not want to meet. Andy was chatting, about the house, about the children in the photographs. Two boys and a girl. Names were mentioned, but Jill did not take them in. The voice was a soothing background, protecting her from the thing that was trying to get at her.

'You've two, haven't you?' Andy asked.

Jill tried to concentrate. Yes, she did have two children. Who were they?

'Yes,' she heard her own voice say, 'Robin and Emily.'

Andrea asked about them, Jill answered, but the black thing at the door was scratching, whining, pulling at her attention. Soon it would break in. Robin and Emily. She tried to think about them. Robin and Jen—

'Jennifer!'

She started up, knocking over the teacup. She had to get Jennifer.

'It's all right.'

Andrea pushed her gently back into the chair, picked up the cup and saucer, knelt in front of her holding her hands. She sounded reassuring, but her eyes were apprehensive.

'The others will be here soon. Penny's on her way. In a minute I'm going to ring for a taxi for Carol.'

Jill relaxed a little. Penny, Carol and Andrea. With the three of them round her, she was better protected against Jennifer.

'Yes,' she said.

'Carol and I have been running a little business,' Andrea was saying. 'We call it Designs Unlimited. Do you remember I sent you a brochure about it?'

Jill could not understand what she was talking about. What business? Carol was going to art school, Andrea was going to university. She heard what Andrea was saying about decorating rooms and planning gardens, but it did not sink in. She had her own plans for her friends. Penny was going to be a famous actress, Carol a great painter, Andrea – Andrea was going to achieve something brilliant in the academic world. Even Jennifer could not do all that. With the help of her friends, she would defeat Jennifer at last.

She hardly noticed the ring at the door, the prolonged muttering in the hall. Then Carol came in.

'Hello, Jill. Long time no see.' Her voice was shrill with nerves.

Jill hardly recognised her. Instead of the pretty eighteen-year-old with the blonde flicked-up hair and pale pouting lips there stood an ill-groomed, overweight woman approaching forty. It jolted Jill back to the present as nothing else could have done.

'My God,' she said. 'Whatever have you done to yourself? You used to be better-looking than Jennifer.'

'Yeah, well— ' Carol gave a flickering smile and perched on the edge of the chair furthest from Jill. 'We're not kids any more, are we? You look different, too.'

This time Andrea's efforts at making conversation were unable to reduce the tension in the atmosphere. Carol either answered in monosyllables or gabbled. It was obvious even to Jill in her self-obsessed state that she was trying to cover something up. Both Carol and Andrea were visibly relieved when the bell went again. More mutterings in the hall, then Penny appeared.

'Jill, darling— '

In a waft of Mystère, Penny kissed her cheek.

Penny was a credit to her. Slim, poised, beautifully turned-out, she was every inch the successful actress.

'I can see you're doing well, Pen,' she commented.

Penny gave an ironic smile.

'The career's going splendidly,' she said, with the emphasis on 'career'.

Andrea hastily interrupted.

'Never mind that now. First we have to talk about Jill.'

'Yes,' Penny agreed. 'Get the committee in order again, shall we?'

Carol took the new pack of cigarettes she had bought on the way out of her bag and lit one.

'I wish someone would tell me what all this is about,' she complained.

Andrea began to speak, but Penny cut in.

'It's what it was always about, surely? The problems haven't changed at all over the years. You and I and Andy are still in trouble over men and careers, and Jill's still screwed up over Jennifer. We parted that last summer with it all unsolved, and we've never managed to sort it out. Perhaps this is our last chance.'

Carol shrugged.

'You sound like someone on the telly.'

'No, she's right,' Andrea agreed. 'She's put into words what I felt. I knew we had to all be together again, not just for Jill, but for all of us. We all need to straighten ourselves out. I know I do.'

Jill found them all looking at her. She was the leader, she was expected to organise them. Yet Andrea, it seemed, had just as much organising ability as she, and Penny had more insight. As for Carol – Jill looked at her again, puffing nervously with a hunted expression on her face – Carol had more experience, just as she always did have, though whether it had done her any good was doubtful. Jill felt lost. They always expected her to come up with the goods, and she couldn't do it. Not with Jennifer to compete with. It was too much.

'Jill.'

Penny was crouching by her knee.

'Jill, you were out at the reservoir this morning, looking for Jennifer. Why don't you tell us about it?'

She could see the reservoir, the red sails against the scudding clouds, the grey shifting water, but she could not see Jennifer. She knew she was there, though. She was always there.

'Come and sit with me,' Penny was saying, pulling gently at her. 'On the floor. You two as well. We must all sit together.'

There were reluctant noises from Carol, but they all complied, sitting in a tight circle on the hearth-rug.

'Closer,' Penny insisted. 'We must touch.'

Jill could feel Penny's thigh on one side, Andrea's knee on the other.

'Now,' Penny's voice became softly coaxing, 'we're all going back to that Saturday in August. We'll each say what we were doing, and what we remember.'

'Oh yes,' Andrea breathed. 'That's it. We must live it again.'

'Get on with it, then,' Carol suggested. 'You first, Pen. It's your idea.'

Penny paused a moment, getting back into that time, trying to recall the details.

'On that morning, I went and called for Andrea,' she began. 'I was wearing hipsters and a pink polo-neck. I had a packed lunch and swimming things in a carrier with yellow plastic handles. My mum had gone to work and my dad was still in bed, so after I'd done my share of the chores I'd nothing to keep me at home. I was early at Andy's, and she wasn't ready. I waited in her front room, which was always dark, even on a bright day, and I could hear her parents fussing. She finally appeared looking flushed and cross. She hardly said a word to me as we walked up to the bus stop, but once the bus came she relaxed. We were the first of our group to arrive, so we bagged a good place on the bank and staked it out with our towels, and then we helped launch some of the dinghies. Someone asked me if I'd like to crew for him for the first race. That drippy boy, what was his name? With the gingery hair? Anyway, I didn't accept, because I was hoping Phil Marshall would ask me. But when he came, he just said, "Hi, Pen," and went out with one of his friends. I was really sick. I can remember that so clearly. I was sick with disappointment.

'Then Andy went out with someone, and Carol and Smithy arrived and we all wondered where Jill had got to. It's all a bit of a blur after that. I suppose we watched the races and larked about, like we always did, and ate our lunches. Then at about two o'clock, Jennifer and Jill finally turned up.'

Jill remembered that all right, being released from the dreadful lunch party her parents had insisted that she and Jennifer attended, only it was later than two, for she had watched the hands of the clock turning and ached to get away. That was clear enough.

'Jill was spitting feathers. She'd missed the race she wanted to enter. She raved on about capitalists and abolishing the *bourgeois* family unit, then we got *Allegro* into the water and she went off by herself. I'm not sure where Jennifer went. I suppose she joined some of her friends. I was really more concerned about Phil Marshall. I hung about the dinghy racks hoping he'd notice me, so I didn't even see Jill come ashore and pick Jennifer up. I only remember the shouting, and them bringing her back.'

There was a silence in the room, as they all saw again the limp body, the vain attempts at resuscitation.

'You now, Andy,' Penny said softly.

Andrea began hesitantly.

'I was hoping Penny wouldn't come too early. My parents were being – difficult. They always distrusted you lot. They were questioning me about what went on at the reservoir. It was the boys. They didn't like the idea of me hanging around with a group of boys. "Flaunting yourself in front of any man who comes along," they said. I was really embarrassed when Penny arrived. I tried to get away, but they went on about putting wicked thoughts into men's heads by displaying myself in a swimsuit. I was afraid Penny might hear and tell the others. That's why I didn't talk much when I did get out.

'Then when we got there, and Pen turned the gingery boy down, I could see him coming to ask me next, so I dashed over to Sue Simmonds and asked her if she wanted a crew. I didn't like her much, but at least she was safe. And with Jill not there, we did well, we nearly won. I even invited Sue over to eat her lunch with us, but when she saw Carol and Smithy there, she refused. I remember looking at Carol, so confident, drinking up all the whistles and the admiration, and wishing I could be like her. I could never – enjoy being female, the way she did.

'Well, anyway, Jill arrived and she certainly was furious. She didn't often go out without taking one of us with her. But the sail seemed to calm her, because after a while she came back and picked Jennifer up. I don't think Jennifer wanted to go at first. They talked for a while, but then Jennifer got in and they went off towards the other end of the lake. It was getting blustery, too cold for a swimsuit. I was just putting a cardigan on, so I missed the capsize. I remember Carol saying, "Hello, Jill's gone over," and when I looked again I couldn't see anything, not even the hull in the water. It was too far away. And then – then we saw the sail come up again, and flap around for ages, but we didn't suspect anything was wrong. Someone sailed past, and turned back and fetched the rescue boat, and it was only then that we realised that something had – happened. And then everyone was asking questions, and shouting and – you know the rest.'

Did they? Jill wondered. Did they know how it felt to see your loved, your hated sister lying lifeless on the grass? And all the time knowing that it was your fault? She drew her breath in sharply, trembling.

Penny took her hand.

'We're all with you,' she said. 'Now, Carol.'

Carol lit another cigarette, shifted position, complained about the hardness of the floor.

'I can't say much more than you two,' she said. 'Smithy called for me. He was full of this car he was going to buy. A Mini Cooper. He'd been looking out for one. He didn't want any old car, it had to be a

Mini Cooper, green, with leather seats. He was going to tune up the engine, he said, and we'd go for runs down to the coast. The only thing was, he didn't have enough money and he was afraid someone else would buy it before he could raise the loan. That's all I remember about the morning really. Like Pen said, by the time we got to the reservoir, Andy had gone out and Jill hadn't come. And as for the afternoon, well, I didn't really see anything, did I?'

'You saw the boat go over?' Penny prompted.

'Yeah, well, I suppose I did, but boats were always capsizing, weren't they? I mean, it was no big deal. You just stood on the centreboard and heaved them up. You got wet and got a few bruises, but that was all. I never thought all that was happening out there, none of us did. Like Andy said, it was only when the rescue boat came in – and then I couldn't really believe it, I mean, you don't, do you? You don't think something like that can happen to people you know. But it did. I do remember being sick, after the ambulance had gone.'

There was a general murmur of agreement. They had all been left shocked by the accident.

Jill felt rather than saw them all focus on her. They had told their stories, now it was her go. She had to approach that locked door and turn the key, and it terrified her. All these years she had been unable to do it, paralysed by the fear of finding that she really had done what she suspected of herself, what she had wanted to do that summer's afternoon.

'I can't,' she whispered.

'Penny— ' she heard Andrea say, but Penny silenced her with a gesture.

'Start in the morning, Jill. Why didn't you come then? You didn't say anything the day before about not being able to make it. I remember that because none of us could believe you'd given in after all you'd been saying. What kept you, Jill?'

'My parents,' she said.

She had known about the lunch party. It was impossible not to know. Her mother had been wittering on about it for days. But she had not intended staying for it. She had said as much several times, and both her father and her mother had stated that she must attend.

'They wanted you at this party they were giving?' Penny prompted.

'Yes, they made me be there.'

There had been a terrific row, worse than any for a long time. They had all been working up to it for weeks, all through the summer, as Jill's behaviour became more and more impossible. The party was just a flashpoint.

'I am not staying to act as bait to your lecherous Tory toads, and that is that!' she had screamed at them. 'I'm going out and you can't stop me.'

She marched into the hall and picked up the bag she had left at the foot of the stairs. Her father followed, standing in the entrance to the lounge, jabbing a threatening finger at her.

'If you go out of that door, my girl, I'll see to it you never go to college. Do you hear me?'

His words started a qualm of fear, but she did not let him see it.

'You can't do that,' she flung back.

'I can and I will.'

'You can't. I've got a place.'

Not Oxbridge, like Jennifer. She could not manage that. Instead she applied to the establishment that would most annoy her parents, the LSE. And she had been accepted. She was triumphant.

'But you can't live on the grant, it's not enough.

I have to make up the amount for you. You go out now, and I won't even sign the claim form. You'll have nothing, do you hear? Nothing. No college for you.'

She stared at him, trying to decide whether he meant it. Getting to the LSE was the one thing she lived for, and she knew he was right, she could not exist just on the grant, let alone without it.

'You don't mean that.'

'Just try me.'

'What about all your boasting then? What will you say to your friends? You're forever going on about how your girls can study for as long as they like, you don't need them to bring in the pennies. You'd have to back down, wouldn't you? Then what would you say?'

'Just try me,' her father repeated.

There was something in the way he said it, not shouting now, but with quiet force, that brought her up short. He did mean it. She could tell. The dream of the carefree student life was to be snatched away from her. No late-night discussions over bottles of wine, no wild parties, no protests and sit-ins and Marxist plottings. She would be left out of the revolution. She was staring into the void.

She dropped the bag.

'You can't do this to me,' she wailed. 'I've got to go to college, I've got to!'

Her mother appeared, and put an arm awkwardly round her slumped shoulders.

'Now then, dear, you just be a good girl and do as we say, and everything will be all right. Now run along upstairs, and change into a pretty dress and do your hair, and your father will run you both out to the reservoir after the lunch. It isn't really too much to ask, is it?'

Jill couldn't speak. She flung off her mother's arm and raced upstairs. They had won.

'It was a ghastly lunch,' she said, so low that the others had to strain to hear. 'Six of the Party faithful that my father was trying to woo. He wanted me and Jennifer there to show what a successful, happy family he had. I had to sit there and smile and field their patronising remarks while my father went on about everything Jennifer had done, and how proud of her they were, and how well she was getting on at Cambridge. If he said Cambridge once he said it a hundred times. Just once he referred to me. "And of course, our Jilly's going to university as well." So when they asked me where I was going I had to admit that it wasn't Cambridge like my sister. And all the time I could feel his eyes on me, daring me to put a foot out of line. He knew he had the upper hand, and he was using it. I felt sick, sick with rage. There was nothing I could do. I was powerless.'

On either side of her, Penny and Andrea made sympathetic noises, Andrea patting her hand. Carol coughed.

'Real Victorian, your dad.'

'But he did give you and Jennifer a lift to the reservoir, as your mother promised?' Penny asked.

'Yes. They were going on to a Party do in the afternoon, and it was on their way. They dropped both of us at the end of the road. J – Jennifer just laughed it all off. She could always get along with the old fogies, she just charmed them all. She didn't care about politics, she wasn't committed. She could have argued brilliantly with them, she was intelligent enough, but she played the part expected of her and left them to it.

'Life's too short to get steamed up about it,' she said to me. 'Forget it, it's not worth worrying about. Get *Allegro* out and go for a sail.'

'I just couldn't get her to see that it did matter, that you had to take sides. She didn't have to, you see. She just danced through life, winning all the prizes, loved by everybody.'

'Or so it seemed to you then,' Andrea said.

Jill turned on her with all her old impatience.

'That's how it was,' she insisted.

'OK,' Penny said. 'So you arrived at the reservoir. What did Jennifer do?'

'She went off with a couple of her old friends from school.'

'And you and I launched *Allegro*.'

'Yes.'

She supposed it must have been Penny who helped her, though she did not remember that at all. She only recalled the murderous hatred for her whole situation, for her parents and everything they stood for, for the hold they had over her, for Jennifer – most of all for Jennifer. There was no getting away from her. Even when Jill went to college, even when she managed to build a life of her own, Jennifer would always be there. Every time she came back, every time she so much as received a letter from home, there was sure to be a mention of Jennifer, and her fresh successes. She would never be rid of her.

The small boat lifted and crashed into a steep wave, jarring beneath Jill's body. She was forced to attend to what she was doing. She was acting like a beginner, the sails were flapping, the sheets shaking themselves into a tangle, the boat sliding broadside on to the waves. Swiftly she sorted it out, gathering ropes and helm, leaning out to balance the light dinghy against the pull of the wind. Sailing needed full concentration, a constant fine adjustment to every change of wind and water. She skimmed over the lake, the boat obedient to her command, and the answer to her dilemma slipped into her mind. Perhaps it had always been there, lurking, waiting for the right moment to come out and take over, rising from the unconscious to the conscious to appear, fully formed and ready to be put into action. Jill did not try to fight it, she even fed the rage that drove her, running over all the many humiliations she had suffered as she sailed back to the lakeside.

It was not difficult to locate Jennifer. She was at the centre of a group, talking to some girlfriends while a couple of young men vied for her attention. The fitful sunshine gleamed on her blonde hair. She smiled and waved when she caught sight of Jill.

'Hello Jilly!'

Someone said something and they all laughed. Jill knew it was because of her. Some joke about the dumb kid sister. In front of Jennifer's friends she felt the contrast more than ever. Hiding her pain, she ignored them, speaking to Jennifer alone, inviting her to come for a sail. And in the end Jennifer agreed, not because she wanted to particularly, but because she was sorry for her sister, for the dreadful lunch party, for the A-level results that had not been as good as hers, for the constant comparisons between them. And Jill hated her for her pity.

They headed out towards the far end of the lake, beyond the marker buoys for the morning's racing, away from the gaggle of boats chasing round close to the clubhouse. Many of them were going in now, for the wind was blowing up squally and treacherous under the piled black clouds.

At first Jennifer found it exhilarating, laughing in the wind, but after a while she became worried.

'Don't you think we ought to reef her down a bit?' she asked anxiously. 'It's blowing pretty hard at times.'

'Hard? It's no more than four or five,' Jill told

her. 'She's safe as houses. We'll hardly move at all if we go taking sail off her.'

'But we're not racing,' Jennifer pointed out.

Jill just laughed. She was wild and high on the speed and the spray, on the awful intoxicating prospect of what she was going to do. At last, at long last she was going to triumph in the race she had been running and losing all her life. Ahead was a towering storm cloud, promising rough weather. She turned the boat until they were running before the wind, dark rollers surging beneath them, sails spread wide to catch every last ounce of power.

'Hold the jib out, Jen,' she called. 'Goosewing her!'

Jennifer moved forward to hold the foresail on the opposite side of the boat to the larger mainsail, and the small boat strained under the force of the elements. Jill was exultant. She was at one with the wind and the waves, as mighty and irresistible as they. She could no more be stopped than the storm that was coming. Above her a seagull, miles from its natural home, rode with effortless grace on the thermals. Jill sailed with it, two creatures of air and water, beyond thought, jubilant with the fierce joy of being.

'Careful, Jilly, for heaven's sake. You'll gybe her!'

She had all but forgotten Jennifer as a person. Now she glanced at the hunched figure and white, frightened face looking back at her and was amazed. Jen was scared!

'It's all right,' she cried. 'I know what I'm doing!'

Jen was scared. She couldn't believe it. Bright, beautiful Jennifer was huddled aft of the mast, wanting only to be on shore again, and safe. Jill felt a great surge of pity for her. Never to know the thrill of riding the wild wind! What a huge, terrible gap in her life. And for the first time ever she was glad to be herself, to be Jill Somers and nobody else, with all the wonderful possibilities that that entailed. Of course she would never be Jennifer. She would never be as pretty, as charming, as clever, never win tennis tournaments or play Chopin preludes. But Jennifer would never be her. She would not know what it was to fight and win, to grapple with impossible odds and come out triumphant. Her path was too smooth, too pleasant, she would never appreciate her good fortune, for she would never know what it was like to be a loser, to be second best. She would never know the fire and the passion, for despite her intellectual gifts she would always skate on the surface of life, serene and contented, only half-seeing the great events and desperate issues around her. Jill did not want to be like that. She wanted to be there, where it was happening, protesting, waving a banner, showing the way. She wanted to live, to experience everything, to be a voice in the power that shaped the lives of others, not just smile sweetly as it all drifted by. It was all there, and she was going to march out and take it by the throat and make it submit to her, for she was not Jennifer, she was Jill, unique and free. She threw her head back and laughed at the sheer wonder of it.

And the wind, seizing that brief moment of inattention, gusted and caught behind the sail, bringing it slamming across the boat. Jill saw it just in time, ducked and called a warning, but too late. The wooden boom cracked against the back of Jennifer's head and the boat tipped over, floating helpless in the white-topped waves.

Jill surfaced, gasping for air, and grabbed at the first thing that came to hand, the rudder, just as another wave broke over the boat and washed it out of her grasp. She swam forward a couple of strokes and this time caught hold of the floating boom. Jennifer. Where was Jennifer? She could not see her sister at all.

'Jen!' she screamed, and a wave swamped her, filling her mouth with water.

Beneath the bright scarlet of the nylon sail was a lumpy shape. With sick horror, she realised that it was Jennifer, and she was not moving. Fighting down panic, she tried to heave the boat off, but *Allegro*, so light and obedient the right way up, was nothing but a wallowing hulk when capsized. Desperately she reached underneath the sail, trying to catch hold of an arm or a leg, but the surge of the waves kept washing Jennifer just beyond her scrabbling fingers. Her mind cleared in answer to the extremity of need. Get the boat up? No, that would take precious minutes. She must reach Jennifer now, before it was too late. All that mattered was that Jennifer should live.

She took a deep breath and dived, forcing herself to open her eyes under water. She was a good swimmer, and the desperate need gave her extra strength. She saw something dark in the dim water, and caught hold of Jennifer's suntop. She pulled, but only the fabric moved, shifted and got an arm round Jennifer's waist, pulled again but still she hardly moved. Something must have got caught up. She was running out of breath. Her lungs ached, crying out for air. She gave a last despairing heave, swallowed a great mouthful of water and let go, fighting frantically back to the surface.

Two spluttering breaths and she dived again. Jennifer must be tangled in the floating rigging. She must get her free. Thinking more clearly now as the seconds ticked away, she felt along the limp limbs, found the rope twisted round one wrist, managed to ease it off. Head and chest throbbing to bursting point with the pressure of holding her breath, she grasped Jennifer under the arms, kicked frenetically and finally pulled her clear of the smothering sail.

Coughing and choking, it was several moments before she was aware of anything but the life-giving air. Then she looked at Jennifer. Her eyes were horribly half-open, and she was not breathing.

Fragments of first-aid lessons, half attended to and mostly forgotten, rose in her mind. Kiss of life – Holger Neilson – recovery position – but none of that could be done in the water. She looked around wildly. They were about as far from the shore as they could be. There was one other dinghy a couple of hundred yards away, but that was all. She tried to wave and shout, but they did not seem to hear her.

'Help!' she screamed. 'Help. Please!'

The sail shivered and shifted as the boat changed tack, then, mercifully, came the answering cry.

'Hold on!'

But the wind was against them, it would take them minutes to reach her. She must make Jennifer breathe. Get the boat up. She could do nothing while still in the water. She remembered the lifesaving classes. Hold the victim under the chin. Swim backwards. That made it slightly easier. She worked her way round the boat till she came to the centreboard. Now what? She was faced with a horrible dilemma. To right the dinghy, she needed both arms and all her strength. She would have to leave go of Jennifer. Oh God, why had she not let her get her lifejacket? She spent agonising

W.L.H.F.M.F.—14

moments trying to decide. Leave go or hold on? She must get the boat up. She let go. Jennifer drifted helpless.

Hands on the rim of the hull, feet on the centreboard, Jill scrambled upright, heavy and clumsy with her clothes clinging sodden to her body. A frantic heave, throwing every ounce of weight and straining muscle against the hold of the water. Nothing, not a movement. Another effort, and then the boat answered, the sail lifting slowly out of the waves at first, then coming up with a rush. With the automatic action of long practice, Jill rolled into the waterfilled hull. The boat lifted sluggishly to the grey waves. the wet sails flapped. Jill looked back to find Jennifer, but already she was just out of reach. She jumped back in.

The other dinghy arrived. Jill's leaping hope was crushed when she saw two fourteen-year-old boys. No use at all. Appalled, they stared at Jennifer's limp body.

'Get the rescue boat!' Jill shrieked at them.

'Right, right.'

Relieved at being sent away, they headed for the shore.

The rescue boat would be too late. Jill knew that with a terrible certainty. No kiss was ever going to bring life back to her sister now.

CHAPTER TWENTY-TWO

They came slowly out of suspended time, as if waking from an intense dream. Jill was weeping silently, the tears running unchecked down her face. Penny, easing her hand out of the manic grasp, put both arms round her and cried with her while Andrea and Carol, released at last from the spell, shifted their cramped legs and wiped their eyes. Though the tension flowed away with the tears, none of them dared speak. They each went over what they had heard, rearranging memories in order to fit this new view of Jennifer into the picture of the past, trying to work out how it related to themselves.

As Jill and Penny calmed at last and pulled apart, Andrea fetched a whisky bottle and four glasses.

'To us,' Carol said, with a weak giggle.

'To us,' they all responded.

There was a slight pause, then Penny added the second part of the toast they had always used then.

'And the future.'

They all looked at Jill.

'And the future,' she whispered. She drank, took a shuddering breath and smiled faintly round. The smile reached her eyes, and a glimmer of the real Jill was there again, ready to pick herself up and go on. 'The future, and all it may bring to us.'

They mumbled in chorus again, each looking now into the uncertainty ahead of them. Even together, even after the trauma they had just lived through with Jill, they could still not recapture the heedless optimism of half a lifetime ago. Too much had happened in between. Only Jill could at last see her way with confidence.

'If only I had known,' she said, but there was no passion behind the words now, just an aching regret for all those tortured years.

'You mean you didn't?' Carol asked, startled. 'You really thought you'd killed her?'

Jill shook her head slowly.

'I just didn't know. I couldn't remember. There was a – a wall, a shutter. I knew I wanted to. I could still feel that. It was all very clear up till then, the lunch, sailing by myself, picking Jennifer up. I knew I wanted to do it, to hold her under, to get even. Every time I tried to remember, that was as far as I got, as far as wanting desperately to get rid of her for ever. I was so afraid, so very afraid that I had done it, that I couldn't – couldn't get beyond that wall, to see what really happened.'

'All this time?' Andrea said softly, appalled at the thought of living with that guilt.

'All this time. Mark helped. He really put me together again. He's been wonderful, he backs me up all the way, he believes in me. But even he couldn't make me face it. Only you three could do that.'

'The lost pieces of the jigsaw puzzle,' Penny said. She was glad for Jill, happy that they had somehow managed to let her look at herself, but try as she might to focus on Jill's problems and their solution, she could not help wondering whether there was some message here somewhere for her. What was she going to do with the rest of her life?

Carol had been thinking along the same lines. She drank back the whisky, put her glass down and reached for the bottle to refill it.

'You know,' she said, 'I always blamed you for Sam and everything. I mean, I thought that if Jennifer hadn't died, I would never have gone and got myself pregnant and married Smithy and all of it. But I guess it was all just a dreadful accident. The drowning, I mean. Just a dreadful accident. It was my own stupid fault getting in the club. I'm always doing it, getting myself into a mess. It's men, I can't resist them. I mean, I like them, I can't help it. And anyway, there's nothing wrong in that, is there? It's the only thing I'm good at, sex. Lots of women aren't. They say they like it, because it's the thing to do, but they don't really, and then they're surprised when their old men want a bit on the side. It's no wonder, is it, that they come to people like me for a bit of fun? But they always go back to their wives. They want it all, you see. They want the security and the home and family and all that, and they want some excitement as well. Selfish sods.'

She looked at Andrea, on the verge of spilling it all. The atmosphere was all too conducive to confessions. Jill had had her turn, now it was Carol's.

'That's why you've been having trouble with your Robert,' she said, and gasped as Penny pinched her viciously on the calf.

'But how did you – ? I didn't – I mean there's no – ' Andrea was protesting.

Unwillingly, Carol caught Penny's eye, and met a look that told her to shut up or else.

'Stands out a mile, sunshine,' she said, in her most worldly-wise tone. 'But don't worry. Like I said, they always go back to their wives. Tell you what, though— ' Beside her, she could feel the waves of disapproval emanating from Penny, but ignored them. What she had to say was for Andy's own good. After all, she always had known more about men than any of the others. 'You ought to turn on the seductive bit every now and again. Soft lights and sweet music, you know? Low-cut dress, slit skirt, that sort of thing. Go to town, try the old stockings and suspenders. They all love it, you know. Fall for it every time. Just because you're married to a fella, doesn't mean to say you should take him for granted. Give him a little thrill.'

Andrea gaped at her.

'I— I— ' she stuttered, 'I don't think Robert goes for that sort of thing. At least – well, not from me, anyway.'

Carol gave her a pitying look.

'Don't you believe it, mate.'

'Well, I— '

'She's right,' Penny broke in unexpectedly.

'Well, perhaps you – I'll think about it.' Andrea took a gulp of whisky. 'Maybe I ought to rethink things. I don't know, it's been such a strange day. I don't seem to be able to think at all'. She looked round at them all anxiously. 'But we will meet again, won't we? Now that we've all got together at last, we won't let it fall apart again.'

'Not me I'm afraid, Andy.' Jill was adamant.

'But why not?'

'There's nothing to keep us now. You were always my defence against Jennifer. Between the four of us, we could do anything she could do, and better. But now – now I've finally realised that I never had to beat her. She was different. She would not have done what I have, if she had lived. We would have gone our different ways. I don't have to prove anything, I don't have to compete with her, or try to be her. From now on, I'm just going to be myself, doing what I can as well as I can, but for me, and Mark, not to show my parents that I'm as good as Jennifer. I don't want to be like her.'

She looked round at each of them, the skills of public life coming readily to her aid, drawing them all into her conviction that she was right.

'I owe it all to you, and I'm deeply grateful. I'll never be able to tell you just how grateful I am. Thanks to you, I can finally put the past behind me. And it's because of that that I feel we shouldn't meet again. Our little alliance is part of the past as well.

I'd like to keep it as it was, and be able to look back on it as something very meaningful, not have to pick it up again in quite different circumstances.'

Andrea was disappointed. The gathering of the three of them at the first reunion had proved to be the start to a new and more interesting phase in her life, so she had hoped that drawing in Jill as well to complete the foursome would have an even more powerful effect. Especially now, when she was so confused over the state of her marriage. She looked at Carol and Penny, expecting them to feel the same way.

'Yes,' Penny said slowly. She held Carol's eyes. 'We're not altogether good for each other now. Not the way we used to be. We've all grown apart. But I am glad we met this one last time.'

Andrea turned to Carol as a last resort.

'We've still got Designs, haven't we?'

'Well – er – ' Carol felt pinned down under the clear messages she was receiving from Penny. Designs had been a lifeline to her, even though she disliked being made to be efficient. But she had been dreading meeting Andy again. And supposing she was to run into Robert? He would be sure to give the game away, he was that stupid. Perhaps it was better to get out while the going was good.

'I – er – I don't know, Andy. It's only the garden side that's working at the moment, and that's all yours. The interiors never really took off, did they?'

'We only started a few months ago. You haven't given it long enough, Carol. I know we can make it work.'

Carol felt torn. She was tempted by the prospect of easy money doing something she was good at, but balanced against that was not only Penny's continued pressure to leave Andy and Robert alone, but the niggling fact that producing exact designs to someone else's specifications was very hard work.

'Sorry, Andy,' she mumbled. 'But you know me. I'm not a sticker. I'm not really cut out for running a business.'

Andrea argued for a while longer, but Carol wriggled out of it.

'I think it's for the best, you know,' Penny said at last. She could sense the pit of anticlimax they were all sinking into, and wanted only to get away, to return to her own life. She was strangely suspended here, cut off from reality. 'Jill's right,' she decided. 'This is a part of the past. It's about time we all grew up.'

As if operated by the same strings, she and Jill both got up. Penny looked at Carol.

'I'll run you home, if you like,' she offered.

Between them, they managed to avoid Andrea's offers of further drinks, of coffee, of food. At the door they paused. It was a historic moment. The magic foursome was breaking up. They turned to Jill, to their leader, for the parting words.

'Andrea— ' She hugged Andy with real warmth, and they kissed cheeks. 'How can I ever thank you for bringing me here and arranging this? You've given me back my sanity, do you know that? I couldn't have lived with Jennifer's shadow for much longer. Now, thanks to you – to all of you – I've brought everything into perspective. You've changed my life.' She gave that quick, approving nod they all remembered. 'And keep this design business of yours going, won't you? I know you can do it. You always were good at organising.'

She turned to Penny, embracing her.

'Pen, you're a credit to us all. I've always watched your career with interest. I'm sure you'll go on to do great things.'

Penny gave a cynical smile.

'Will you make me a Dame when you're PM?'

'Of course,' Jill promised, taking her seriously.

'I'll hold you to that.'

It ran unheeded off her politician's back.

'And Carol— ' Another hug, another swift exchange of kisses. 'I'm so glad you came. It's marvellous to see you again. It wouldn't have worked if we hadn't all come together.'

They parted in a flurry of waves and good wishes, Andrea taking Jill out to the reservoir to pick up Jill's car, Carol and Penny getting into Penny's car for the ride home.

Penny got in and slammed the door, waiting while Carol struggled with the seatbelt. She watched in the rear-view mirror as Andrea started up and moved out of the driveway. They all waved again.

'Patronising cow,' she said.

Carol looked at her, lips twitching.

'Too bloody right, mate.'

Giggling like the schoolgirls they used to be, they set off.

CHAPTER TWENTY-THREE

Andrea returned to a silent house. At the reservoir, Jill had gazed once more at the restless water, said goodbye to Jennifer, and after another speech of thanks to Andrea, driven off with an eager heart to the brilliant future she had mapped out for herself.

Well, that was something achieved, surely? Andrea thought, as she looked out at her sunny garden. To help another human being out of a nightmare she had been living half her life? We were all put on this earth to help each other, after all.

But what about me? asked the little voice that had become stronger each day since the reunion lunch. If Jill had spent half her life agonising over Jennifer and trying to compete with an impossible ideal, then Andrea had spent most of hers trying to please others. First her parents, then Robert and the children. The only thing she had done for herself was Designs Unlimited, and now that was finished.

She wandered into the dining room and touched the desk with its neat trays and files, the typewriter under its dustcover. She couldn't do it without Carol. Carol was the creative one, Andrea was just the organiser. Perhaps she had known all along that it wouldn't last. As Carol had said, she wasn't a sticker, and Andrea had realised that when they started. She had just hoped that Carol would be interested enough to stay the course, that success would come quickly enough to keep her going.

She took out the sketch plans she had been making for the latest garden project, and frowned over them. They were creative. And they were good. There was no doubt about it. She might not have any formal training, but she was sure these would stand up against those done by anyone who had been to horticultural college. Then she sat down suddenly as a new thought struck her.

'Why not?' she said out loud.

Why not indeed? There was nothing to stop her. The children were at school. All the difficulties she had raised when Camilla had nagged her about working she disposed of with the wave of a hand. She could get a cleaning lady in to do the house. She could batch-bake every fortnight or so, stock up the freezer, buy a microwave. That was easily arranged, it just needed a bit of organisation. But what about Robert? What would he think?

He would have to take her seriously. Designs was just a game, as far as he was concerned. Something to keep her from being bored without distracting her from the task of looking after him and the house. But if she went on a horticultural course, took a diploma or whatever the qualification was, he would be forced to sit up and take notice. It would shake him, and that would be no bad thing.

With new vigour, Andrea went into the hall and found the Yellow Pages. The agricultural college out at Enderby might run something suitable. She found the number, rang the secretary, discovered they were offering just the thing, and asked for forms and information to be sent. It was as easy as that.

'There!' she said. 'That'll show you!'

She was doing something on her own at last. What was it Penny had said? That it was time they all grew up? Andrea had considered herself an adult for years. After all, she was the mother of three children. But maybe, she thought with something like surprise, she had been using them as an excuse not to venture any further. She turned her mind back to the practical problems. Enderby was about thirty miles away, out in the real country beyond the suburban sprawl, but she had a car of her own, it would not be difficult to drive there each day. Not knowing exactly where it was, she went upstairs to find the road atlas, which Matthew had been studying in his room.

But as she passed the master bedroom, her new found confidence failed. Supposing it did not make any difference? What if, instead of making Robert take notice of her, having a career of her own just drove them further apart? She paused in the doorway, chewing her lip. She really wanted to try the horticultural course, she knew it was just the thing for her, something she could do well. But when it came down to it, her marriage was what mattered most. Robert had promised that this particular affair was over, but what if there were others? A paltry diploma would never compensate for the knowledge that her husband was looking elsewhere for sexual fulfilment. She glanced at the double bed, neatly made with old-fashioned sheets and blankets, as Robert did not like duvets. Under her pillow was a prim cotton nightie, on the dressing-table a small selection of understated make-up. She had always thought that that was how he liked her. His words of last night came back to her, his account of what he had done with that woman. That was what he really wanted, it seemed. But she couldn't do that sort of thing. Could she? Inhibited Andy, whose mother did not approve of her wearing a swimsuit in front of the boys at the sailing club?

'I got away from you, Mother,' she said softly. 'I married Robert even though you thought he was too old for me, and divorced into the bargain. And I don't go to chapel any more.'

If she could do that, surely she could take this last step away, and grow up? Slowly she sat on the bed, then lay down, and imagined herself and Robert doing the things he had spoken of, touching, playing . . . and instead of disgust, there grew a small thrill of excitement. With dawning amazement, she realised that she might actually enjoy it, that she had been missing out all these years. Time hung suspended as her viewpoint on herself subtly shifted. She did not have to be ruled by her early training, she could learn to enjoy her own body, as Carol did.

She reached for the nightie, got up and bundled it into the bag of jumble in the bottom of the wardrobe.

'Goodbye, Andy Pandy,' she said.

Penny drove Carol through the maze of new streets with their carefully unalike houses.

'Well,' Carol said at last, 'that was a turn-up for the books, wasn't it?'

'Sure was.'

'You're not still mad at me about old Robert, are you?'

'If you'd have told Andy, I'd have murdered you.'

'Yeah, I know.'

'But you were right about what you said to her. I wonder if she'll take any notice?'

Carol considered.

'Dunno. Difficult to tell with Andy. But she does love Robert. Perhaps she will. Do them both good.'

'Mm.' Penny drove onto the dual carriageway and headed for the council estate. 'Do you want to get married again?'

Carol had thought about it often, but come to no definite conclusion.

'Not really. Not yet, anyway. I mean, it's nice to have a proper wage coming in each week, and a man about the house can be useful, but the moment they marry you they stop being nice to you, don't they?

When I'm old, perhaps. Not much fun being on your own when you're old. Nobody else is going to fancy you then, are they? So you might as well have a husband around. But not now.' She gave a short laugh. 'I'm not on the scrap heap yet. What about you? You're doing all right on your own.'

Penny's knuckles whitened on the steering wheel.

'Oh, I want to,' she said. 'I want to desperately.'

Carol patted her knee.

'Don't worry, sunshine, you might do. Who knows?'

She sighed, thinking of her own immediate future. There were bills waiting to be paid at home.

'I suppose I'll have to get another grotty cleaning job.'

'You could set up your own design firm, like you said you were doing at first, remember? You've proved you can do the artwork.'

'No, I'd get in a right mess. Besides, it wasn't working. Andrea's gardens were far more popular than my interiors.'

She expected Penny to argue with her, to tell her to get out there and hustle, but she didn't. They fell silent, each occupied with her own thoughts. Everything had been said now. They wanted only to get away.

'You can drop me off here,' Carol suggested, when they got to the small parade of shops near her house. She had managed not to let the others see her place so far, she was not going to display it now. 'I got to get something for tea.'

'Right.' Penny drew in, turned to look at Carol. 'I guess it's goodbye, then.'

'Yeah.'

They both felt awkward, wanting to say something profound, finding only the usual worn-out phrases. Carol picked up her bag, reached for the door-handle.

'Well, so long then, Pen. All the best.'

Penny leaned over and kissed her.

'Take care, Carol. Be lucky.'

Carol climbed out and stood on the dusty pavement, waving as Penny pulled away. The car went round the corner and out of sight, taking the past with it.

She wondered what to do next. The house did not particularly call her. Then she remembered that she really did need to get something for tea, and wandered into the minimarket. In a curious state of release, she bought a few odd items of food and a plastic carrier to put them in, came out again and stood gazing dreamily at the last of the cakes in the breadshop window. Wasps gathered on a jam tart. Gradually, thoughts began to surface. Poor old Pen, all screwed up over a man. Poor old Andy, stuck with that boring Robert for the rest of her life. What a drag! And most of all, poor old Jill, nutty as a fruitcake and forced to sit in Parliament. Carol had heard them all carrying on on the radio. Hear! hear! Sounded like feeding time at the zoo. And to think that she had been so envious of them at that first lunch. They had all seemed to have so much compared with her, especially Jill, the cause of all her troubles. Now she found she was profoundly glad not to be in any of their shoes.

She drifted along, thinking of Satisfaction Smith, of Keith, of the many other men in her life. God, it had all been fun. You could bet the others hadn't enjoyed it like she had. She'd had her downs, but boy, had she had her ups as well.

The scruffy cafe at the end of the parade had put a couple of tables on the concrete forecourt in a feeble attempt to lend a continental air to the place.

Carol found that the whisky had given her a thirst. She bought a Coke and sat down on a rickety iron chair. The late afternoon sun streamed over the marching rows of tiled rooftops. Carol relaxed, closing her eyes and letting the sun warm her face. A sense of peace stole over her.

So she had thrown away the chance to become a designer in a flourishing business. Well, never mind. It wouldn't have suited her. She would have got bored and missed deadlines and annoyed Andy. And she had blown it with Robert. No more cosy meetings in the flat. He would go home and be a good boy now, terrified that he might lose Andy. At least she hadn't messed things up too badly there. She would have been sorry afterwards if she had spilt it all and upset Andy. She was a nice girl and Carol didn't really want to hurt her. She hoped Andy would take some notice of the advice she had offered. She was certainly welcome to Robert. He had been a generous lover, but when all was said and done, that was about all he had in his favour. How dull to be Andy, lumbered with him for the next twenty years, with life going smoothly on its calm predictable course, and nothing more exciting than a new car or a coffee morning to look forward to. How much better to be Carol, and not know what was going to happen next.

She thought vaguely about going home, but it was so pleasant, sitting in the sunshine, that she did not feel like moving. The house would be in the same mess when she got back, but what the hell. She might not always live there. After all the disasters that had fallen lately, she must be due for a change of luck pretty soon. A nice rich widower, maybe, with a lovely place out Andy's way, or on the Heights. A double garage, she thought happily, and a swimming pool. Yes, that would be nice. She could just fancy lying at the side of a swimming pool with a long cool drink in her hand. And then he would pop off suddenly from a heart attack or something, and she would be really upset for a while, because she'd been fond of the old thing, but he would leave her stacks of money and she'd be able to jet-set it around the world. White beaches with palm trees by day, wild clubs and parties by night. Heaven!

Enjoying her fantasy, she envied nobody. It did not matter that she had no money, no job, no man in her life and four children to keep. What was the use of planning and worrying like the other three did? It didn't make you any happier.

A shadow fell across her face, and she opened her eyes in mild annoyance. A large man in a t-shirt was grinning down at her.

'Enjoying the sun, darling?'

'I was.'

With one practised sweeping glance, she took him in. Merry eyes in a battered, lived-in face, muscular arms and shoulders, slight beer gut above the tight jeans, easy, confident stance. Beyond him, a delivery truck was drawn up outside the hardware shop. With that old quiver of recognition, she knew that she liked what she saw.

'Nice day for sitting around,' he remarked.

'Sure is.'

She did not allow him a smile yet, but her whole body altered subtly without her even moving, sending out receptive signals.

'Too nice to be stewing in traffic jams. You got the right idea. I got to drive all the way back to Milton Keynes.'

'So what did you do to deserve that?' Carol was not ladling out any sympathy yet. 'I expect you've got a wife that doesn't understand you and all.'

'Not me, sweetheart.' With an expansive gesture of the arm, he demonstrated his lack of shackles. 'Free as a bird, me. Come and go as I like.'

'Fly from tree to tree,' Carol elaborated for him.

'That's it.' He looked down at her empty glass. 'What are you drinking? Like another?'

Carol looked at him with withering lack of interest.

'Last of the big spenders, aren't we?'

'That's me, baby. Come on, what is it? Coke? Lemonade? Be a devil – have a cup of tea. For you, I'll even throw in a doughnut.'

'Wow.' Carol close her eyes again. 'Big deal.'

She heard him chuckle and walk into the cafe, not put off an inch by her attitude, taking it for what it was, part of the game. She waited till she heard him ordering Cokes and buns for two, then allowed herself a smile, and laughed inside, secretly hugging the growing bubble of excitement. Here we go again.

Penny drove into the parking bay behind her block of flats and found the familiar dark green Morgan waiting there. The state of suspended emotion that had gripped her the length of the journey home was drowned in a flood of joy. He was here! She stopped untidily in her space and scrambled out of the car. With the pleasure came the tension, and the renewed and strengthened certainty that she was coming up to a crossroads. She had avoided making decisions for too long, had run away and refused to face them. Now she was going to be forced to choose. The knowledge did nothing to slow her down. She hurried across the cheerless tarmac and in at the back entrance. Duncan, Justin, the new play. They raced round and round her head. Carol, Andrea, Jill and Jennifer. That was over now, they were free to go their own ways. They could sink back into the past where they belonged. She ran up the stairs, too impatient to wait for the lift, hastening towards the future.

Duncan came into the hall at the sound of her key in the lock.

'Darling.'

He caught her in his arms.

'Where have you been? I've been trying to reach you for hours.'

'Out to Andrea's. I'm sorry, if I had known, I'd have left a message for you.'

Duncan looked at her with total lack of comprehension.

'I don't know what you see in those dreary suburban housewives.'

'They're not dreary,' Penny said loyally. 'But I shan't be seeing them again. That was what it was all about. The break-up of the alliance. The dispersal of the forces. Goodbye yesterday.'

'Oh.'

He still could not understand why she had disappeared on such an important day.

'I'm here now,' Penny pointed out, and kissed him. But though he responded as passionately as he always did, she could sense a tension, an unease about him as great as her own. She pressed against him, drawing strength from the feel of his body, and took his face in her hands. 'What is it?' she asked. 'What's up?'

He did not answer immediately, but led her into the living-room. There on the coffee table was a bottle of champagne nestling in a silver ice bucket. Penny gave a cry of surprise, looked from it to Duncan, waiting for an explanation.

'For our star,' he said.

Something was wrong, something in the way he said it. He was not as pleased as he pretended to be. Buying the champagne was what he thought he ought to do, not an expression of what he really felt. Penny found herself doing the same, behaving as she should in the circumstances.

'The play? I've got the part?' Breathless delight.

'You've got the part. Lewie phoned, he didn't know where to find you either, so I said I'd tell you.'

'Oh Duncan! Isn't it *wonderful*?' Arms round his neck, huge smile.

'Wonderful, darling. I've really pleased for you. You deserve this.'

'Glasses! I'll get some glasses, you open the bottle. We must celebrate! It was lovely of you to buy champagne, you always think of the right thing.' She kissed him briefly on the cheek. 'I do love you.'

He watched her bounding across the room to the drinks cabinet to fetch the glasses.

'I love you, too, Pen,' he said, almost to himself.

The cork popped, the drink fizzed, Penny squealed with a hilarity she did not feel, they drank to a long and successful run. Then they sat on the sofa and drained another glass each. Despite the drink going rapidly to her head, Penny was finding it more and more difficult to keep up the pretence. She had to find out what was bugging him.

'There's more, isn't there?' she asked. 'Something you haven't told me?'

'Clever girl. You're quite right. I've had some good news as well. We can make it a double celebration.' Avoiding her eyes, he leaned forward and refilled the glasses. 'I've got the job I was after. An arts and entertainment programme. With Granada.'

'*Granada*?' It hit her like a kick in the stomach. Granada. The north. He was going away. The hollow bubble of her pleasure over the new role burst. And then she really had to start acting.

'Darling, how wonderful!' Big hug, ecstatic kiss.

'An arts and entertainment programme! Of your own? You'll be terrific at it. It's what you're really good at, you'll have a chance to use all your talents. I'm sure you'll be a huge success. What's it going to be called? When's it starting?'

Yes, when is it starting? How soon are you going to leave me? How long can I go on being bright and supportive and not scream and rage and be the jealous, clinging, draining woman that drove off all her other lovers? Why can I never win? Hold on to them with every hook at your command and they resent it and leave, let them feel they're free to go and they do just that. They go. But not this one, please God. Not Duncan. Don't let it be over. I couldn't bear it.

'. . . as I work out my notice,' Duncan was saying. 'Then there's the setting up to do, although a lot of groundwork has been done already. The guy who had my job had to leave, so I'll have to pick up the threads, work on what he's done and put my own ideas and style onto the basic frame. It's scheduled to start running in the autumn, so I'll have a lot to do. I don't know quite how much until I get there and see just how much of a mess has been left behind.'

Through her own pain, Penny thought she caught a shadow that should not have been there. There was a flatness to his enthusiasm. This was a great opportunity for him, he should be sparking with excitement, glowing with the prospect of all he was going to achieve. But something was missing. Something was dragging down the moment of glory for him, just as it was for her. The suspicion started a small hope. She nursed it for a few moments, hardly daring to bring it out lest it be dashed. She focused on Duncan's hands, long fingers turning the stem of the half-drunk glass of champagne. Concentrating on keeping her voice level, she said,

'I – I shall miss you, when you move.'

The silence of the room pressed round her.

'Me too.'

They both stopped trying to be heedlessly happy.

'When will you be going? Soon, I suppose.' She fought to keep the ache out of her words.

'I'll put my place on the market tomorrow, then I thought I'd go up at the weekend and have a look at properties. I probably won't get it fixed in time. I'll have to find something on a short let, or I might just stay at a hotel.'

'I see.'

There was so much she wanted to say. She could feel it building like a huge tidal wave, but tried to hold it back, terrified that once she let it go she would force him into admitting what she least wanted to know – that she had never meant as much to him as he meant to her, that it was just another passing phase, great while it lasted but not the overwhelming love of his life.

And then she saw that the glass between his fingers was shaking. Abruptly, he put it down.

'Our timing is appalling, isn't it?' His voice was taut. 'I knew this was coming up, but I didn't know whether I'd get it. I couldn't say anything till I knew, it wouldn't have been fair to you, not with that audition to go to. To tell the truth, I— ' He stopped, shook his head impatiently. 'No,' he said to himself.

Penny could hardly breathe. Her first instinct had been right. His pleasure at her success was all a sham. But instead of being outraged, she felt the small glow of hope begin to flare.

'You hoped I wouldn't get it?'

'Yes,' he admitted.

Her mouth was dry.

'Why?' she managed to ask.

'No point in discussing it now.'

'Yes there is,' she insisted. It was not like Duncan to switch off like this. It underlined how important it was.

'No, Pen. There's nothing worse than might-have-beens. Let's face it, we're both ambitious people. I know you're not going to throw away this chance. I meant what I said, you do deserve it. You've worked hard and you've got it in you. What right have I— ' He broke off, jumped up and walked over to the window.

She saw the choice then, he did not need to spell it out. Leave London, turn down the part, probably leave Justin with Mike and Wendy – or run the risk of losing what they had found together. She looked at him, standing with his back to her, tension in every line of his well-made frame, and knew what her heart told her to do. The events of the day rolled swiftly through her mind. Jill and Andy and Carol, still ruled by the past. Jill had finally shaken it off and come to terms with herself. Andrea might well be able to, she certainly had the incentive. Carol – she wasn't sure about Carol. She probably lacked the necessary will to change. But Penny could do it. She could step out of the never-ending spiral of failed relationships. If she was willing to pay the price.

She hurried across the room and put her arms round Duncan, forcing him to look at her.

'What right have you to do what?' she asked. And when he did not immediately answer, 'To ask me to go with you?'

For a long moment, he gazed hungrily into her eyes, and to her joy she saw a longing that was a mirror of her own.

'Yes,' he said at last. 'That's what I wanted. And I wanted it to be something permanent, not just one of these enjoy it while it lasts arrangements. But I guess the time's not right. I can't ask you to walk out on the best break you've ever had. I respect you too much for that. And— ' he paused, closed his eyes briefly, then came out with the hard truth – 'and I'm not willing to give up my new job either. I don't want to lose you, Pen. If we've really got something going, it can stand the test of a few months.'

A few months. Anything could happen in that time. Penny knew she had to snatch at happiness while it was still within her reach.

'I'm not taking that risk,' she told him. 'There are plenty of good roles around, I'll get another. But there's only one you, and you're what I want.'

And before he could argue, she ran back to the table and poured out the last of the champagne.

'Now we've really got something to celebrate.'

She handed him a glass, raised her own.

'To us, and the future.'

Duncan laughed, kissed her, willingly gave in.

'To us,' he repeated.

THE END